"McCarthy always does an excellent job of
combining laugh-out-loud humor with sizzling,
steamy passion."
—*Romance Junkies*

Praise for *A Date With the Other Side*

"Do yourself a favor and make A Date With the Other Side."
—*Bestselling author Rachel Gibson*

"Fascinating."
—*Huntress Reviews*

"Fans will appreciate this otherworldly romance and want a sequel."
—*Midwest Book Review*

Praise for the other novels of Erin McCarthy

"Will have your toes curling and your pulse racing."
—*Arabella*

"Erin McCarthy writes this story with
emotion and spirit, as well as humor."
—*Fallen Angel Reviews*

"Both naughty and nice . . . sure to charm readers."
—*Booklist*

High Stakes

Erin McCarthy

BERKLEY SENSATION, NEW YORK

THE BERKLEY PUBLISHING GROUP
Published by the Penguin Group
Penguin Group (USA) Inc.
375 Hudson Street, New York, New York 10014, USA
Penguin Group (Canada), 90 Eglinton Avenue East, Suite 700, Toronto, Ontario M4P 2Y3, Canada
(a division of Pearson Penguin Canada Inc.)
Penguin Books Ltd., 80 Strand, London WC2R 0RL, England
Penguin Group Ireland, 25 St. Stephen's Green, Dublin 2, Ireland (a division of Penguin Books Ltd.)
Penguin Group (Australia), 250 Camberwell Road, Camberwell, Victoria 3124, Australia
(a division of Pearson Australia Group Pty. Ltd.)
Penguin Books India Pvt. Ltd., 11 Community Centre, Panchsheel Park, New Delhi—110 017, India
Penguin Group (NZ), Cnr. Airborne and Rosedale Roads, Albany, Auckland 1310, New Zealand
(a division of Pearson New Zealand Ltd.)
Penguin Books (South Africa) (Pty.) Ltd., 24 Sturdee Avenue, Rosebank, Johannesburg 2196,
South Africa

Penguin Books Ltd., Registered Offices: 80 Strand, London WC2R 0RL, England

This book is an original publication of The Berkley Publishing Group.

First edition: August 2006

Library of Congress Cataloging-in-Publication Data

McCarthy, Erin.
    High stakes / Erin McCarthy.— 1st ed.
        p. cm.
    ISBN 0-425-21013-8
    1. Vampires—Fiction. 2. Casinos—Fiction. 3. Las Vegas—Fiction. I. Title.

PS3613.C34575H54 2006
813'.6—dc22

                                                        2006007264

PRINTED IN THE UNITED STATES OF AMERICA

10 9 8 7 6 5 4 3 2 1

Prologue

Dental hygiene was important to a vampire.

Or at least to Ethan Carrick, who had been born before the bubonic plague, when simply having teeth in adulthood was considered an achievement.

Since his human death and rebirth nine hundred years ago, his teeth and body continually rejuvenated themselves, and he wasn't exactly in danger of gingivitis. But he liked the clean, silky feeling of his teeth after they'd been polished, and the crisp minty smell of professional toothpaste.

He smiled at the perky dentist as she strolled into the room. "Am I going to live?"

She laughed, her sleek, dark hair bouncing on her shoulders. "For now. But I wish you'd let me take some x-rays. It's a little challenging to see cavities with the naked eye sometimes."

But not difficult to view vampire fangs on an x-ray film. He'd pass. "I'm sorry, but I have an irrational fear of radiation. I just can't do it without falling out of this chair in a total panic attack." He capped this off with a smooth smile, reclining comfortably in the squeaky, hard dental chair.

She cocked her head to the side and smiled back. "You're teasing me."

It was true. And he was flirting with her, because this woman was exactly the type he'd been searching for—sweet, pleasant, intelligent, but very feminine, very pliable. Innocent.

A quick shift through her mind showed nothing but rainbows and puppies, cotton candy and baby cheeks. Such a cheerful and refreshing change from so many modern women, whose minds raged like warriors, and whose rampant aggressiveness turned Ethan off.

No, Dr. Brittany Baldizzi was exactly the kind of woman he'd been looking for. His campaign manager would seek to find some flaw in her, a smear in her background, and it would all be shot to hell, but for now, Ethan felt cautiously optimistic.

"I am teasing you. But I'm still not getting x-rays. Now don't leave me in suspense—tell me if I have to revisit this torture chamber again within the next six months or if I get to join the Cavity-Free Club." He pointed to the wall of honor, which boasted Polaroid pictures of gap-toothed children grinning in pride.

She leaned against the sink and folded her arms across her chest. Her scrubs were too bulky for Ethan to get an accurate perception of her figure, but she had a pleasing, bouncy walk, and a fresh, shampoo smell.

"You don't have any cavities."

"See? I told my mother it didn't matter if I ate all those sweets and never brushed." Ethan sat up in the chair and ripped off the little bib with the metal clip. "I believe this is yours?"

Dr. Baldizzi took it, her hands still in latex gloves, and pitched it into the metal garbage container. "You're kind of funny, you know that?"

Charming was the adjective he preferred, but it was a start. He probed her mind a little deeper, looking for clues to what she liked, how he might seduce her.

Then he sensed it. It was buried deep, almost undetected, but there it was.

Lazy teasing was forgotten. His eyes sharpened, muscles tensed, mind scanned and processed.

Well, this was an interesting twist.

Time to speed things up a bit.

"You'll have dinner with me tonight." It wasn't a question. And he knew what her answer would be because he was guiding her to give the right one.

Brittany stared at him, her smile drifting off into confusion. "Yes, yes, of course I will. I'll have dinner with you tonight."

"And you're going to pack an overnight bag so you can spend the night."

Not that Ethan was going to sleep with her—he really wasn't interested in her sexually—but he wanted her in his hotel, The Ava, under his watch, while he discussed with Seamus the new little revelation he'd just uncovered.

Glassy-eyed and a little droopy, his dentist nodded. "Okay. I'll pack a bag so I can spend the night."

Ethan stood up and removed his file chart from her hands and tucked it under his arm. He smiled and gave her warm fingers a squeeze. "Perfect."

One

"I'd like to speak to the owner of this casino." Alexis Baldizzi flashed her prosecutor's badge at the door minion, and fought the urge to just shove past him and start screaming her sister's name. That wouldn't get the results she wanted.

The guard showed no emotion. He just stared down at her from his foot-and-a-half height advantage. "Mr. Carrick is unavailable."

Well, no kidding. He had no appointments open for the next three months, which was why she was flashing her badge. Mr. Carrick could be in the middle of packing away a sushi dinner, schmoozing his way through a shareholders meeting, or reading the latest John Grisham on the commode, and she couldn't care less—she was going to talk to him. Now.

"Look." Alexis fought the crick in her neck from staring up at tall, dark, and dumb. "I can talk to Mr. Carrick now or I can come back with a warrant for his arrest on kidnapping charges." You know, she really loved her job. Power was a beautiful thing. Especially since it was her lovable but naive sister, Brittany, who was the victim she was rescuing this time.

One thick, black eyebrow went up. Then without a word, the guard turned and went to the reception desk a few feet away and spoke to the woman sitting there. They put their heads together and murmured while Alexis rocked on her heels impatiently, scanning the quiet lobby.

Both the guard and the receptionist were tall, with dark hair and luminous, ivory skin. The woman in particular was gorgeous, the perfect accessory to a well-decorated office building, and Alex was annoyed even further. She had a personal grudge against tall women who looked good in sleek black pantsuits and red lipstick, since they embodied everything that was lacking in Alexis's own appearance.

It also creeped her out a little that the pair looked like twins escaped from a Goth concert. They blended with their surroundings, the modern black-and-white furnishings cool and sleek, industrial design. The entire room—including its inhabitants—had about as much color and appeal as a skunk.

Alexis simultaneously cursed Brittany while praying she was okay. It was typical of her sister to get coaxed into something like this, and while Alexis didn't think she had been harmed in any way, she didn't like that Brittany was living with an eccentric, rich casino owner as his personal blow-up doll.

Really, really didn't like that.

The very thought sent her striding forward, right past the desk.

"Where are you going?" the startled receptionist called.

"To see your boss." Duh. Alexis picked up the pace when she heard the security guard's heavy tread following her.

Obviously Mr. Carrick's office was right down the hall, since she had been told at the reception area on the twelfth floor that Mr. Carrick's private offices took up the entire twenty-second floor. Goth Guy was gaining on her, yelling, "Hey!" so Alexis kicked it into gear and started running, looking for a door that seemed appropriately impressive enough for a self-important rich bastard.

Double doors. Bingo. Alexis reached for the handle and turned it right as the guard reached her. He touched her shoulder, and before Alexis could even figure out what was happening, she was sailing through the air like water tossed from a bucket. She landed with a bone-crunching smack—nerves firing, muscles jarring, face grinding into the gray carpet.

"Ow," she said. Damn, double damn, she had broken every bone in her frickin' body. Including her nose, which she grabbed, eyes watering. Like she didn't have enough problems at the moment—now she was going to have to suffer through rhinoplasty to fix a broken nose.

"I'm sorry, Mr. Carrick. I tried to stop her," Big Stupid Jerk said.

"Apologize to the lady, James, and help her up. I'm sure you didn't mean to trip her."

First of all, she hadn't been tripped. He had pushed her, though she didn't see how one little shoulder shove could toss her five feet across the room. Second of all, that voice just sent shivers down her probably broken spine. Dang, no wonder the guy was successful. He sounded commanding and cultured, confident and calm.

Which pissed her off.

"James can keep his goddamn hands off of me," she said, peeling her face from the floor like old wallpaper.

Doing so brought legs into her line of vision. Not just one pair. Or two. But a dozen pairs of legs, some in dress pants, some wearing pantyhose, one lone rebel in jeans.

Whoops. Looked like Carrick was having a dinner party. She felt so bad for interrupting. *Not.*

Thick hands touched the back of her own pantyhose-covered calves and Alexis kicked out in reflex, making contact with a hard surface. Perfect. It was Stupid Jerk James's chest, she saw with satisfaction as he grunted in what she hoped like hell was pain.

"Hello? Keep your hands off me!"

"I was just going to . . . uh . . . flip . . ." He was making motions with his hands like he was folding a tortilla in half.

Alexis glanced down. Lovely. Her suit skirt had ridden up during impact and the bottom of her buns were peeking out. This was why she hated girl clothes. Couldn't do a damn thing in them, couldn't look like a heterosexual without them.

James, who apparently had a death wish, yanked her skirt back into place quickly. But not so quickly that he missed getting cracked on the hand when Alexis reached back and popped him one.

"I said, keep your hands off me." Alexis pushed herself up onto her knees.

"Mr. Carrick," James whined, "I was just—"

"Let her alone, James. She obviously doesn't appreciate your gentlemanly assistance."

There was humor in Carrick's voice, and Alexis felt her already tested temper flare. She stood up, adjusted her jacket and skirt, and turned to her audience. "He's the one who pushed me in the first place!"

Her gaze floated from the receptionist to James and on past, trying to find the source of the voice that was pissing her off. Well, they were all pissing her off, but Carrick more so because he was laughing at her. No one laughed at Alexis Baldizzi or her baby sister, Brittany. Okay, so people probably laughed at Alexis Baldizzi. But never so she could see or hear it.

Prepared to rip the bastard's face off, Alexis dismissed an aging hippie in jeans, passed over a brunette in a cocktail dress, and landed on a man in the center of the room, one hand casually in the pocket of his gray pants. Damn it, he was gorgeous.

Not that she had expected her sister would run off with a mutant, but this guy was hot. Tall, blond, blue-eyed, well dressed, muscular but not too pumped up . . . crap. It might be harder than she'd thought to drag Brittany away from this guy.

But no matter how difficult, or how well Carrick's pants fit, Alexis was going to succeed. "Carrick?"

"I am Ethan Carrick, yes. And to whom do I have the pleasure of speaking?" He took several steps closer to her and smiled.

The calm, casual tone he was using was unnerving. But Alexis readjusted her mental strategy. She was a prosecutor and she knew how to switch gears based on people's reactions to her. So she stood a little straighter and stuck her hand out. "Alexis Baldizzi, county prosecutor. I need to speak with you for a minute." *And rip your nuts off.*

Face, nuts, something needed to be ripped off.

He stopped in front of her. Took her hand, and slowly, slowly shook it, clasping her tightly in his grip. "Right this moment?"

"Yes." Shake, shake, her hand still went up and down in his. She gave a little tug, but couldn't escape the contact. He wasn't letting go of her, which was just weird. Tugging again as he smiled—an innocent Botticelli blond angel smile—she asked, "Do you have an office we could step into?"

There was just a slight pause, then he dropped her hand so quickly, her whole arm careened into her leg. "Certainly, Ms. Baldizzi." He turned to his ten or so guests. "Excuse us momentarily. I'm so sorry for the interruption."

Then he gestured for her to walk in front of him. "I have a private office right down the hall. Would you like some coffee, water, wine?"

"No, thank you." Alexis adjusted the strap of her handbag on her shoulder. His aplomb was really starting to bug her. He didn't look the least bit curious as to why she had barged into his reception room at six o'clock on a Friday night. In her job, she was used to people reacting to her with suspicion, yet this guy was completely unconcerned.

"Are you perhaps any relation to Brittany Baldizzi?" he asked conversationally. "She's a dentist."

Weeelll. Slick Rick. Bringing Brittany up first. Alexis had to give him credit. He was smooth, and oh-so-polite. Charm personified. He had gone on the attack, making the first move, which put her on the defensive. And she hated him all the more for it.

"She's my sister." Alexis stopped walking toward the door and whirled to face him, temper getting the best of her rationality. "And I want to know where the hell she is."

His eyebrow rose. "Sister? Really? You don't look a thing alike, though you're both lovely. And at this exact moment, I couldn't say where Brittany is, but I would guess she's in her room. She's planning on joining me at the informal dinner I'm having."

Not if Alexis had to kill him first. "Where's her room?" she asked through clenched teeth. Good thing her sister did her dental work because she was probably cracking a filling.

"Suite twenty-three twenty. There's a private elevator from this floor. Is there a problem? A family emergency? Perhaps I can be of assistance."

"You can assist me by getting the hell out of my way." Alexis was upset. Really upset. Like her eyelids were twitching and her hands were fisting and her legs were jiggling. Brittany had abandoned her dental practice, moved into a Las Vegas casino that looked remarkably like a giant dildo, had not spoken to her sister in three weeks, and this guy was acting like they were at a goddamn Meet and Greet.

As far as she was concerned, Brittany had been kidnapped and brainwashed, and this man in front of her was responsible for the whole nightmare.

"Is there something wrong with your eye?"

"No. Now show me the elevator." Alexis headed back toward the hall, barging past him. Her shoulder clipped his forearm, and instead of stumbling back, he never moved an inch. She, on the other hand, bounced back like a tennis ball making contact with a racket.

"Will you get out of my way?" Alexis brushed at her jacket, not wanting any part of him touching her. "Give your guests Brittany's apologies, but she won't be attending any dinner party."

"Why would that be?"

His faint British accent was as annoying as his perfect good looks. Alexis knew his type. He was like a poster child for Sin City. Come to Vegas and get swept off your feet by a tasteful, rich Brit who will make you a star . . . or more likely, charm you out of your panties and leave you a pregnant cocktail waitress.

"I would have thought it was obvious, but since you need it spelled out—she's leaving with me," Alexis tossed over her shoulder, heading toward the door, hoping the location of a private elevator to the twenty-third floor would be obvious. That exit line would sound just plain old stupid if she couldn't figure out where she was going, but sometimes acting confident was more important than actually knowing anything.

"Brittany doesn't want to leave. She's quite happy here."

That smug, arrogant tone had Alexis jerking to a stop, thoroughly irritated. She whirled around. "You're an asshole." With that, she stomped to the elevator, hit the up button, and gave him her back.

Ethan watched Alexis Baldizzi punch the elevator button a second time, her foot tapping impatiently, her hand clutching her purse. A few moments earlier, he had been thinking that perhaps just one hot little affair before he settled down would be a really smart idea, and that the feisty Alexis was a damn good candidate for such a partner. He'd been thinking that she was sensual, passionate, erotic, and would taste juicy and feel soft as he took her.

But that was a few minutes in the past.

Before she'd called him an asshole.

Now desire had been replaced by annoyance. No one in nine hundred years had called him an asshole. To his face anyway. Who talked like that? Well, he did, but what woman said that to him? It was crude and unnecessary and he completely failed to see what he had done to inspire such rudeness.

Seamus came up behind him as he leaned against the doorframe of the reception room.

"Who the hell is that?" he asked in a low voice audible to vampire ears, but not mortals. "And why are you letting her go upstairs?"

Ethan forced himself to relax. For several hundred years, he had been gaining steadily on his temper, displacing his passions from the battlefield to the bedroom, and he wasn't going to let one ill-mannered woman destroy that progress. "She says she's Brittany's sister. But I can't say I see the resemblance."

His dentist was tall, slender, with fair skin and dark, straight hair. This Alexis was flat-out short, not much higher than his shoulder. She had wispy blond hair that had been escaping from a twist at the back of her neck. She was curvier, too, if that glimpse he'd caught of her backside when she was sprawled out on his carpet was any indication.

She was the complete genetic opposite of Brittany.

"That can't be Brittany's sister." Seamus adjusted his red tie and shook his head, dark eyes clouded with disbelief. "Brittany is . . . sweet."

"Yes, she is," Ethan said, rather grimly. "Brittany is pleasant, naive, cheerful . . ." And got on his everlasting nerves. Being with her was rather like ingesting too many sweets in a short period of time.

But that was his problem, not hers. He clearly was a bloody ingrate, and not nearly as civilized as he liked to think. Yet he still didn't see how a woman like Alexis—pushy, impatient, short—could share the same DNA with Brittany.

"That woman is a harpy," Seamus said firmly, as Alexis slapped the elevator door with her hand and swore eloquently at it.

"That's a little harsh, don't you think?" Ethan spoke with little conviction. Alexis had been, well, harping at him. But what puzzled him—or rather irritated him—was the realization that Brittany in all her sweet feminine perfection got on his nerves, while Alexis, who certainly had shades of the harpy about her, stirred his blood.

Just a little.

Enough to puzzle him.

Well, hell, actually a lot.

Which infuriated him. He was supposed to be giving up on women. He had promised Seamus and the entire Vampire Nation that his randy days were over and he had grown serious and wise with age. He was supposed to chose a suitable wife and get on with it, not visualize a most unsuitable woman lifting her skirt for him.

"Harpy's not quite the right word for her." Luscious . . . sexy . . . edible, maybe.

"Bitch?" Seamus asked with a grimace.

Ethan laughed loudly, earning him a glare tossed over Alexis's shoulder. "No. Not what I had in mind. And I suppose she has the right to feel put off, you know. That was a nasty spill she took when James pushed her."

"I thought you said James tripped her on accident. I wasn't looking . . . too busy checking the latest exit polls on my Sidekick."

Holding his hand up, Ethan prevented Seamus from spewing

out a half-dozen statistics that meant nothing to him. One of the downsides of his career choice. "Later on the exit polls, please. And James didn't push or trip Alexis, technically. I think he was reaching out to get her attention and forgot that he is much stronger than he used to be."

"Ah, to be a young vampire again." Seamus shook his head. "When all the world was new and exciting and everyone looked like a meal . . ." He grinned. "It's hell to get old. Now it's all responsibilities and shaping a new world order. I haven't even put the bite on anyone in a hundred years."

"Whine to me when you hit your five-hundredth birthday. Until then I don't want to hear it." Especially since Ethan was distracted at the moment. "So why do you think Alexis is here?" he asked quietly, aware that mortal ears had severe limits, but not wanting to chance Alexis hearing him.

"To save her sister from your evil clutches, I take it."

That was what concerned Ethan. His mild interest in Brittany had become much more when he had realized who she was. What she was. And Seamus had been ecstatic. Neither one of them wanted to give up the idea of Brittany.

"I don't have any evil clutches. Haven't since at least the sixteenth century. But if they are well and truly sisters . . . is Alexis an Impure like Brittany is?" He wasn't sure if that was a plus or a minus, or if it mattered in the slightest. Alexis was not a woman who could be easily persuaded or guided.

During the time he had been with her, Ethan hadn't been able to pick up on any of Alexis's thoughts. Not that he had really been trying to probe her mind, but nothing had come across to him.

"I don't know. I didn't sense anything from her, but I wasn't focusing on it. I was focusing more on staying out of her firing range. Not my kind of woman, Ethan, seriously." Seamus shuddered.

Ethan looked at his friend and campaign manager, suddenly curious, and unable to resist the chance to give Seamus a hard time. "What *is* your type of woman? I haven't seen you with a female since that little French girl tried to get you to take a turn on the guillotine. Are you saving yourself for marriage or something?"

Seamus scowled. "With all due respect, Mr. President, mind your own damn business."

With a laugh, Ethan clapped Seamus on the back, as the elevator finally opened for Alexis. "Let's go back to the guests. Brittany won't leave, I can guarantee it."

Because Brittany could not leave. As an Impure, she was his ticket to reelection for the presidency of the Vampire Nation. She would appease his minority constituents, and lend credence to his claim that he was older, wiser, less inclined to violence than he had been in his youth.

Which was true. He did see the value of negotiation and democracy now, whereas at one time he'd thought the only solution to a problem was to raise his sword. Now he was ready for diplomacy, and Brittany would make a truly valuable first lady.

"Are you sure? You haven't exactly been, uh, aggressive with Brittany. You're usually much more, well, successful earlier on with women." Seamus cleared his throat.

"I'm wooing her, Seamus." Ethan glared at his friend. "This is a serious venture, not a hot tumble in the barn. I'm being delicate."

Which was a laugh in itself. Ethan hadn't wooed any woman with the intention of doing more than getting her out of her clothes.

This was different, and he was having a little trouble adjusting himself to the prospect of a monogamous relationship. Marriage. Jesus. He got vampire sweat in his armpits just thinking about it. And with Brittany an Impure, their marriage could last some sixty years or more.

"Well, pick up the pace on the wooing. It looks like you're not interested in her. If I were a girl, I wouldn't think you were being delicate, I'd think you wanted to be 'just friends.' " Seamus made quote marks with his fingers.

Everyone was a critic. "If you were a girl, I wouldn't be pursuing your platter-face. But do you think you can do this better? You woo her. Let's see how far you get, Mr. No Date This Century. At least I'm still having sex."

"You're having sex? You're not supposed to be having sex!" Seamus looked instantly alarmed. "You're supposed to be convincing Brittany and every other undead that you've reformed. You can't be whoring around at the same time you're 'wooing' Brittany."

"Will you quit with the damn quote marks in the air? And I didn't mean I was having sex this minute. I just meant I have recently. You know, more recently than you, who last had sex when Napoleon was alive."

"Kiss my arse." Seamus's brogue, which he had lost over the centuries, reappeared in his anger.

Ethan laughed. "Relax. If you want to be a monk, that's your business. And I'll turn on the charm with Brittany if you feel things are moving too slowly. I agreed to get myself a wife, didn't I? My word is sacred."

Yet for some reason, instead of picturing serene Brittany at his side, a vision of her obnoxious sister rose in his mind.

And his thoughts regarding her had nothing to do with marriage and everything to do with arousal.

Shit. Seamus was right. He wasn't trying to charm Brittany. Not with much enthusiasm anyway. Because the thought of bedding Brittany left him cold.

And the thought of Alexis made him lava-hot.

Which was one more reason to avoid Alexis.

It didn't matter if she had challenged him by her dismissal and insult. He was a Master Vampire, elected president of all undead registered voters. He knew plenty of women who would sleep with him willingly and with great pleasure. Scores of women.

Her attitude was not a reflection on his manhood in any way, and he did not need to prove himself to her.

Ethan grimaced. Liar. It mattered a hell of a lot that Alexis Baldizzi had looked at him like he was a troll.

Which wasn't a positive thing at all.

He had sworn to give up violence and casual sex, and in ten minutes Alexis Baldizzi had him contemplating doing both to her.

Two

Alexis impatiently watched the elevator open, annoyed that she'd had to stand there pacing for five minutes while Carrick had stood in the doorway and watched her. He had spoken too low for her to hear his words, but when he'd laughed, she'd had the annoying suspicion that he had been amused by her.

Ready to charge onto the elevator, Alexis saw Brittany standing in it, smoothing the stomach of her black cocktail dress.

Alexis sighed in relief.

Brittany was alive, even if she had been brainwashed. And leave it to her baby sister to thrive under the circumstances. She looked gorgeous—all high cheekbones, glowing eyes, and glossy hair. Money and sex were good for the complexion, apparently.

Not that Alexis would know, since she had neither, but Brittany looked great.

"Alex!" Brittany smiled and threw her arms around her for a hug. "What are you doing here?"

Saving her from a heated sexual affair with a rich man, of course.

Alexis was going to have to come up with a better argument than that to get Brittany to leave.

Hands on her hips, she frowned as Brittany moved out of the way of the elevator door. "Hello? I was worried about you! This is totally not like you, Brittany."

Her sister just laughed. "Actually, yes, it is. I'm the impulsive one who thinks with her emotions. You're the one who plans everything to the last detail. I think it's because my biological father was a drifter, you know. I just go with the moment."

Alexis winced as Brittany grabbed her hand and tried to pull her down the hall, toward Ethan and his stone-faced friend. Alexis was uncomfortable whenever Brittany discussed her father, and frankly, she didn't know how a man who had seduced a married woman, then abandoned her pregnant, could have produced her sister, who was one of the sweetest women in Vegas.

Which probably wasn't saying much, given the grading curve of divas and strippers, but Brittany still deserved a special shout out for being damn nice.

"Ethan! Look who's here!" Brittany called in her cheerleader voice. "My sister, Alex!"

"I've had the pleasure of meeting her," Ethan said, his deep voice carrying the length of the hall. "Why don't you bring her in to join the rest of the guests?" With a smile, he disappeared from the doorway, retreating into the reception room.

"Awesome idea," was Brittany's opinion.

Sucky idea, was Alexis's opinion.

Before Alexis could formulate a reply that would involve fewer than nine swear words, her sister stopped walking and turned to her. Gave her a quick hug and a perky hand squeeze.

"I'm fine, Alex. I told you that when I called you. I left you two voicemails and three e-mails telling you what I was doing, and you can always call my cell phone if you need to talk to me. If you would answer your phone once in a while, we could have actually discussed it."

Guilt rose up in Alexis. "It's this case I've been working on . . . I tried to call you at home, but you weren't there, and your cell was turned off, and . . . hey, wait a minute." She crossed her arms, annoyed that she was so quick to defend herself. "Don't turn this around and make me look like the bad guy. You're the one who disappeared."

"But you're better at being the bad guy than me." Brittany gave her a pretty, dimpled smile.

It was hell to be responsible for another human being. Alexis had been doing it since Brittany was thirteen. Alexis had been eighteen, and their mother had taken one last big drug trip, straight into an overdose and her death. Unlike their selfish mother, Alexis loved Brittany with a fierceness and complexity that sometimes startled her, and she would do anything for her. Had sacrificed and worked very hard to keep her attractive and wonderfully naive little sister safe, happy, and successful in the career of her choice.

Alexis wouldn't have it any other way. But at the moment, she wanted to shake Brittany. How could she just throw over her dental practice for the first sexy, rich guy to glance her way? And why couldn't a sexy, rich guy glance at Alexis?

Not that she'd do anything more than laugh in his face, but it would be nice to be *asked* once in a while. The last guy to ask her out was Hansen at the bagel shop, who had expressed interest in her unique mind and her love of strawberry cream cheese.

But this wasn't about her—it was about Brittany ruining her own life. And how that would affect Alexis.

"So what is going on? Are you in love with Ethan Carrick?" Alexis could barely keep the fear out of her voice. A guy like that didn't love—he consumed. He purchased a product, kept it for his entertainment and pleasure, then moved on when he was tired of it.

There were many men like that, and Alexis had bumped against more than her fair share of them as a prosecutor. Cold, calculating men, whose every motive revolved around selfish want, and Alexis didn't want them anywhere near her sister.

Brittany's red lips opened in astonishment. "In love with him? Of course not! I'm here for business."

Alexis would bet what they were doing sure in the hell wasn't tax deductible.

Her eye started twitching again.

In Brittany's world, men invited attractive women in their twenties to their overthemed hotels for business purposes. In Alexis's world, they did it because they wanted a little sumthin' sumthin'.

"What kind of business, Brit?" She gave a nervous glance over at the door and made sure the man in question hadn't returned.

Brittany's little nose wrinkled. "My business, of course. I zoomed Ethan and he asked me to do the rest of his staff."

"You zoomed him?" she asked in shock. That sounded like space sex or something. Or like a motorized blow job. Holy crap, she needed to have a talk with Brittany.

Maybe her sister could teach her something.

"Yes. Teeth whitening."

Oh. Teeth whitening. Of course. That made perfect sense. Not.

"He offered me a lot of money to do it, and I might have said no except I realized that it was important for me to spend time with Ethan and his staff, because I need to save them from eternal damnation."

Huh? Alexis stared at her sister, waiting for anything about that sentence to make sense. "Umm . . . eternal damnation? Baby, what are you talking about?" Brittany had always led with her heart, but she'd never shown signs of insanity before.

Brittany tossed her long black hair over her bare shoulders and nodded. "Yes, eternal damnation. They're all vampires, Alex."

"Vampires? Vampires. Vam-*pires*?" Alexis felt her blood pressure rising like an elevator. She'd started out on the fear floor and was heading straight toward furious. A headache was brewing behind her eyes, and she wished that Brittany wasn't six inches taller than her, so she could just grab her sister and haul her ass home where she belonged. "You mean like Dracula? Bloodsucking demons with bad breath, nocturnal habits, and an aversion to crosses, stakes, and garlic? That's crazy."

"Yes."

"Yes, what?" Alexis rammed her hands into her suit pockets. "Yes, it's crazy, or yes, they're bloodsucking demons?"

"Both. I know it's hard to believe, but Ethan is a vampire, and he needs our help."

Our help? The only thing Alexis was going to give him was a flying roundhouse kick in the crotch.

Not only was he a rich casino owner, but he got his jollies

running some kind of goofy club/cult of creepy pale people who all had her little sister believing they were freaking vampires. Dead people. Undead. Double dead. Whatever you wanted to call it.

They weren't any of it. And what they wanted to do on their own loser time was their business, but since they had dragged Brittany into their weird hobbies, Alexis was not happy.

In fact, she was so angry her mouth went hot and the hallway spun a quick tilt.

"I'll help him, Brit." She jammed her purse back onto her shoulder. She'd help escort him to the police station to answer a few questions.

And prosecute his ass away from her sister and straight into prison.

Ethan heard the moment Alexis and Brittany stopped speaking by the elevator bank and headed toward the reception room. Even while chatting with Peter Federov about his winnings at the Bellagio's elite poker table, Ethan sensed the angry footsteps marching in his direction long before he saw Alexis.

She was muttering, though he couldn't decipher the words, in an irritated way that amused him as he sipped vintage blood from a champagne flute.

"Thirty grand in one hand," Peter was saying. "Like taking candy from babies, since I can sense everything going on in their minds."

"That's not exactly ethical, Peter," he said automatically, though he was distracted.

Now he could smell Alexis, a warm blend of vanilla lotion and the natural scent of her skin, a salty anxiety. The steady, rapid beat of her heart echoed in his sensitive eardrums, and the cadence of her walking drummed in harmony with the pulsing of her veins. With chilled, aged blood on his lips, the taste a sharp, dry, subtle satisfaction, he suddenly wanted more. Sweet, warm, immediate blood, like a bubbly Riesling wine, straight from the source into his mouth, where it would roll over his tongue and fill his cheeks and make his eyes slip shut with pleasure.

"Screw ethical, Carrick. Why do we have these talents if we cannot use them? If we want something, we should take it."

Take it. Ethan could take it. He could draw Alexis to him and take her thick, rich blood, and she would never know. It had been a long time since he'd fed straight from a mortal, and he was suddenly very thirsty for the experience.

Peter ran his hand over his bulging middle. When turned, Peter had been a Russian diplomat under the czar, and he still had the physique of a man who loved his borscht. Very unappealing at the moment, when Ethan was suddenly aroused by Alexis Baldizzi.

"Excuse me, Peter. I do believe Brittany is coming into the room." He clapped his hand on Peter's shoulder and started toward the door, curiosity and hunger for Alexis compelling him to move more than any consideration for Brittany.

"That mortal girl is too nice for you," Peter called after him in his thickly accented English. "She will bore you in a decade."

Ethan paused. Why did he think Peter had the absolute right of it? He felt the need to grimace at the thought of marriage to Brittany, but he controlled himself. "It's not about entertainment. It's about politics."

This was something he and Seamus had strategized. He needed

a wife. Choosing an Impure was a brilliant move, one that would keep his opponent, Donatelli, from gaining too much ground on him. It didn't matter if there were no sparks. Sparks had burned down London. Sparks didn't build nations.

"Hah," was Peter's opinion.

There was no time to reply before Alexis burst in through the door. Wildly, she scanned the room, blond hair escaping from the twist at the back of her neck, chest heaving from exertion. And possibly indignation.

Brittany stood behind her, half a foot taller, her body and style elegant and smooth, yet it was clear who was the power partner in their relationship. She hovered behind Alexis looking worried, waiting for her sister to take action.

Which didn't take long. Ethan barely had time to give a smile in greeting before Alexis locked eyes with him and attacked.

"What the hell is the matter with you?" she demanded, her short legs eating up the distance between them.

"I beg your pardon?" He could handle this without getting angry. It didn't matter if she made a scene in front of his reelection team. He had self-control, gained over many years of grappling with his temper.

Nor would he let her arousing scent distract him, even as his nostrils flared slightly and he calculated that it had been a very long six months on the campaign trail since he'd last had sex.

"How can you live with yourself? It's bad enough that you own a glitzy over-the-top casino that breeds vice and preys on human weakness, but to lure young women here on the pretext of business just makes you a bastard."

Since he supposed he had lured Brittany, he couldn't really

dispute that, though he was not going to apologize for owning a casino. It was Las Vegas, for God's sake. The whole point of the place was to make money off of sin. Or fun, however you cared to look at it. "A bastard, too? I thought I was an asshole."

Her cheeks flushed red. "You're both."

"I think perhaps this is something you need to discuss with your sister, not me." Never once in three weeks had Brittany indicated she wasn't happy with their business arrangement, and while Ethan had not made much of an effort to seduce her, she seemed to enjoy his company.

Well, if you wanted to be annoyingly technical, the first few days he had exerted a slight mental influence on her, but he hadn't done that in weeks. So he felt no guilt.

"I did discuss it with Brittany. And it confirmed that you're a freak loser."

Brittany was biting her fingernail. "Alexis, I don't think you should . . ."

Freak loser. She thought he was a freak loser. Funny, that. He could take a lot of insults, but he could not believe for one second that this woman, this little tiny *imp*, could find him so completely lacking. Or that he could even care what she thought.

Ethan clenched his fist. "Would you care to elaborate on that statement?"

Her chin came up, dimple first. Her blue eyes flashed with anger, her breathing anxious and fast. "Brittany told me that you all think you're vampires."

There was a gasp from the room. Ethan thought it was Isabella, the head of the council for the preservation of the undead. Otherwise the room was still, silent, everyone waiting for him to speak.

Alexis stared at him defiantly.

Ethan was a little surprised by this turn of events. He hadn't suspected Brittany of guessing their identity. What he'd sensed from her in recent weeks had been more of a sympathetic kindness, not that she'd concluded they were vampires. Long term, this was good news. If Brittany thought they were vampires, and was still hanging about of her own free will, it should be but a few weeks' work to convince her to fall in love with him and marry him.

Hooray. Somehow he wasn't as excited by that as he should be.

"I don't *think* we're vampires." He knew they were. Big difference.

"Look, we all have our hobbies. If you want to drink tomato juice and call it blood"—she gestured to his champagne glass—"and surround yourself with bad Elvira impersonators, that's your business. But leave my sister out of it. She's a sweet girl and she actually believes you're the walking dead and wants to save your souls from hell."

Save their souls from hell? Where had that come from? Astonished, and holding a glass of human blood in his hand, he looked over at Brittany, dug around in her head a little. She was easy to read, wide open to him most of the time if he wanted to go looking.

Alex is too cynical, wish Alex could be happy, know they can be helped, Ethan is sad and lonely . . .

Her thoughts rolled like a teleprompter and Ethan was appalled. She thought he was *lonely*? Here he'd been trying to woo Brittany slowly and surely and she felt sorry for him. That was a kick to the ego.

Neither sister found him attractive.

Losing his touch with women was unacceptable. He was not going to slide into old age a vampiric Mister Rogers. Zip-up sweaters and soft smiles. Good God.

He had sworn he would marry and settle down, but he didn't want to be undesirable to women.

While he was having a mental crisis, Brittany was shrugging her shoulders in apology, hands up in a conciliatory gesture. "You probably didn't want me to know that you're a bloodsucking demon, but I couldn't help but notice. And I like you and don't want to see you spend eternity in hell."

Alexis rolled her eyes. "Personally, I'm okay with him going to hell. But he's not a vampire, Brittany. Vampires don't exist! He's disturbed, he's a cult leader, he's a self-important rich bastard, but he is not a vampire."

Ethan drained his glass, the blood having warmed to room temperature. But it wasn't what he wanted to take the edge off his desire, to quench the thirst that raged hotter and hotter in him as Alexis stood face to face with him and confidently insulted him.

"Seamus, please escort Brittany and the other cabinet members down to the private dining room. I'll join you shortly after I finish speaking with Miss Baldizzi."

There was movement around him as his guests politely moved to do as he had asked. Alexis made a squawking noise. "Brittany is staying with me! In fact, she's leaving with me, right now. And that's *Ms.* Baldizzi to you."

But Brittany evaded the hand that reached out to grab her. "Alex, you don't understand. I *have* to stay." She latched on to Seamus's arm and headed for the door. "Please don't be mean to Ethan. He can't help what he is."

She made it sound like he was gay or something. Ethan snorted in annoyance before he could prevent himself.

Alexis made to follow her sister, but Ethan put his hand on her shoulder and stopped her. "I am sorry you're displeased with my arrangement with Brittany."

"That's a big-ass understatement." She struggled to wiggle out of his touch.

But he was strong, so strong that it was no effort to keep her pinned. "She's an adult. Anything she does is her choice."

Over her shoulder, she gave him a look of utter disdain. "You've taken advantage of her naiveté and manipulated her. You make my skin crawl."

She'd managed to push the right button. His anger exploded, irrational and hot. "What would you say if I told you I really was a vampire . . . and that I fully intend to marry your sister?"

The words hung in the air for a sickening second, her gasp of outrage loud in the silence.

He saw her movement, a slight shift, but even with his heightened senses he never guessed her intention until he felt the impact and the sharp pain jolt through his chest.

Now that was a first.

The crazy woman had actually hit him.

Three

Alexis thought she was handling herself, keeping it cool, until Ethan wouldn't let go of her shoulder. His touch was firm, powerful, and effortless, reminding her that she was stuck in a puny woman's body. She hated that she had to spend her entire life at eye level with most people's nipples.

Alexis didn't like to feel powerless, and that's what Carrick's grip did to her.

Added to that was his annoying statement that he was going to marry her baby sister, and she lost it. Snapped. Did what instinct, anger, and years of Korean karate training had taught her.

With a yank, she pulled his arm forward, then used her elbow to drive into his chest. It was a satisfying way to lose his grip on her shoulder. Letting out a *"Ki-Hap!"* she whirled around and faced her opponent.

Okay, so *opponent* was an exaggeration, but it still felt good to see the surprise on his face.

"Look, Alexis . . ." He raised his hand.

She went in with a knife-hand block that deflected his movement. Annoyance pinched his features. She struggled to make sure pain didn't show on hers. Dang, the man was hard. Solid. Making contact with his palm had been like blocking a slab of concrete. Which only increased her determination to show him he could not physically or metaphorically push her around.

Waving both his hands toward her face, he said, "I'm not trying to—"

Alexis got him with a double maneuver, right then left.

Ethan glared. "What the hell are you doing?"

"Sang Dan Mahk Kee. High block, front stance." She eased back just a little, but stayed in ready position.

"Oh, my God." Ethan rolled his eyes. "There's no reason to pull out your little martial arts techniques. I'm just trying to resolve this to our mutual satisfaction."

That would mean he would drop dead in front of her. He wasn't hitting the floor, so she went on the attack, giving him a spear hand to the arm just for fun. "I'm a Dan member, which is the Korean equivalent of a black belt. Don't mock me, Carrick."

"Stop hitting me. I'm not going to fight back, it's completely ungentlemanly. Besides . . ." He smirked at her. Actually smirked. "I don't wish to wrinkle my shirt restraining you."

Pompous and British, that's how he sounded to her. "I am seriously a woman on the edge here. Just give me one more reason, one more asshole remark, and I'm going to pop you. And enjoy it."

Alexis bounced on her feet, wishing she weren't wearing a

business suit. It was going to be a little tricky to get her foot into his chest, but she had outrage fueling her. Stepping out of her shoes, she kicked them aside, and was annoyed when she dropped another two inches.

Ethan just eyed her, took a deep breath, and unclenched his fists. "Look, I think we got off on the wrong foot here. There's no reason to be hostile. And I fail to see what's so objectionable about me. I'm sure Brittany could do worse."

Hello? "You just told me you're a vampire! Which means you're insane. I don't want my sister involved with a lunatic, because she'll think it's her job to save you, and I know, as sure as the sky is blue, that you can't change people. Once a nut, always a nut."

Alexis saw violent criminals every day in her job as an assistant prosecutor specializing in sexual crimes. Men who took advantage of their power and position and hurt women, children. She'd do anything to protect Brittany from the pain and suffering she had seen.

"I'm not a lunatic. In fact, I'd argue that I'm more sane than you are. You've barged into a private business, insulted me, hit me, all to rescue a sister who doesn't want to be saved." Ethan Carrick took a step closer to her, got in her face, and smiled tightly, his eyes cold and triumphant. "She likes it here with me, wearing pretty dresses and strolling through the casino on my arm, a rich man's girlfriend, and she likes it in my bed. Just as you would."

The pleasure he was getting from rubbing the victory in her face was more than Alexis could handle. Hey, she could admit it—she was a control freak. She liked to win. She didn't like to have any man get the better of her, and she didn't like that Brittany had insisted she couldn't leave.

So she jabbed Ethan in the gut with her elbow and kicked his leg out from under him. He went down hard, with a surprised grunt and a loud thud when his back connected with the floor. It was a shame the carpet was so plush—ceramic tile would have really made an impressive smack.

It was probably wrong to feel as satisfied as she did, but she'd worry about that later. Like when she died. Right then she fought a battle not to laugh, and lost. But she only got one snort out, watching him wince, before she suddenly heard a whooshing sound, and felt the air move around her.

Confused, she saw darkness coming at her, then before she could blink, she was the one on her back on the floor, Ethan Carrick on her chest, his knee wedged between her legs.

"*Don't* do that again," he said tightly.

Alexis sucked in a breath and turned her head to the side, disturbed by how close his face was to hers. How the hell had he pinned her? It had to be the business suit. She couldn't move in it.

"Do what?" she asked in irritation, lifting her shoulders a little to test how tightly he held her. She moved a whole eighth of an inch. Damn, whatever else he was, Ethan was in shape.

"Hit me. I've lost patience with you." Gripping the lapels of her jacket, he stroked the fabric with his thumbs, his breath on her cheek. "Go home, Alexis. Leave your sister to her choices. Perhaps if you got a life of your own, you wouldn't need to interfere in hers."

That was a direct hit. It touched on all Alexis's vulnerabilities, her fear that without Brittany she'd wind up alone, cynical and bitter. And she'd be damned if she'd let Ethan know that.

"Bite me," she said, shifting her leg just a little so she could position herself better.

Ethan's eyes darkened. "Now there's a thought."

Oh shit, she knew that look, recognized that sound. Felt the heat of his leg pressing into her skirt, watched his eyes drop down to her lips. Pervert. Men were all the same.

So were women apparently, because her body was doing the whole arousal thing. Faster breathing, tightening nipples, arching neck. Slow burn beginning deep between her thighs.

That seriously pissed her off. Betrayed by her own hormones.

"Would you like me to bite you? I bet you taste good, Alexis. Hot and passionate."

"Is that smoldering look supposed to be turning me on? Because it isn't working," she lied.

"Be honest here." Nostrils flaring, he leaned closer, running his finger over her lip. Alexis tried to ignore the very real jolt she felt, blaming it on long-term celibacy.

"You can sense there's something between us." His hands were roaming over her sides, brushing past her breasts.

What she sensed between them was a massive erection pressing into her groin.

Instead of ignoring it, like an obedient body would, her inner thighs responded with an enthusiastic greeting of warm wetness in her panties. That quick exhalation of air came from her own lungs, too. Alexis was appalled that her body was actually liking what he was doing, even as her mind rebelled.

He was going to kiss her. It was so obvious. His eyes were half-closed, his mouth a hairbreadth from hers, his thumb stroking over her nipple like he was sure of her positive reception.

Holy crap, she was letting him touch her chest. She was going to let him kiss her. She was going to like it.

That horrible thought sent her into action.

"I do feel something between us," she whimpered, impressed that she sounded so legit. Reese Witherspoon had nothing on her.

"What's that, love?"

"My knee." With a swift movement up, she nailed him in the nuts, then rolled out from under him as he jerked back in shock.

"Don't ever do *that* again," she said, scrambling to her feet and yanking her skirt back into place. "If you do, I won't hold back like this time."

Because she was very much afraid if he tried to put that move on her a second time, she just might let him finish it.

Which meant insanity was catching, and she didn't have a prayer of saving Brittany from him.

"Hold back? That was holding back?" Ethan hunched over and fought a wave of nausea. While it was nearly impossible to injure his body, he still felt pain, and Alexis had delivered him a hell of a kick. Right where it counted. Good thing vampires didn't procreate—at least they weren't supposed to—because she had probably maimed him.

Good God, a woman hadn't gotten the best of him in over seven hundred years. He must be losing his touch. He had actually fallen for her capitulation. He'd thought she'd felt the same urgent and suffocating lust he had experienced when he'd found himself over her, in the perfect position to invade her body with his own.

It was humbling to realize how much he had come to rely on reading people's thoughts. That, with quick reflexes, always kept him in control. But Alexis had a mind like a bank vault, and the door was shut tight to him. Without sensing her thoughts and actions, he was as vulnerable as a mere mortal.

He hadn't known that kick was coming until it landed right on his testicles, and if he didn't want that to happen again, he was going to have to be much more alert.

The challenge of that had him strangely aroused. Excited.

Which was pathetic. Had his life become so staid and boring that a woman abusing his bollocks had him horny? Given the erection in his pants, it seemed so.

"That was just a little demonstration, Carrick. I could break your nose, knock out some teeth, pop you in the eye if you'd like."

Let her try. Feeling a grin split his face, he decided he'd been working too hard on his reelection, and had expended a lot of energy worrying about Brittany's reaction to him. Or nonreaction. She treated him more like a friend than a potential lover, and she was just as perky and cheerful with Peter and Seamus as she was with him. That lie about Brittany enjoying his bed—while childish and boastful—had been to provoke Alexis.

Clearly it had worked.

And he was enjoying the challenge Alexis presented far too much for a man who was supposed to be responsible and focused on business.

"I'll pass on having my eye poked out, thanks, but how lovely of you to offer." Besides, his body would just heal the damage and he didn't think Alexis was ready to see vampire restoration.

"Lovely. That's me." Alexis gave a snort, undid her hair from its twist, and scraped it back into a new makeshift ponytail.

Ethan stood up. "You are rather lovely, Alexis, if one ignores the bad temper, foul mouth, and monstrous stubbornness."

She glared at him as he brushed off his pants.

There was a look in her eyes he didn't trust. "What? Are you going to hit me again?"

"I'm thinking about it."

He could hardly wait. "Let's just skip that, shall we? Look, I'm sorry that you are displeased with your sister, but I think that is for the two of you to discuss."

It was a good thing he was an experienced politician, well versed in persuasion. He'd been delivering the same rhetoric to Alexis for thirty minutes. Now if only she'd actually listen to him.

"So why vampires?" she asked. "Why not werewolves or demons or druids? Shapeshifters or wizards? Is it because vampires are supposed to be sexy?"

Yes, he based everything he did on the desire to be sexy. Good God.

Though she had a point, he supposed. He didn't imagine morphing into a chimp would be attractive to women. And Ethan did like attracting women.

"I guess I can see that, if you take out the whole sucking blood thing. The werewolf attraction I never got—I mean, they have fur and crawl on all fours." She bit her lip. "Though my boyfriend in law school could pass for that on a bad night after drinking vodka. So what do you call your group? A family? A coven?"

"Conservatives."

She didn't seem to hear him. Retrieving her shoes, she said, "So who are you supposed to be? Angel? Lestat? Dracula?"

Those pansies? None of them had seen battle in the Crusades. None of them had fought through a wall of human flesh to defend God and country, women and children.

He was a bit insulted that she thought he was playacting, pretending to be a vampire. And he certainly would never pretend to be any of the men she had named.

"I'm not supposed to be anybody."

"You should go for Drac. After all, he had three wives and one true love . . . what more could a guy ask for? As long as you leave my sister out of it, you can vamp to your heart's content." She glanced around the room, high heels dangling from her fingertips. "Do you have a coffin?"

"Maybe," he said cautiously, not sure which answer she would prefer. He had the bizarre, primitive urge to impress her. To force her to admit she found him attractive.

"Must be nice to have so much time and money that you can just goof around. It's like war games, isn't it? Or playing paintball."

She had reduced nine hundred years of living to being hit in the thigh with a blue paint pellet.

"Do you like blackjack?" he asked, a bit off-kilter and fumbling to regain some control.

The question stopped her bizarre tangent.

"Huh? Blackjack?"

"Yes." He kept a supply of chips behind the bar. He grabbed a pile and held them out to her. "Why don't you go try your hand at the tables? I'll send Brittany to talk to you."

Win points by sending the sister, giving her exactly what she wanted . . . yes, he was very clever.

Alexis narrowed her eyes in suspicion, but she took the chips from him. Their fingers touched, and Ethan felt a wave of human emotion that shocked the smile off his face. He couldn't read her thoughts, but he could feel her loneliness passing into him through her skin.

What was even more shocking to him was how easy it was to recognize. Because the low, trembling tenor of it matched his own.

☾☽

Brittany discussed the Westminster dog show with Seamus Fox and wondered if she had the courage to drive a stake through his heart. She really doubted it.

But the problem was, she really liked Seamus, just like she was fond of Ethan, and she hated to think that their souls were bound to rot in hell. It seemed like she should either find a way to convert them or kill them, freeing them from an eternity of damnation.

"I bred terriers for years," Seamus was saying, sipping a glass of red wine.

She knew it was really blood, even though it was bottled up as a Merlot. When she'd asked for a glass, she'd been discouraged that it didn't match the meal, and had had a Chardonnay shoved into her hand.

"Oh, I love terriers. I had a Jack Russell, but he died of cancer two years ago. Brownie was a present from my sister, Alex, for my sixteenth birthday." Alex had always tried to compensate for their lack of parents, and she'd made Brittany's birthdays special.

She hoped Alex wasn't mad at her, but she really couldn't go home. Aside from the fact that she still had dental appointments with some of the hotel and casino staff, she needed to figure out if there was some way to save the dozen people who were in Ethan's inner circle and who were all clearly vampires.

"Your appointment with me is tomorrow," Brittany reminded

Seamus. "I think it's really generous of Ethan to provide on-site dental services to his staff."

Seamus grimaced. "We can give my slot to someone else. I don't really need a cleaning."

"Afraid of the dentist?"

"No, of course not." He looked affronted, his dark eyebrows drawing together. "I'm just busy, and I think that I saw the dentist recently."

"When? In this century?" Brittany nudged his arm, and wished they would just admit to her that they were vampires, so they could discuss their salvation. But every time she had broached the subject with Ethan or Seamus that first week in the hotel, she had suddenly found herself confused and talking about something else. They were obviously controlling her thoughts—vampire trick—but in recent days she was sure she'd been successful in locking them out.

"No, probably not," he admitted with a grin.

Now that it had all come out in the reception room, Brittany didn't see why Seamus and Ethan didn't admit the truth—that they had probably both been alive when dentists and barbers were one and the same.

"How long?" she asked. "I mean, specifically."

The sudden urgent need to use the bathroom overcame her. Brittany shifted uncomfortably in her seat.

"Not long enough," Seamus said.

Obviously, she wasn't going to get a straight answer. She glanced around the room. There were ten or so of them dining in this private room tonight, though she was convinced she was the only one really eating. She suspected Seamus of sipping the wine and bisque and dumping the salmon in his napkin, since she hadn't actually seen a single bite go past his lips. Yet somehow it was disappearing from his plate.

"I wonder what's taking Ethan and Alex?" she asked. "I hope Alex isn't giving him a hard time. She can be very overprotective."

"I'm sure Ethan can handle the situation."

The pressure on her bladder overcame her good manners. "Will you excuse me for a minute, Seamus?"

"Certainly." He stood up when she did, which always startled her a little.

Most guys in Vegas wouldn't know chivalry if it bit them in their gambling arm.

"How old are you?" Maybe his good manners were the result of being reared in Regency England or something.

"Thirty-seven." *Times ten.*

Brittany heard the words as if they'd been spoken, but they hadn't. She was sure of it. Dropping her napkin to the table, she said, "Times ten?"

Seamus's eyes went wide. "Pardon me?"

"Times ten. What do you mean?" She knew what he meant, she just wanted to hear him say it out loud—that he was somewhere in the neighborhood of three hundred and seventy years old.

Still standing, Seamus just stared at her. "I don't know what you're talking about."

Jiggling in place, Brittany decided she couldn't pursue it. She was going to wet her pants. Or cocktail dress. Did she have a bladder infection? Good grief, things felt urgent.

"Never mind. I'll be right back."

Walking as fast as she could with a cramped abdomen, she headed toward the hall. There was a powder room down three steps to the left. She'd been in there once before. It was very small, for use with the private dining rooms, and it had the feel of a glamorous forties dressing room.

As she rounded the corner, Brittany came to a startled stop. Reclining on the sofa was a couple, the man making like a throw rug on the woman. Lots of draping and clinging and soft murmurs. Embarrassed, Brittany hung back.

She should just leave, but the closest restroom was in the main dining room, a heck of a hike from where she was. And she really had to go, but Embrace on a Couch over there were a foot from the door she had to open. Maybe if she just sort of slid past them, they'd never even notice.

The man was petting the woman's hair, tilting her head up. Her eyes were closed in ecstasy and Brittany found herself staring way longer than was appropriate. It should have been tacky and base, getting it on splayed out in front of the ladies' room, but instead they looked sensual, even arousing to her. There was something artistic and worshipful about the way he touched his lover.

Until he swabbed her arm with an alcohol pad.

What the hell?

He murmured to the woman, running his lips over hers even as he inserted a syringe into a vein near her elbow, and slowly drew blood into a vial.

Oh, God, she was watching a serial killer. Brittany panicked, frozen against the wall. What should she do? If she screamed, he'd kill her, too. She hadn't brought her purse and there was no one hanging around. Maybe she should just run for help.

Slowly, slowly, she took a step back so she could flee without him noticing.

The man, who was dressed in a suit of all things, reached into his pocket, pulled on some latex gloves, set the vial into a lab tray, and started to dip little strips into it, like they used at the gynecologist to test her urine.

What the . . . ?

Freaking out. She was freaking out. She wished Alex were with her. Alex would kick the guy, break his nose, haul the poor woman out, and demand attention from someone in about two seconds. Brittany was a wimp. She couldn't think, didn't know what to do.

The woman groaned, but her eyes still didn't open.

He shushed her with a soft little sound, then kissed her again, moving down her neck. Then he bit her.

Bit. Her. Oh, ick, she was watching a vampire feed. He was sucking the woman's flesh, drawing her body up toward him, and Brittany felt her legs start to give way.

Knowing they were bloodsucking demons was one thing in *theory*; to see it was another. She made a sound of horror before she could stop herself.

His head snapped up. There was blood, a wet crimson stain, smeared on his pale lips.

Eew. Eew, eew, eew. Brittany felt her face go hot. "I . . . I . . ."

"Leave," he said, in a deep, rich voice, with an accent she didn't recognize. "You never saw me."

That whole vampire mind control thing again. It was starting to bug Brittany. Like she was just going to leave this poor victim bleeding on a hotel couch.

"No. Not until I see that she's okay."

"Pardon?" He looked flummoxed.

He was also French, or maybe French-Canadian, given the way he rolled off his "o" sound.

"Is she okay? Are you a good vampire or a bad one? I've never seen you with Ethan. Does he know you're here?"

Instead of answering her, he peeled off his gloves inside out, inserted the strips and the vial into the fingers of the latex, and tucked the whole neat package back into his pocket. He put his hand out toward her. "Leave."

"Stop that. I'm not leaving. I can help you." Sympathy overcame her fear. How awful it must be to face eternity, soulless and lusting for blood. It must be like fighting a drug or alcohol addiction.

He tilted his head, stared at her with brilliant green-gray eyes. "It's nothing like drug addiction. Now tell me who you are and why I can smell vampire all over you."

She smelled like vampire? That was kind of gross. She should shower again before she went to bed.

"Um . . . I'm Brittany Baldizzi." The confused and frightened. "Why did you test her blood?"

"I cannot talk to you." He shook his head, smoothing his hand over the woman's forehead. "You belong to Carrick."

"What do you mean?" she asked, inching toward the woman, afraid he was going to crush her skull. She wasn't sure how she could protect her, or even if the woman was still alive, but she had to do something.

But he leaned back over, murmured into the woman's ear, and disappeared. Suddenly, he was just gone, and Brittany let out a shriek.

"What?" The woman sat up and stared at her in confusion. "What's the matter?"

"I'm sorry . . . I was just going to the restroom and I saw you . . . and him . . ." She was practically incoherent.

"Oh!" The woman flushed, but gave a sly smile. "Is that why he ran off? He's trying to be discreet. No matter. I'll hook up with him later."

"Did he, uh, hurt you?" Brittany asked, rubbing her sweaty palms on her dress.

"Hurts so good." The blonde ran a hand through her tousled hair, and tugged at the bodice of her dress. Leaning on the wall, she sighed with satisfaction. "That was a first for me. I've never come just from a man kissing me before."

"Oh!" Well. Um. Getting her blood drawn had never once made Brittany feel orgasmic. "Does he do that often to you?" *Suck your blood and make you climax?*

"No. I've been flirting with him for weeks. I'm a waitress in the Shadow Lounge and he comes in most nights. Tonight I pretty much threw myself at him, and I'm so glad he caught me. Though it sucks he left. Things were just getting good."

"Sorry."

The busty blonde, her curves bursting out of a shiny metallic top, laughed. "No biggie. You just had to pee, right? Can't fault you for that."

Brittany looked at the woman. "Right." Only she didn't have to go to the bathroom anymore. That urge was completely gone as if it had never existed.

Now she was strangely hungry instead.

Four

Alexis knew her ass was bigger than Buffy's, but she had to go with what she had. If Ethan Carrick wanted to play vampire games, she'd give him his little thrill for the night. If he wanted to be a vampire, then she would be a vampire slayer.

Now wearing jeans and a silky camisole top that attempted to make the most out of her breasts, she did a slot machine here and there on the main casino floor, moving closer to the elevator banks. After letting Carrick think he had persuaded her to give it all up, go home, and leave her sister to him, Alexis had, in fact, gone home. But only to change her clothes and formulate a plan.

Five minutes alone with Brittany. That's all she needed to convince her sister to return to her normally scheduled life, sans Ethan Carrick and his creepy Goth crew.

Alone was the key. With Ethan hovering all the time, making her lips tingle, Alexis knew she was going to have problems convincing

Brittany to leave, so she had to get to her sister when no one else was around.

Winning two dollars on a slot, Alexis printed her ticket and tried to look nonchalant. Casually, very casually—she was so good at this subterfuge thing—she inserted herself into a crowd of drunk, laughing women getting on the elevator. At least she thought they were drunk, but maybe the giggles were just from having a good time. Since Alexis didn't really know how to have a good time, she wasn't really sure.

She pushed the button for the twenty-second floor.

"Dang, I shouldn't have worn a bra," one woman said, reaching into her dress with both hands and tugging.

Alexis guessed her accent was from Texas, her dress from New York.

"So take it off," one of her companions suggested. "Since you had your lift, you should be fine without it."

"There are other people on this elevator," the woman said with great dignity, before dissolving into giggles.

Other people must mean Alexis, because they all seemed to know each other.

"I don't care if you do," Alexis told her. "But there's probably a camera somewhere in here."

"Really? I never thought about that." And the woman proceeded to peel down the front of her bodice, rip off her bra, and shake her ta-tas in a slow three-sixty. "Got to catch every angle. I'm not sure which is my best breast side."

Her three girlfriends screamed and laughed. Alexis watched with horror, and oh, my God, envy. When in her thirty years of life had she ever done anything impulsive, goofy, shocking?

Never, because it always seemed like frivolity belonged to her mother, and not since she was five years old had Alexis wanted to be anything like her mother. But there was a difference between her irresponsible mother and these women, who were just having fun. In their forties and looking fabulous, they were clearly enjoying life.

Did Alexis enjoy her life?

Sort of.

She liked her job, felt satisfaction when she won a case and a person who had committed a crime was forced to serve time for that.

She was proud of Brittany, that she had become a dentist, and was happy and well-adjusted, and normally didn't do anything to give Alexis worry. Normally.

But did Alexis enjoy her life?

She wasn't sure.

The elevator opened on the nineteenth floor and the women got off, the brazen one having pulled her dress back up. But she left her bra lying in the middle of the floor with a "that should get people talking."

Alexis moved gingerly around the black lace bra, hoping no one would get on the elevator and think it was hers. She couldn't imagine ditching a bra—that was like throwing thirty bucks on the floor of the elevator.

Brittany was right. She was wound too tight.

Feeling a little melancholy and edgy, she got off at the twenty-second floor, looked around, gave a startled, "Oh! This isn't right," in case anyone was witnessing her, and turned to the private elevator.

Hitting the up button, she hoped James, the ham-fisted security guard, wasn't hanging around. He would recognize her. She didn't think he was swift enough to figure out what she was doing, but nonetheless, he'd probably call Carrick.

But no one yelled or grabbed her shoulder, so she figured she was safe. The door slid open, she rushed on, and saw this elevator only went to floors twenty-three to twenty-six. Bingo.

She wasn't sure what she would do if Brittany refused to come with her. Probably have a cow. The whole situation was disturbing on many levels, not the least of which was that in the past, Brittany had always looked to her for advice. Alexis had been able to influence Brittany, guide her, help her make the right decisions. It was really scary that suddenly her baby sister seemed to be thinking on her own. And not very well, given that she was hooking up with a Gothic cult.

"Twenty-three twenty . . ." She scanned the hall, heading left when she saw which way the room numbers went.

The carpeting was thick, with black-and-white Art Deco squares, but it still felt like her footsteps were echoing loudly in the hushed hallway. Since this floor was private, the space between doors was farther, and each suite was tucked into a little alcove, with a gunmetal gray placard affixed to the wall next to it with the number on it. Alexis had to admit, as far as tacky casinos went, Carrick's wasn't so bad. She kind of liked the Old Hollywood theme, with its sleek furniture and plush glamour.

Just for one day, it might be nice to trade in her short, big-in-the-booty body, and her tough-talking prosecutor lingo for long legs, a slinky dress, some wicked red lipstick, and a sultry voice that made men drool.

Yeah, like that was going to happen.

And she sure in the hell wouldn't want to live like that for more than one day. Smoldering looks would get exhausting after a while.

But a date here and there would be nice. Only the men she came into contact with were either smooth-talking defense attorneys or criminals. She wasn't willing to take a chance on a repeat offender, no matter how attractive he might be in a beige jumpsuit. And defense attorneys made her gums itch.

A man stepped out of the alcove directly next to her. "This is a surprise."

After swallowing a scream, Alexis glared at Ethan Carrick. Damn it, she was one freaking door away from Brittany's room. Which meant Carrick's room was next to Brittany's, which kind of made her want to throw up. How could her sister be having sex with this man?

And why couldn't she be having sex with anybody?

"Hello." Even though her heart was beating just a wee bit faster than normal, she gave him a casual smile and started on past him. Not doing anything here . . .

"I thought that you went home." He stepped in front of her.

"I did." She moved left to get around him.

He shifted, blocking her way. "Then why are you back?"

She moved right. Again he blocked her.

"Look at us, we're dancing," she said in exasperation. "Will you just move?"

Ethan had changed into jeans and a black T-shirt, which showed every one of the well-defined muscles in his long and lean chest and arms. An expensive watch, with a diamond here and there, flashed on his wrist. There was a darkness in his eyes that she didn't understand, and didn't like.

"Tell me why you're here and I'll move."

Might as well be honest. They were going to get into it whether she told the truth or made up some bullshit story. "Okay, here's the thing. You like to pretend you're a vampire. So I'm pretending to be a vampire slayer. And I'm going to get my sister and take her back to her apartment, where she belongs, away from this freaking fun house."

She expected a little more of a reaction. He didn't move, except for his left eyebrow, which rose half an inch. "You don't look like you have a stake tucked in that slinky shirt you're wearing."

Jerk. "Maybe I have holy water and I'm going to throw it in your face."

"If you'd like, go ahead. I'm sure it would be refreshing."

"I really think that I hate you," she said, his flippant attitude getting the best of her.

"And here I thought we were getting along so well."

And she didn't understand why being around him reduced her to a frustrated eight-year-old.

Yet it did, and she faked to the left, then ran to the right, in a move any football player would be proud of.

Only Ethan didn't fall for the fake. He quickly stuck his hand up to block her passage. It was a block, all right, but he also succeeded in grabbing her breast. Just a perfect lineup—his hand, her breast, like a ball and a glove, and she made some kind of startled yelp like a tortured yeti.

For the first time all evening, Alexis actually saw Ethan Carrick lose his cool. While she felt her face flame, and her entire body went stiff, he dropped both his hand and his lower jaw.

"I apologize . . . that was not intentional . . ." He frowned, obviously at a loss for words, and man, oh man, did that make her happy.

So what that she'd had to get accidentally felt up to reduce him to this? It was worth it, and so amusing to see him struggling and embarrassed. She suddenly felt a whole lot better about old Ethan. It said a lot to her that he could have the decency to turn a little craven after grabbing her boob.

She couldn't stop herself from grinning. "Well, that was good for me. How about you?"

Astonishment crossed his face, but quickly turned to laughter. "You have an interesting sense of humor. Wittier than your sister."

The mention of her sister should have restored her anger, but it didn't. Not really. Alexis felt she had regained the upper hand, or at least stood on even footing with Ethan, and that made her less inclined to violence. "Brittany is very naive. Her mind doesn't go in the same lowly directions mine does. Which is why she's completely wrong for you. Once you get tired of sleeping with her, you'll be done with her, and I don't want to see her hurt."

"You do know that she wants to stay." Those pale blue eyes of his darkened to denim. "And I think, despite your denials, you can understand the attraction."

Alexis worked a heavy eye roll. "So you've said Brittany wants to stay. But I'm not convinced of that. And I was being sarcastic when I said I enjoyed your touch. It was a joke, Bite Boy."

The smile that played around his lips was smug. "You liked it."

"No, I didn't. I don't find you even remotely attractive. You're like my driver's license. I can't avoid you, you cost me time and money, and no matter what I do, you make me look bad. You're a necessary evil. For the moment."

"There's nothing evil at all about me."

She was so ready to move on. "I would have thought that was the attraction to the whole vampire club—'Look at us, we're evil, we're so bad, don't mess with us.'" Alexis ducked under his arm to get to Brittany's room. "Give me a break."

Ethan let her take two steps, then found himself speaking. "I'll cut Brittany loose if you'd like. Tell her to go home."

He leaned against the wall, knowing he was taking a risk, but intrigued by Alexis Baldizzi. He saw shades of himself in her—the determination, the righteousness, the absolute indignation. As a more experienced vampire now, he had suppressed the wildness, the fiery crusading of his youth, and had vowed to use diplomacy to seek the changes he sought.

After nine hundred years he well understood the world was not black and white, the way Alexis saw it.

Yet despite that difference, Alexis stirred passion in him, roused an urge to do something asinine and showy, like leaping off the top of his hotel just because he could, or flying to Paris without the use of a plane just to feel the wind rushing past him. He wanted to tear her clothes off, roll around in a sweaty mass of sheets, and bite her all over her body.

Fortunately, she didn't look willing.

Or unfortunately, because he couldn't stop himself from wanting to convince her she wanted him. Or to admit she wanted him, if she already did want him. It was absurd. But then again, no woman had ever looked him straight in the eye and told him he was unattractive before, and it felt a little like he'd sat on a burr. Not a pleasant feeling.

Pride could get him into trouble with this one.

"Why would you tell Brittany to leave?" she asked cynically. "Because you want me to beg you to do it? Forget it. I'll kick your ass before I beg."

It would be interesting to let her try to kick his ass, as she so eloquently put it, but unnecessary. "No, no begging required. Just that you play the game in Brittany's place." If she thought it was some kind of rich man's hobby, playing vampire, he'd let her believe that. For now.

"What?" Her hands went on her hips. "What the hell have you been smoking? I have a life, a career, court cases. I can't play Barbie. Besides, I don't have the legs for it."

"I don't expect you to forsake your career." He still had a bit of an old-fashioned fascination with a woman doing man's work, but he could certainly see how Alexis would be successful. Lawyers were argumentative, tenacious, and convinced they were right. That was an accurate assessment of Alexis.

"What I'm suggesting is you return here at the end of every day. You have dinner with me, stroll the casino with me, entertain guests. Sleep in the room next to mine."

"You want me to have sex with my sister's lover after she gets dumped by him? By you. That's sick. Twisted."

He supposed he should have clarified that earlier. "I have never taken your sister to my bed. We have a platonic friendship, and I apologize for misleading you earlier."

She rolled her eyes. "Whatever."

"Can we discuss this in my room? Brittany could step out into the hall at any moment, and I don't imagine she would appreciate this discussion." He opened the door to his suite and smiled.

"Don't close the door behind us."

Obviously not trusting him to follow that order, she actually picked up a ceramic hound statue he had standing sentry to his living room, and plunked it down in front of the door. It held the door wide open, and she surveyed her work.

"Nice dog."

"Thanks."

She pointed. "Go first."

To humor her, he did, but he hovered in front of the sofa. He would not sit down until she did. There were childhood lessons, inherent manners, that just couldn't be erased, no matter how long he lived.

"It looks like a British hunting lodge in here."

That was rather the point. "I tried to emulate my home in England."

"From what? The nineteenth century?" She flopped on an easy chair and turned sideways in it, so her legs hooked over one arm, and the other acted like a backrest.

Inviting her in had been a stupid idea. Now his suite was going to smell like her—like her smooth, human flesh, and her pulsing, hot blood. That was his favorite chair and he was probably going to have to burn it now. Otherwise every time he sat in it, he was going to be hungry. For Alexis.

He never had mortals in his room. Even his maid was a vampire, because she could clean at night when he was out and about, and she wouldn't balk at the blood stored in his refrigerator.

"So if you don't believe me, you can ask Brittany. We haven't . . ." He searched for a delicate phrasing. "Been intimate."

"You're trying to tell me Brittany has been living right next to you for three weeks and you haven't once banged her?"

So much for delicate. "That's what I'm telling you. Not even a kiss. As I said, I apologize for misleading you about our relationship earlier." Ethan knew when to be honest, and if he had any chance of coaxing the delicious Alexis into his bed, he had to reassure her that Brittany had not been there first.

What the hell was he saying? He was not supposed to be sleeping with anyone. He was wooing. He was mature, responsible, a post-randy vampire president ready to settle down into marriage.

Right after he banged Alexis.

"Then why the hell is she here if you're not 'intimate'?"

She used Seamus's habit of quote marks in the air, which irritated him since Seamus was yet another reminder of all his responsibilities, all that was expected of him.

"Because I'm a Master Vampire, over two hundred years old and therefore eligible to run for the presidency. Brittany is a half-vampire, the daughter of a mortal mother and a vampire father." That was more than he'd intended to tell her, but he wanted to see her reaction. Wanted to fish around for information since he still didn't have any access to her thoughts.

But Alexis just snorted. "Brittany's father was a prick, but he wasn't a vampire."

"You would say that about your father?"

"Not my father. Brittany's father. We have the same mother, but different sperm donors. Neither father is worth dwelling on. My mom had appalling taste in men."

That explained quite a bit. It also meant that Alexis probably had no vampire blood in her. He couldn't know for sure, since he couldn't get inside her head, couldn't sense anything about her, but it seemed likely she was pure mortal.

"But this is a game, remember? And Brittany is a half-vampire. I intended to recruit her to the position of my wife, first lady of the Vampire Nation."

Alexis just stared at him. "You don't really believe in this stuff, do you? Because I'm going to call the cops and tell them you kidnapped my sister if you do. A weird hobby is one thing, but if you're delusional, I'm calling Metro Police."

"I know the difference between truth and fiction," he said in a soothing voice. He didn't want her bolting and taking Brittany with her. Nor did he want any close encounters with the police. While he could fool most humans, he didn't want to test his ability to hide his vampire traits long-term in a jail cell. Dining on the guards wouldn't earn him any early release points.

"But I'm up for reelection, and as I've been known in the past as a bad-tempered vampire, prone to certain playboy tendencies, my campaign manager and I agreed I needed a woman by my side. To soften my image."

"Well, Brittany would be good for that. I would suck at it." Her feet kicked up in the air as she lounged in the chair.

That little scrap of nothing shirt had slipped to the side, exposing the swell of her breast. He could sink his teeth in there, with a firm bite, and his fangs would puncture like into a soft apple. He wished that when he bit, there were sound, sort of a crisp, powerful crunch instead of soundless sliding into flesh.

Chomping on Alexis would be very satisfying.

He crossed his legs, uncomfortable now that he had a raging erection.

This was not the original plan, coaxing Alexis into Brittany's place, but already he liked this one much better. The thrill of the chase, the satisfaction of finally catching her—he looked forward to both with an anticipation that wasn't befitting the staid middle-age vampire he was supposed to be. "Actually, you would be even better. Sister of an Impure and a career woman. Perfect. If I have a confident businesswoman by my side, they will see that I have really matured if I allow my partner to have equal say in our relationship."

Not that he was feeling very mature. He was acting more along the lines of a teenage boy looking to score than a responsible adult vampire. You'd think he'd been having Seamus's dry spell the way he was behaving.

"So, you've always been a dictatorial asshole and now you want people to think you're more willing to compromise?"

Not the words he would have chosen, but he was trying to be charming and agreeable. He wanted this woman. Despite the fact that Seamus would kill him, and his spontaneous plan was less than foolproof, he had to have her. Would have her. "Exactly."

"So you play pussy-whipped and I play bossy girlfriend? That could be fun." She grinned, tucking her blond hair behind her ears.

He was having a midlife crisis. That's what this was. There was no other explanation for why that statement suddenly made him feel like the horniest vampire in North America. Lusting after much younger women, good God. Next he'd be buying a sports car and getting a tattoo.

"I think a lot of things between us could be fun."

"One week. I'll stay for one week if you agree to let Brittany leave and never have any future contact with her, personal or professional. I get my own room, with a master key so no one else can enter at any time. If I have to work late, I have to work late and you'll just have to get over it, but I will be here from eight P.M. to eight A.M. every day for seven days. I'll depart at midnight on Friday, the seventeenth, because tonight counts as night one. You provide me access to dining in the casino restaurants for free and dry-cleaning services. I'll draw up a contract for you to sign and failure to comply with any of my terms will result in me identifying you as a cult, potentially holding people against their will. Do you understand and agree to all terms?"

And here he'd been worried he was taking advantage of her concern for Brittany. Alexis could take care of herself. He drummed his thumb on his knee. "Anything else?"

"Yeah. Just so we're clear, I'm not having sex with you. I am not interested in you as anything other than a means to an end. This escort service has no fringe benefits other than me smiling at your weirdo friends."

That's what she thought.

So she found him unattractive, did she?

Well, he would just show Alexis Baldizzi that Ethan Carrick was a man who knew how to treat a woman.

"I had no intention of using you in such a crude fashion. I confess myself shocked."

She rolled her eyes and sat up. "Somehow I don't think a whole lot would shock you. You're like me that way—I've seen everything and then some."

"You're a prosecutor, right?"

"Yes. Sex crimes. There are a lot of sickos in this world, Carrick, and I've met quite a few of them. So your vampire games don't surprise me. As long as you're not biting people or something whacked out like that, what you do is your business. But not with my sister around. That's the bottom line—Brittany goes home."

"I agree to all your terms." This was probably one of the worst ideas he'd gotten since that time he'd gone coffin sledding in France nine hundred years ago, but it was done.

And he found himself really looking forward to getting to know Alexis better.

Maybe then he could shake off the boredom and discontent that encircled him like a tight leash, growing tighter and tighter.

Maybe an affair with Alexis would satisfy his growing tactile urges and prevent him from doing something bizarre like dying his hair, dating his secretary, or getting his chest waxed.

He was *not* having a midlife crisis.

Five

Brittany was starting to think she shouldn't have let Alexis talk her into leaving. They were driving on U.S. 95 toward Alexis's house in Summerlin and all she could think about was that man—that vampire—and how he had caressed the woman outside the restroom, suckling her, making her moan with pleasure while he drank her blood.

It had been like watching two people have sex—embarrassing, arousing, shocking. Exciting. And that disturbed her . . . What those people were was wrong—soulless, evil—yet she was fascinated by them, and she had to do something.

"I need to go back." She had agreed to leave only because Alexis had threatened never to speak to her again—which they both knew was a lie, but if Alexis was worried enough to say it, Brittany knew it was serious. She never wanted to cause Alexis worry. Her sister had had her childhood yanked away from her way too early, and she'd spent a lot of years stressing about money and Brittany, when she should have been dating and having fun.

So Brittany had left the hotel because she didn't want to see that look in Alexis's eye, the frantic concern that made her look older than she was. But she couldn't get the image out of her head of the man with the expensive suit, rich caramel hair, and a little lab kit in his pocket.

There had to be a way to form an intervention or something. But first she needed to know everything about Vegas vampires. If she understood them and their ways, she could figure out how to save their souls. And the only way to learn about them was to spend time with them.

"Over my dead body," Alexis said, turning into the driveway of her stucco house, the garage light glowing in the dark. She opened the car door and cursed. "Flipping yucca bush! I hate this ugly, spiky plant. I can't believe the landscaper put it right where I park the car and need to get out. I hit it every single time."

She forced her way out of the car.

"Alex . . ." Brittany bit her lip.

Her sister stopped whacking at the foliage with her purse and bent over to stare at her suspiciously. "What? You've got that pretty girl wants something voice going on."

"I have to go back." Lives depended on it. She might be just a dentist, and too trusting, according to Alex, but there was a reason she had met Ethan Carrick. A reason he had invited her to his hotel, and she didn't think it had anything to do with oral hygiene.

It was a cry for help, and she had to answer it.

Alexis saw the stubborn tilt to Brittany's chin, and the very impressive pout her lower lip was creating. She knew that look. Had caved under it many, many times. But this she couldn't compromise on.

"No."

"I'll go on my own."

"I'll lock you in my spare bedroom."

"No, you won't." Brittany scoffed.

Shit, she was right. Alexis would never do that. "You're serious?"

"Very."

"You'd go back without me?"

"Yes."

Then Alexis had no choice. She sighed. Leaned on her car door. Crossed her arms.

Despite her earlier conversation with Ethan, once she had Brittany out of the hotel, she had rethought the whole staying with him thing. If she had Brittany out on her own powers of persuasion, what did she need him for?

Nothing. Her whole willingness to stay had been based on his offer to kick Brittany out. So when that became unnecessary, she had figured their little agreement was just null and void.

Brittany's one-eighty changed things again.

"Alright, how about I go back? You stay here and I'll take your place at the hotel and keep an eye on them." That was a little vague, but she was just feeling Brittany out for the time being.

Brittany wasn't buying it. "Alex. I want to find a cure for their vampirism. Not prosecute them."

Here's where it got dicey. "Who said anything about prosecution? I could do that—cure them." Maybe a high kick to the head would solve their problems. "I'm persuasive."

"If that's what you want to call it." Brittany still wouldn't get out of the car, just sat there in her cocktail dress, long legs crossed.

Alexis couldn't imagine where Brittany got her stubbornness. Alexis would have thought she herself had drained the family gene pool of that particular trait long before Brittany was born.

"Okay, here's the thing." Alexis wiped her hands on her jeans and prepared to eat crow for her sister's sake. "Ethan, well, he, uh, invited me to dinner. As his date."

Brittany's face lit up. "Alex! That's wonderful. When was the last time you went on a date? Like six years ago?"

It hadn't been that long. Surely there had been someone . . . like Jim back in law school . . . okay, so that had been six years. Damn. "I was thinking maybe I need to open myself up to new experiences." There, that sounded like Brittany-speak. All warm and fuzzy and full of self-realization.

Brittany got out of the car finally, thank God, and winked at her. "That's not all you're going to be opening, if you know what I mean."

"Brittany Anne!" Crap, she was blushing. Mostly because she'd had a flash of memory of being under Ethan, her body hot and humming. She had so been lying when she'd said she wasn't attracted to him.

Brittany grabbed her suitcase out of the backseat and giggled.

"It's dinner, not a night of wild monkey sex."

"I bet vampires have great stamina."

"I'm sure they do." But Ethan wasn't a vampire, because vampires didn't exist, and she wasn't going to sleep with him anyway. "And if you really think he's a vampire, you shouldn't be encouraging me to have dinner with him."

"Why not? He's a great guy. Very charming, with loads of manners. You could do worse."

"What if he sucks my blood?" Alexis asked.

"He hasn't sucked my blood yet." Brittany carried her suitcase toward the open garage door. "Besides, vampires put a glamour on you when they do it. You don't feel anything but pleasure."

"That sounds like kinky shit to me, and I don't do kinky. Nobody's putting a glamour on me if they value their life." Not that they could, because they weren't really vampires. It. Was. A. Game.

"If they want to put a glamour on you, they can. But don't worry, I don't think he would do that to you. If Ethan invited you to eat dinner, he's much too well mannered to *make* you dinner, you know what I mean, sweetie?"

Jesus. Brittany was making her head spin. And the words *eat* and *Ethan* in the same sentence weren't a good direction to be sending her libido in.

Alexis opened the interior door in the garage and walked into her white-on-white kitchen. "All I know is that someday you're going to settle down and marry an accountant and have cute, black-haired babies, and a little house in Boulder City, and I am going to breathe a huge sigh of relief." She tossed her keys on the counter and wondered what was appropriate to pack for a week with a bunch of psychos playing an adult version of Dungeons & Dragons. Her wardrobe was sadly lacking in velvet capes.

Vampires. Please.

Brittany startled her by throwing her arms around her from behind and giving her a big hug. "Alex, you know I love you. You're the best sister in the universe, and I don't mean to make you worry."

She patted Brittany's arms and felt the sudden embarrassing rush of hot tears to her eyes. "I love you, too, Brit. And I mean it about the accountant."

"Yeah, right." Brittany let her go and laughed. "The day I marry an accountant is the day you marry Ethan Carrick."

Alexis winced. Damn, she really hated to let go of the Brittany-accountant fantasy.

From his vantage point at the blackjack table, Ringo watched Ethan Carrick emerge from the private elevator with his right-hand man at 10 P.M. just as he did every night. Carrick was a creature of habit, and Ringo appreciated that.

Made his job easier, that Carrick took his so seriously.

Ringo took his job seriously, too, and could be considered a workaholic by some. But he didn't do anything stupid, and what Donatelli wanted was stupid. Nodding to the dealer, he kept an eye on Carrick as he moved around the casino floor, chatting to an employee here and there. Ringo inhaled from his cigarette before resting it in the glass ashtray.

Another reason he loved Vegas. He could smoke wherever the fuck he wanted. None of that huddling around a garbage can with twelve other people outside a crowded restaurant freezing his balls off. Here he could blow his secondhand smoke in anybody's face he felt like, and he appreciated that.

"You look like you're doing pretty good," a perky voice said next to him.

Glancing to his left, he noticed that a skinny brunette had taken the vacant seat, previously occupied by an ancient oil refinery owner. This woman was easier on the eyes than old Arthur had been, he'd admit that, but he didn't like to chitchat when he was working.

"Not bad," he said in a cool tone.

"Enough to buy me a drink," she said with a giggle.

Ringo stifled his irritation. He hated women who giggled. It was like air escaping from a tire, a signal that, once expelled, nothing but an empty shell would remain.

This girl definitely didn't look too heavy in the IQ department, even if she had a pretty face, shiny black hair, and breasts that were too large to be natural on her thin frame. Yet he didn't think she was a hooker. There was too much genuine mischief in her eyes, a lusty sort of hunger hovering around her face.

Probably one of the girls who were dead broke, and enjoyed milking men out of meals and drinks, then leaving them panting and desperate. Ringo wasn't desperate for anything. Hadn't been since he'd left the Marines and half of his humanity behind.

With a flick of his wrist, he flipped a twenty-dollar chip toward her. "Go buy yourself a drink, gorgeous. And leave me alone to concentrate before I lose this whole pile because I'm staring at you instead of the wheel."

She took the chip, wrapping her fist around it and caressing it with her thumb. "Thanks. I'll be back with your change, cutie."

Yeah, right. Giggles was going to pocket that change, no doubt in his mind. But he didn't care, because she was blocking his view of Carrick. As he picked up his cigarette and took a hit, she blew him a kiss with moist, cherry red lips, and sashayed off.

Damn. He couldn't see Carrick anymore. He'd left the floor.

Not that it mattered, really. Carrick did the same thing every night, and he never left his casino. Ever. He was a rich, young, reclusive nut-job. And contrary to Donatelli's crazy decapitation request, Ringo was going to plug the casino owner with a bullet, right to the heart. Dead was dead, and a bullet was cleaner than that mess Donatelli wanted.

The Italian was an eccentric client—he supposed they all were—and demanding, but Ringo knew his job, and he'd do it the right way. The low-risk way.

"I'm back. Did you miss me?" Giggles reappeared a minute later, a martini in one hand and a five-dollar bill in the other, which she set in front of him.

"Not at all," he told her truthfully, taking a hit from the dealer on his hand.

She giggled. "I'm Kelsey. I work here."

If she started singing for him, he was going to shoot himself.

"Yeah?" He might as well have said, "I don't give a shit," but that didn't stop Kelsey.

"I'm a receptionist. Bet you thought I was a dancer or something, didn't you?" She winked at him. "I know how men are. But seriously, I'm a receptionist. For Mr. Carrick, the casino owner. I answer the phones," she added helpfully, like he lived under a rock and might not know what a receptionist was.

Stabbing his butt out in the ashtray, he turned a little and gave her half of his attention instead of a tenth. "You like your job, Kelsey? Mr. Carrick a good boss?"

He had no intention of involving Kelsey in his plans, but maybe she could tell him the layout of the private floors, and where Carrick went for dinner every night, since he didn't seem to eat in any of the hotel restaurants.

And if she was his receptionist/lover, why was she trolling his casino for sugar daddies? Carrick was a big-ass sugar daddy in his own right with his two-thousand-room hotel and ten-million-a-day casino.

"Oh, he's the best boss. I'll never leave him," she said solemnly.

Ringo could practically hear the rocks in her head rattling. "You're doing it again," he reprimanded, going over twenty-one on his hand. "Distracting me from my game."

"Sorry." She laughed, her lips around a swizzle stick, licking martini juice from the tip. "I'll be a good girl and behave." With a twist of her wrist, she made as if she were zipping her lips shut.

It was too easy. Carrick's receptionist landing in his lap. Maybe she had been sent to distract him.

That seemed far-fetched. Carrick didn't know who the hell he was.

But it made sense to keep an eye on Kelsey. "Never behave, gorgeous, that would be a waste on you. Let me close out here and we'll go grab a table and get to know each other a little better."

Zipped lips were forgotten. "Cool!" She leaned over and kissed him quickly. "I like the way you smell," she murmured against his mouth.

Then she giggled again.

Six

Alexis stared at the itinerary in front of her and decided Carrick was weirder than she'd given him credit for.

7 P.M.   Assemble in Sinatra room for reception line.

8 P.M.   Fundraising dinner, open only to conservatives supporting President Carrick's reelection.

11 P.M. Benefit concert with special guests, The Suckers, to support campaign financing.

There was then a long list of what she could and could not do, including an insistence that she wear pantyhose—like her underwear was anyone's flippin' business but hers—and the pearls provided for her in the room safe, key on the dresser.

If this were a bid for the U.S. Senate, or a gubernatorial race, she could hang with it. It would make sense.

But none of this was real. They were pretending to elect a president of a Vampire Nation that was a flipping figment of their seriously corroded imaginations. She was so glad Brittany was safe at home, far away from this bunch.

Brittany hoped she didn't bump into Alex. Her sister would kill her if she found out she had come back to The Ava. But she couldn't stop herself. She had to understand what was going on. She had to help them, even if she put herself at risk.

Which didn't really explain why she was back in the hallway by the bathroom, where she had seen that man and woman the night before. Biting her lip, she looked around the empty space.

Had she really thought he'd just be standing here? And why was she so anxious to see him?

Okay, that was obvious. She thought he was hot. Sexy. A hard body.

But he was also a vampire, and she had to remember that first and foremost.

Which was why she screamed—just a little—when two seconds later he came around the corner.

He started, then stopped in front of her. Studied her. "You are ze woman from last night. Carrick's woman."

French accent wasn't helping her stay focused. Brittany clenched her legs together and nodded. "Yes. But I'm not Carrick's woman . . . my sister is." Sort of. But she didn't want tall, dark, and Francophile to get the wrong idea about her.

"Who ez your sister?"

"Alexis Baldizzi." Brittany swallowed. Maybe this wasn't such a brilliant idea after all. They were kind of alone here. "She's a lawyer. A *prosecutor*."

"You are Brittany then?"

All she could manage was a nod.

"I was born in Brittany, in France, you know." With that, he turned as if to leave.

"Wait! Who are you? Why aren't you at Ethan's parties? And why did you draw that woman's blood like that?"

One second he was three feet away, the next he was flush against her, his finger over her mouth. Her breath left her nostrils in startled gasps, blowing down on his flesh. His finger jiggled on her warm lips, tickling her.

"Hush, Brittany. Use some sense about where we are."

Then she was flying backward, wind rushing past her ears, eyes stinging, legs completely off the ground.

Alexis opened the door to Ethan's polite request and glared at him. "I'm not wearing these pearls."

"Why not?" He entered the room with confident strides and glanced at her chest, she hoped just to study the offending necklace.

"I look like Barbara Bush. And no offense to Babs or anything, she seems like a lovely woman, but she has about forty years on me."

The dress she was wearing was blue, and normally she thought it was flattering to her blond hair, but tonight she felt dowdy. Short-legged.

"The pearls probably would look better with a black dress."

And he was the fashion police? Hell if she was changing now. "Tough. This is the only evening dress I brought. I didn't know you all were so serious about this crap. This isn't *Buffy the Vampire Slayer*, it's more like *The West Wing*. Only with weirdos instead of actors."

"I just meant perhaps we should change your necklace." He went over to the safe in the closet, looking damn dapper in his tux.

Alexis grimaced at herself in the full-length mirror and sucked in her gut. Could you say *pear*? Ugh. Or blueberry, given the color of her dress. And why couldn't her hair just once cooperate and lay down straight without frizzing? And why in the hell did she care?

She was driving herself nuts.

Ethan's fingers on the back of her neck didn't help either. Sometimes he moved too fast for her taste. She couldn't gauge his next movement. Now he was all fingers here, and touching there on the back of her neck, whisking off the pearls and draping her in diamonds.

Hel-lo. Somehow it seemed like she should reject the necklace, given that it made her feel a little bit like a paid companion. But at the same time, she liked it. She liked the way his eyes changed to match the depth of the blue in her dress as he leaned over her shoulder, brushed her hair aside, watched her in the mirror for her reaction.

Bad news, that's what Ethan Carrick was.

"Since you're staring so intently, can I assume you like the diamonds?"

"No. I was just trying to figure out which was more nouveau riche—the necklace or you."

He chuckled. "Cute. Very cute."

That was a word just made to irritate her. Cute was for puppies and bunnies and little things. So when his lips brushed the back of her neck, she cracked the side of his face with her knuckles.

"Knock it off, Carrick." She stepped away from him. "Now let's go downstairs and get this farce over with."

Ethan looked neither surprised nor upset by her backhand or her words. "You're quite skilled at this bossy girlfriend role."

"Don't you forget it."

🦇

Ethan smiled and greeted a South American dignitary whose title suddenly eluded him, and pressed the small of Alexis's back.

"I'm Alexis Baldizzi, it's a pleasure to meet you, Mr. Raul-Fortunato. Did you have a pleasant flight to Nevada?"

"Absolutely." Mr. Raul-Fortunato beamed.

They chatted for a minute, Alexis wearing a serene smile and murmuring platitudes like she'd been born a politician's wife.

Yet when Mr. Raul-Fortunato left them to join the other guests, Alexis muttered, "Freak."

And for J. P. Montmarte, the French engineer, she shot, "Chez psycho," at his retreating back.

"Stop it," Ethan told her. "Someone is going to hear you."

"What?" She turned that faux innocence on him. "I'm being perfectly pleasant. Just be sure to wind me up again when the next guest arrives." Moving her arms like a robot, she tilted her head toward him. "See? I'm a windup toy."

He struggled not to grin. "Better windup than blowup."

"This is where I smile at the room and call you an asshole under my breath. See? Doing that right now . . . smile at the pretty guests, Ethan's an asshole . . . yes, I can multitask with the best of them."

An older gentleman Ethan didn't recognize gave Alexis a little wave as he caught her eye from across the room.

Alexis waved back with cheery enthusiasm as she said, "Hi there, Loon. Wacky-Willie. Crazy with a capital C, all of you. And I am, too, for being here with you."

Seamus was glaring at him from the head table, and yet Ethan wanted to laugh. "Alexis, I suggest you relax and enjoy yourself." He couldn't stop himself from stroking his hand across her back. "You look beautiful tonight, by the way. I like the way your back-side looks in this dress. My hand is itching to touch it."

Or smack it with a nice resounding slap on bare skin. Either way would work for him.

"Do it and you die."

"Oh, come on . . . admit you want me to, just a little."

She glanced up at him, eyebrows slightly raised. "Nope. Sorry. Not at all."

It was a lie. It had to be. No woman had ever dismissed him so out of hand. It was starting to irritate him. Well, it had been irritating him since the moment they had met, but it was even worse now because he was wearing a tux, had given her a diamond necklace, and she still looked at him like he was bacterial slime.

"When is the food being served? I'm starving."

Time for her to accept some realities. "There is no dinner. We're vampires. We don't need food to sustain us." Blood was what he needed, and he was starting to suspect he wouldn't be satisfied until he drew some straight from Alexis during a slow sexual mating.

"No food? That sucks." She gave him a sour look. "I'm going to faint if I don't eat something. I only had a yogurt at lunch because I thought this was a real dinner—I mean you called it a dinner—which would mean food to any normal human. You should have told me you all were eating before the party."

Clearly, sex wasn't the first thing on her mind.

Turning, she snatched champagne off a passing waiter's tray. "Geez. No food. What a rip-off."

"I'm sorry. It didn't occur to me to tell you. I'm sure I can get you something sent up from one of the restaurants downstairs. What would you like?"

"I want Frank Sinatra's pepper steak. And a mixed-green salad. Am I going to have to sneak into the bathroom to eat it so I don't embarrass you?"

"The bathroom?" Ethan laughed. "God, no. You can eat in the room down the hall designated for the serving staff to take breaks in. I'll tell everyone you're freshening up."

"While I scarf my food down. Great, just great, Carrick. Thanks for being such a fabulous host. Don't know why I thought I wouldn't enjoy myself."

That was sarcasm, obviously. "Would it make you feel better if I kissed you?" He tried to draw her closer to him.

"Get away from me, pimp." Alexis could turn glaring into an art form. She gave him an inspired look of hatred.

"I like the way your lips part when you're angry," he teased.

"You're a sick man. Go order my food." She left him standing there and went to mingle, which meant tilting her head and doing beauty pageant impersonations for anyone who would talk to her.

Realizing he was just standing there staring at her firm little bottom, Ethan pulled out his cell phone and ordered her food. Frank Sinatra's pepper steak. What a smart-ass.

He liked that about her.

Seven

Alexis was debating the rules of chess with a kooky Russian when Ethan reappeared at her side. "Look, Peter, with all due respect, you can't castle after moving your king."

He shrugged with that cool nonchalance all Russians seemed to have mastered. "Says who?"

"The rules!"

"What rules? Do you have these rules? Can you prove these rules to me?"

"I don't have them right this second up my dress, but I can prove it to you."

"That's a shame there are no rules up that dress, because now I can call you a liar."

Alexis laughed. Peter amused her. He was like an arrogant walrus.

Ethan took her elbow. "I have something to show you, my dear. Please excuse us, Peter."

"Yes, yes, young passion." Peter waved his arm in a grand sweep. "There is nothing like the first flush of mutual sexual desire . . . you go show her your secret something, Carrick, this old Russian understands."

Oh, that was subtle. "Did you pay him to say that?" Alexis asked Ethan. Somehow she wouldn't put it past him.

"No! And I'm quite shocked that he did say that." Ethan nudged Peter. "You're going to get me in trouble here, old chap."

Peter winked at Alexis. "Or laid, which would be better."

"In his dreams," Alexis said before Ethan could reply.

But instead of laughing or getting annoyed with her, Ethan gave her a smoldering look, like the one he had when he'd pinned her on the floor. "Yes, that is definitely a dream of mine. Recurring frequently, I might add."

Damn it, she felt the beginning of a blush rising up her cheeks. "Down, boy. Take me to my dinner." At Peter's smirk, she added, "Food. My pepper steak."

Ethan's shoulders were vibrating as they moved toward the door, like he was having trouble containing an obnoxious laugh. Alexis couldn't even reprimand him because she was having trouble not cracking a grin herself.

They stepped into the hall and a tall, skinny mass of long black hair and legs came at them in a blur.

"Kelsey!" Ethan put his hands up and stopped the blob. "Where are you going in such a hurry?"

A gasp left Kelsey's mouth.

"Calm down," Ethan said. "What's wrong?"

Oh, great, there was going to be some scene with an ex-girlfriend. Just what she wanted to witness while her food was getting cold in some unknown break room.

The brunette gave a sob, than flipped her hair back, exposing her alabaster cheeks and red lips. Really red lips. Like bloody red lips. A wet sheen covered them, and she must not use color stay, because that lipstick had feathered out in the corners of her mouth and . . .

"Wipe your mouth, Kelsey." Ethan pulled out a handkerchief and gently cleaned her off, like she was a child.

"Oh! Sorry, Mr. Carrick." And she burst into tears, great big loud sobs that produced no actual moisture, but made her chest heave and her shoulders shake, and her cleavage come perilously close to bursting out of the tiny black dress that could have doubled as a hair ribbon.

Alexis glanced right and left, wondering where her dinner was and if it would be rude to ask Ethan. She really didn't want to hear whatever conversation was about to ensue.

"What's the matter, Kelsey?" Ethan returned his handkerchief to his pocket and squeezed her hand.

"Mr. Carrick, it's just so awful . . . I'm so glad I found you . . . I was with him and I was, um, eating, and then I heard it. He's going to kill you!" This was capped off with another round of crying.

Very dramatic. And bizarre. But Alexis wouldn't expect anything less from Ethan and Company. "Kill Ethan? A man gave a verbal threat against Mr. Carrick? Does he have a weapon? We should call the cops."

"That isn't necessary," Ethan said, rubbing Kelsey's arms and staring at her.

Kelsey's brow furrowed, and she tipped her head like she was thinking hard or listening to something. "Okay," she said. "I know I'm not supposed to, but he was . . . sorry, Mr. Carrick. I won't do it again." She shuddered. "It was gross. It was like he was empty in there, you know what I mean?"

"Shh. Why don't you go get a drink in the reception room? Find Seamus and tell him what you told me. How did you leave him?"

Kelsey flushed, her pale cheeks staining red. "I just left him. By my desk. I wasn't thinking . . ." She covered her face with her hands and groaned. "I'm so stupid!"

Alexis was getting impatient. "If someone threatened you, we need to call the police. People lose their whole life savings in these casinos sometimes, and then go nuts and shoot the owner or half the people on the floor. You can't dismiss this."

"I'm not dismissing it." Ethan let go of Kelsey and turned to Alexis. "I'll handle it myself with my own casino security. Go back into the reception room with Kelsey, please, and I'll be along shortly."

Without another word or waiting for any response, Ethan headed to the elevators, already flipping open his cell phone and punching in a number.

Alexis looked at Kelsey, still a little confused and uneasy about the whole thing. "Hey, aren't you the chick who sits at the front desk? I remember you from yesterday."

Kelsey nodded. "I'm Kelsey."

"Hi, Kelsey, I'm Alexis. Where did you leave the guy? By your desk, you said? Did you tie him up or what?"

Kelsey bit her lip and shook her head slowly.

Alexis watched the elevator numbers go from twenty-six to

twenty-two in a smooth thirty seconds. It stopped at twenty-two. Ethan was going to confront the man himself, the dumb ass.

"You going to stay here, Kelsey the receptionist, or are you going down with me? Because I'm following Ethan."

So she didn't really like Ethan all that much—that didn't mean she wanted him to get beat up or killed or anything. He could use Alexis "Ball Buster" Baldizzi covering his back with a few quick maneuvers. She had been trained to deflect an attacker, and while she knew Ethan was strong, the odds would be better if she went with him.

"Mr. Carrick told me to go get Mr. Fox. I have to do what he says or I'll get fired. Besides, I don't want to see him again . . . that man."

Alexis pushed the down button on the elevator. "Who is he?"

"I don't know. He didn't tell me his name. I met him down in the casino at the blackjack table and we came up to the office to, uh . . ." Kelsey had the grace to blush.

Putting her hand up, Alexis said, "I don't need details. I know what you mean." She got in the elevator. "Sure you're not coming?"

Kelsey shook her head violently. "I'll get Mr. Fox."

"Suit yourself. See you in five." Alexis waved as the door shut. She slipped her high heels off, leaving one on the floor and wielding the other as a weapon.

Twenty-two was quiet when the door whooshed open, and at the last second, self-preservation made her hang back. Maybe she should leave this to the experts. Then when she glanced out of the elevator, she saw Ethan lying on the floor in front of the reception desk.

"Shit!" Dropping the shoe, she sprinted the twenty feet and fell to her knees. "Ethan? Are you okay?" The room was dim, the office overnight spots on, but not the regular fluorescent day lights.

She crouched over him, heart in her throat. His eyes were closed, and he was very, very still. There was a strange smell in the air that seemed familiar before her brain told her what it was. Blood. Oh, God, that was blood. Patting his head, she didn't see any injury, so she moved down his shoulders and peeled back his black jacket.

"Oh, Jesus." Her stomach rolled over as her hand touched his sopping wet dress shirt. "Ethan?"

He'd been shot. Right near the heart, if the rip in his shirt and the growing circle of blood were any indication. Maybe two times, because it looked like there was another hole slightly right of center and raised. Covering him back up with his jacket, Alexis pushed down on the fabric to stop all that blood from gushing out.

A hot, panicked taste filled her mouth. She didn't have her cell phone. But the reception desk was right behind her. "Hang in there, Ethan, I'm calling 911."

Scrambling up, she tripped on the hem of her dress and hit the desk. Grabbing the phone, she picked it up and hit the buttons. A squawking sounded in her ear. "Damn it!" Maybe she had to dial nine for an outside line or something. It didn't work. The phone yelled at her again. The third try dialing nine plus the number, she got through and breathlessly explained the situation and her location in the casino to the operator.

"Does he have a pulse? I don't know." Stretching the phone cord, she picked up Ethan's wrist and felt around. "I don't feel anything." She didn't feel anything. That was bad.

"Someone will be there momentarily."

"Thank you." Alexis hung up the phone and started digging around in Ethan's neck for a pulse. She had to find one, there had to be one somewhere. He couldn't be dead. That just wasn't believable.

He had been pissing her off five minutes ago and now he couldn't just be dead.

"Where's your pulse, damn it! I really don't like you, you know, but shit, Ethan, I don't want you dead."

There was no pulse or heartbeat, and she could see clearly that his chest wasn't rising and falling either. The tears came then, which shocked the hell out of her. She never cried. And unlike Kelsey, her tears were loud and wet. They blurred her vision as she pressed her hands hard over Ethan's wound, feeling helpless and a little frantic.

"Okay, I'm lying. I do like you . . . in fact, I've been lying when I said I wasn't attracted to you. Every time you look at me, I get that weird sort of tingling sexual awareness. And you may be insane, but you're always polite, and you seem to treat your employees well, so I guess you're not a total pig, and you shouldn't really die. I mean, you're not dead." She waited a second, well aware that Ethan was exhibiting all the obvious signs of death, and that his entire shirt, jacket, and waistband were now drenched with his blood.

Closing her eyes tightly and pulling her hands back, she begged, "You're not dead . . . are you?"

"No. Could you please call Seamus for me? He's number two on my cell phone. It's in my pants pocket."

Alexis screamed and opened her eyes. Ethan was sitting up, resting on his elbows, eyes wide open. "Ethan! How? What . . .

oh, shit, I'm hallucinating. I fainted, didn't I? See, I didn't eat dinner and I drank that champagne, and now I've let my wants replace reality." She had never been unstable before or prone to delusions, so that was the only explanation.

"Never mind, I'll call him myself." Ethan dug his phone out with jerky movements and flipped it open. He pushed a button. "It's me. Can you intercept 911, please? I was shot and Alexis called the EMTs in. Yeah. I'm fine. Thanks."

"Um . . ." Alexis bit the inside of her cheek and tried not to disintegrate into hysterics. "How are you sitting up? Talking? You didn't have a pulse a minute ago!"

Ethan was stripping off his jacket and his blood-soaked dress shirt. When he bared his chest, she gasped. A nasty flesh wound gaped wide open above his heart.

That was absolutely sick looking, all puckered flesh and slimy, coagulating blood. "Oh, crap, that's like a science lab. Dissection 101 . . . God, you must be in so much pain. And how are you even sitting up, and why did you tell Seamus to intercept the EMTs?" Her voice rose shrilly, because even as she stared at the torn flesh of his pectoral muscle, the wound got smaller.

She blinked. Okay, no more champagne for Alexis. Either that or it had been spiked with a friendly little plug of acid. "I don't feel so good."

Because now when she pried her eyes open, the wound was closed. Just gone. Bye-bye. Like it had never been there.

"Alexis." Ethan wiped the blood off his chest and waist with his balled-up shirt and looked her straight in the eye. "I'm a vampire. For real. No game. No pretend. I am a vampire, and I can't be killed with a bullet."

Everything she'd ever eaten in her life threatened to come back up. "Ha ha. Very funny. This is some kind of trick. A joke. Let's make an ass out of Alexis." But even as she said it, she knew it wasn't true. She was a logical person, and what she'd said was illogical. There was no way Ethan could have faked lacking a pulse.

He'd been shot. In the heart. The wound had closed. Which meant the only thing that made sense was if . . .

"I'm a vampire."

Oh, crap. She'd been insulting a vampire for two days. Yelling at him. She'd kicked him in the nuts. "Well. Okay. Lucky you, I guess." She went for a laugh, but it sounded like a bad hyena impersonation.

"In this case, yes." He winced a little as he touched his chest. "I wasn't trying to mislead you, it just seemed easier to let you think I was playing some kind of game."

"Are you all vampires? Seamus, Kelsey, Peter?" She felt betrayed, like everyone else had a secret and didn't bother to tell her. It was prom all over again.

"Everyone at the reception tonight is, yes. It really is a fundraising dinner. I really am president of all registered vampire voters."

"Cool." If she was going to hang with vampires, she might as well go for the head honcho. Alexis dug her fingers into her thigh. This was going to take a mental readjustment. A big one.

Ethan's eyes briefly closed, and he lay back down on the floor. "Sorry, just a little dizzy still. I think I lost too much blood."

Alexis didn't have a response for that. "Sorry" seemed trite and she had no idea where vampires replenished lost blood . . . oh, yuck. Yes, she did.

Ethan looked pale, his lips parted and still. His face was contorted in lines of discomfort. Alexis rolled her eyes, checked out the ceiling. Wiped her sweaty palms on her dress and pondered why she had for one minute thought her life was unexciting.

"Um . . . would it help if . . . you know, you had like some of mine? Just a little, though!" Alexis felt her cheeks burn as Ethan's eyes popped open.

"You're offering your blood to me?" He studied her, midnight blue eyes boring into her. "You surprise me, Alexis."

Embarrassed, she tried to backpedal. "Well, this is an unusual circumstance, obviously, and it wouldn't be like an open-ended invitation. This is a onetime deal, because you clearly are in pain. You look like shit. I would do it for anyone."

Liar.

He smiled. "It doesn't have anything to do with the fact that you're attracted to me? That you like me and, whenever I look at you, you feel a tingling sexual awareness?"

Ethan struggled not to laugh at the outrage and horror that flooded Alexis's face. He shouldn't tease her, but even in his half-conscious state, he had reveled in her words.

She was attracted to him. He hadn't lost his touch with women. Not that any other women had entered his thoughts since he'd met her. After nearly a millennium of living, he had finally found a woman who intrigued him enough to stay in his head nearly every second since the moment he'd met her.

And she liked him. That was enough to help him ignore the wave of pain the bullet ripping into his chest had caused.

"If you weren't wounded, I'd hurt you right now."

"I know you would. You'd kick my ass, right?"

"Absolutely," she said, even as her lip trembled. "And for the record, people say all kinds of weird things when they're under stress. So don't read too much into that sexual tingling thing."

"Of course, I understand." Ethan stayed on the floor, even though he could stand up now. In fact, he should be getting up and checking the security cameras for the man who had shot him. There would be clips of him in the casino with Kelsey, and going up the elevator.

But he just wanted to lie there and bask in Alexis's sympathy for just another minute. It had been a long time since a woman had bothered to fuss over him. That implied an intimacy that was lacking in his life and relationships.

"So, do you want the blood or not?" Her voice started to sound a little testy, though her hand hovered over him like she wanted to pat him, soothe him.

Ethan stared up at her, trying to get inside her head. But it was blocked, like it always was. "I can't, Alexis. It would be painful for you."

She frowned, tucking her hair behind her ear. "Then how do you feed normally? You can't run around hurting people. It would be on Jerry Springer if vamps were biting people left and right."

There was an image. He sat half up. "A lot of our feeding is done from blood banks. But when we feed from a live source, we make sure they don't feel pain. We either put a glamour on them or give them pleasure to distract from the pain."

Let's see how she took that.

"A glamour? Like a trance? No way in hell anyone is doing that to me."

That's what he'd thought her reaction would be. "I can't put one on you anyway, because I can't read your thoughts. You're the first person who has ever been completely closed to me." Ethan was starting to suspect the reason for that and he wasn't sure he liked it.

"Really? Wow. That's cool, because I totally wouldn't want you getting into my head. That would really piss me off."

"Don't worry. I can't."

She looked thoughtful. "So no glamour. And the pleasure thing . . . I'm not in the mood right now. Besides, I'm not sure you could turn me on."

He snorted, shifting his elbow away from the bloodstain on the carpet. "I most certainly could arouse you. But I'm not really in the mood either, to tell you the truth. I'm feeling a little like I took a bullet in the chest."

Alexis rolled her eyes.

With a laugh, he said, "So why don't we go up to my room and I'll grab a bag from the fridge? I'll order you another dinner since I'm sure yours is cold by now. I'll have Seamus make our apologies to the guests, and we can eat while I have security scan the tapes for the attacker. I want to know how he brought a weapon into my casino."

Alexis swallowed hard, but nodded. "We can eat together? Sounds good. Steak . . . blood . . . they're not so different, right?"

He grinned. "Not really." Alexis had some grit, and he admired that.

"Do I have to call you Mr. President?" She stood up and tugged at her dress just about everywhere she could tug, ending with the straps.

"No, you can call me Ethan. But if you want to hum 'Hail to

the Chief' whenever I walk into the room, that would be appropriate." With a charming smile, he stood up. Not normal vampire speed, since he was low on blood, but faster than a human. Faster than most mortal eyes could follow.

She blinked. "Show off. Last time I offer you blood, geez, you obviously don't need it."

Feeling downright giddy, which must be the lack of blood, Ethan flung his arm over his face and winced. Doubled over.

"What? What is it! Are you bleeding again?" Alexis reached for him.

He dropped his arm and smiled. "No. It's just that I was momentarily blinded by your beauty."

Her jaw dropped and she slapped his arm. "Idiot."

But as he laughed, he saw her struggle not to grin.

Eight

Brittany studied the vampire in front of her and waited for him to explain why he had flown her up to the roof of Ethan's casino.

It had been quite an experience, zinging through the air so fast she hadn't even been able to see where they were going, or even if they were going up or down. Like the world's fastest roller coaster, or like that blissful moment of wild exaltation right before an orgasm. But he had set her down a solid two minutes ago, and she'd already patted down her flying frizzed hair, crossed her legs on the little chimney he'd set her on, and was ready for him to say something.

He just stood there staring out at the Vegas strip.

"Did you want to speak to me?" she asked, trying to be helpful. Meeting new people was awkward sometimes and she had seen him suck a woman's neck. That probably wasn't a standard introduction.

Just a shrug. He was around the same height as she was, lean, with caramel brown hair that was a touch long. Dressed in black pants and a short-sleeve silk shirt, he was stylish, with a European flare that was a little too cosmopolitan for the average guy running around the bowling alley.

Not that she imagined this man had ever played tenpin.

Getting up, she moved to his side and rubbed her arms. The hot desert night felt wonderful up there, like somehow they were higher than the heat, basking in a comfortably warm wind. Brittany breathed in deep, taking in a crisp earthy pull of air, unlike the oppressive atmosphere down on the Strip, with its cocktail of odors—people, food, exhaust fumes.

"There's the Stratosphere. And Excalibur." She pointed out the landmarks, enjoying the view, the magic of a million lights filling the desert sky.

He glanced at her. "Did you grow up here, in Las Vegas?"

"Yes. My mom was a stripper." She smiled. "Alex would freak if she heard me say that. She wants to pretend we were both hatched. But Mom had her moments."

"Who gave you your vampire blood?" he asked quietly.

"No one." Brittany tried to get him to look at her, but he was still studying the cityscape. "I don't have vampire blood." That she could say for certain. Ethan had never once even tried to bite her, let alone given her blood.

"Who ez your father?"

"I don't know. Some guy my mom had an affair with. I think she met him at the club she was working at."

"Ethan Carrick, he tells you nothing."

It wasn't a question. "If you mean that he's a vampire, no, he hasn't told me that. I figured it out on my own."

She couldn't take it anymore. Something about this man was so sad, so quiet and intelligent, that she touched his arm. "What's your name? Why don't you go to Ethan's parties?"

Finally he gave her his full attention. "I am Corbin Jean Michel Atelier." He nodded his head.

"You were going to bow, weren't you? But you stopped yourself."

Again he nodded.

"That's cool. You can bow to me if you want." Brittany thought she would really like that, actually.

"It ez out of fashion."

"That's okay. I don't think drinking blood is really fashionable either. So Corbin, what brings you to Vegas, and why won't you answer my questions?"

"I am here because there is nowhere else I want to be."

Well, that was a nothing kind of answer. "Why did you bring me up here?"

"Because you need to understand you cannot talk about my kind when there are mortals around. You must be discreet. That ez all."

"Okay." But there was something else, something bothering him.

"There ez nothing."

"I didn't say anything."

"I heard your thoughts." He tapped her temple with his finger. "You have very loud thoughts and feelings. They spill out of you like sunshine. I hear everything."

And here she'd thought she'd gotten a handle on blocking out vampires. She hoped he couldn't tell she thought he was cute.

Or that she was thinking of that woman from the night before and the look on her face . . .

"What about her?" He looked sharply at her. "I did not hurt her."

So much for privacy. "I know you didn't hurt her. In fact, she told me that while you were, you know, doing your neck thing . . ." Brittany stared straight at him. "She had an orgasm."

Corbin looked aghast. "You should not talk about these things."

"How else am I going to help you if I don't talk to you?"

Now she'd hurt his masculine pride. He bristled. "I do not need your help. I need you to stay away from my business."

Brittany looked over the edge of the building, down at the street far below. "If I fell, would you catch me?"

His arm came up in front of her like he expected her to pitch herself over the side. "Of course I would!"

With a pleasant sigh, Brittany tossed her hair back. "I thought so."

She is a very strange person.

Corbin's thoughts floated over to her, and she knew, felt, that he wasn't soulless. Humanity beat just as bright and strong in him as it did in her.

She grinned at him. "Takes one to know one. If I'm weird, you're even weirder."

"You can hear my thoughts?"

"That was the first time," she assured him, since he looked so horrified.

"I could kill you," he said.

"But you won't."

"I could drain you of your lifeblood and fill you with mine, making you a vampiress."

"But you won't."

He paused. "I'll take you back. You shouldn't be seen with me."

Brittany looked around the rooftop. It wasn't like the joint was hopping up there. "Who shouldn't see us?"

"Any of them. I am banished."

Ooohh. Brittany sat back down, pulling the snap of her jeans out of her gut. "Now this sounds good. Tell me all about it, Corbin Jean Michel Atelier. What did you do to put yourself in the vampire doghouse?"

She wanted to know so she could help him, of course. And she would not kiss away that tiny frown line between his eyes.

"You most certainly will not!" he roared. "Then for sure we will both be killed."

"You're already dead," she pointed out.

"Real dead. No more on this earth dead. And while I'm many things, suicidal is not one of them."

"That's a relief." She patted her lap. "Come sit down and tell Auntie Brittany all about it."

His eyebrows shot up. He didn't look like he thought she was cute, which was kind of a disappointment. Men usually found her fairly attractive. Brittany felt her lower lip jutting out. She didn't mean to do it. It was just a reflex. Because nine times out of ten it got her what she wanted with Alex.

But not with Corbin.

He shook his head. And stepped off the edge of the roof.

Brittany screamed in reflex. Then remembered he wouldn't get hurt. He would just wing away or whatever he did to fly.

But then she remembered something else. "Corbin! You can't just leave me here! I'm stuck on the roof!"

Alexis sat on Ethan's burgundy leather sofa, listening to the running water of his shower, and tried to get a grip.

Okay, so he was a vampire. So what?

Everyone had their little quirks. God knew she wasn't perfect, and really, was vampirism an imperfection, or more just like having brown hair versus black? There was no reason to flip her wig like some squealer bimbo and run out of there screaming.

Needing blood was like needing an asthma inhaler. Sort of. In a more gruesome, demonic, unnatural way.

But hey, she was no wimp. She'd had defendants threaten her with physical harm. She'd had defendants' mothers fling their three-hundred-pound bodies at her after a conviction verdict was read. Vampires? She was cool with it.

Alexis Baldizzi was stuck in a pixie's body, but she didn't have to act like a wuss.

So she propped her bare feet on the couch and jammed a plaid throw pillow behind her back. She liked plaid. It was the antithesis of the scarlet bordello-like atmosphere she'd grown up in. While every other kid on the block had a mother in seventies' plaid pantsuits, her mother had been wearing short shorts, bikini tops, and high heels.

Thoughts of her mother disintegrated when Ethan walked back into the room, his blond hair dripping wet, wearing jeans and a button-up shirt that wasn't buttoned. Damn it. The last time she'd seen his chest, it had been covered with blood from a gaping chest wound, which had been a little distracting. Now he had nothing but clean, smooth skin, no evidence that a bullet had ever entered his chest.

And without the whole no pulse, rivers of blood thing to distract her, she couldn't help but notice he was pretty damn hot. A little pale, but hot.

"Feeling better?" she asked, crossing her legs out of a survival instinct. If she could erect a sign below the waist of her evening gown, she would. KEEP OUT. DO NOT ENTER. NO TRESPASSING. VAMPIRES NOT ADMITTED.

Because he had that look again—that super sultry, let's make like bunnies and do it look.

"Cleaner. A little tired, but fine, thanks. I'm sorry you had to find me like that. And I appreciate your quick emergency response even if it wasn't necessary." He sat down on the couch next to her and gave her a smile.

"Yeah, well, all in a day's work."

"I ordered a new dinner for you. It should be here in a minute or two."

"Thanks." Alexis stared at his chest. She couldn't help it. She knew what she had seen, believed Ethan was telling her the truth about his unusual genetic makeup, but it was still hard to swallow.

"You can touch it if you want. Feel for yourself. There's no permanent damage."

That was enough to rip her eyes off his chest. "I'm not going to touch it!"

"Scared you'll like it?"

Yes. "No. Please. Get over yourself, Carrick."

He laughed. "You're handling the events of the evening very well. I usually get hysterics when a mortal discovers the truth about me."

Alexis wasn't entirely sure why she wasn't in hysterics, but she was grateful for that fact. "Have a lot of mortals discovered the truth about you?"

Leaning his back against the arm, and lifting a leg onto the couch, he shrugged. "No, not really. Maybe two or three. I've told some. But mostly we blend."

She wished he'd blend his crotch into the couch so she wouldn't have to look at it, all spread out at her like a forbidden fruit. It was a little hard to keep her eyes off inappropriate parts. If she looked at his chest, she pictured touching it. If she looked at his crotch, well, hell, she didn't want to go there. If she looked at his legs, she imagined wrapping her own around them. And when she looked into his pale, cerulean blue eyes, she had an entire mental striptease choreographed in her head.

Either he was doing that vampire mind control thing that he swore he couldn't do on her, or she was a sick bitch who thought vampires were sexy.

Why the hell couldn't he be a werewolf? That wouldn't have done a thing for her, she was positive. Fur had never gotten her going.

"So . . . how old are you? And how do you blend if you have to sleep all day and suck blood all night?" Did he need three pints square a night, or did he have to graze on blood constantly, like a whale shark with plankton, or could he make it a whole week without touching the stuff?

Ethan gave her a look. "I don't suck blood all night. And I was born in 1067, the son of a Norman lord and his new Anglo-Saxon wife."

Alexis swallowed, more freaked out than she cared to admit. "Wow. Dude. That's seriously old. And you don't look a day over thirty."

"Neither do you." He smiled, and nudged her leg with his foot.

"I am thirty." Which had seemed old until an hour ago. "So is nine hundred really like the new thirty then? Do you feel just as perky as ever?"

"Actually, I get stronger with age. We're weak in our youth."

"You should have a millennium birthday party. That would be cool."

"Maybe I will. I hadn't thought much about it. I've been busy with the campaign."

"Can I have a stiff drink now?" Alexis thought it was time for a bottle of gin, just to settle her stomach.

The doorbell rang. "I have a better idea. Dinner."

A minute later, he had her steak dinner in front of her, served with pea pods and roasted potatoes. It did smell good, but she felt rude eating in front of him. "Did you ever, um, eat?"

"No, I was waiting for your food to arrive."

"Go ahead. You must be dying since you lost all that blood." Without even trying, she managed to make him laugh. "No pun intended."

"If you'll just excuse me, I'll grab myself a drink then."

"Sure." Alexis chewed and sipped an ice water, her stomach making embarrassing noises as it embraced the beef enthusiastically.

She was surprised to see Ethan come back into the room empty-handed. "Where's your drink?"

"I had a nip in the kitchen. I didn't want to bother you. The sight and the smell, well, it can take some getting used to."

"I don't think I'd mind. I mean, it's not like you're dragging a bellman in here and going at him like a mosquito. You're just going to like suck it out of a bag, right? How often do you do that?" she asked around a mouthful of potatoes.

"I don't suck it out of a bag. I drink it out of a glass when I am thirsty. Sometimes once a night, sometimes every other day, sometimes once a week depending on my mood and what I'm doing."

"Does it taste different? I mean, do you prefer B positive over O?" Alexis wondered what her blood would taste like. Pepper steak?

Ethan snorted. "In nine hundred years, no one, not a single person, has asked me that."

"I have a curious mind. It makes me a good lawyer."

"Or just nosy."

"Bite me. I'm not nosy." Then she realized what she had said. "Not literally! No biting. It's just an expression."

Ethan laughed. His finger swiped the corner of her lip, scaring the crap out of her. And sort of turning her on. But he only licked his finger. "You had some water dribbling down there."

Alexis felt her face heat. "Don't lick me. That's inappropriate."

"I didn't lick you. I licked my finger, which touched you. I'm getting the feeling that I make you nervous. Is it because I'm a vampire?"

"I'm not nervous. But if I was, yes, it would be because you're a vampire. You have to admit, that's a little odd. I mean, I saw you bleeding like a stuck pig and here you are all cute and casual thirty minutes later." And now that her stomach was feeling much better, she was starting to think it would be a good idea to have some alone time. Far away from Ethan Carrick.

"I'm cute?" He looked pleased by that. "My mother always said I was angelic looking."

Alexis rolled her eyes. Apparently even after nine hundred years of life, men still needed their egos stroked. "Mothers are blinded by love. But you're not ugly, I'll give you that."

"Be still my heart."

"Hey, how come you're blond and all your vamp friends have black hair? You don't fit the raven-haired brooding image."

"Maybe not, but as I said, I'm angelic looking. Trustworthy. Having dark-haired cabinet members is a coincidence, but it does provide a nice contrast. Makes me stand out in the political crowd."

Alexis chewed on that as she chewed on a pea pod. She really should go back to her room. But Ethan was right. She was nosy. She had about three million questions for him.

But first things first. "I'm going to scream if I have to wear this dress for another second. I've got to take it off."

"I have no problem with you taking it off. In fact, the thought rather pleases me." Ethan gave her a lecherous grin.

"Watch it, Carrick. I'm not some White House intern that's easily excitable when a president strolls into the room."

"No? Good. I wouldn't want you to be easy." He stood up. "But if you'd like, I could get you something to change into."

Wear Ethan's clothes? That was a dangerous proposition. It

wasn't like her room was a million miles away. It was right next door. She could run over, change, run back. Which might not look so good. She might look a little too eager to be back in his company. Not to mention that the idea of putting a powerful vampire's clothes next to her undersexed flesh had an enormous appeal.

"Thanks. That would be great."

Brittany would be so proud of her. She had utterly lost her mind and was acting on pure impulse.

"Finish your dinner and I'll go grab something. The pants will be long, though, you'll have to roll them up."

"Thanks. Rub it in. I'm well aware that I'm vertically challenged." Alexis stabbed a piece of beef and watched Ethan walk into his bedroom.

For a vampire, he had a nice ass. How sick was it that she was attracted to a man who was older than the discovery of the New World? Granted, there were lots of things older than Ethan—like dirt and cockroaches—but he was still really damn old. And she was thinking naughty girl thoughts about him.

She should have dated more. Plain and simple.

Ethan came out and said, "I put some things in the bathroom for you when you're ready to change."

"I'm ready. And I'm done with the dinner, it was delicious, thanks."

"You're welcome." He didn't move from his spot in the hallway, which meant she had to shimmy past him, brushing her arm against his.

She shivered.

"Cold? I can get you a sweatshirt, too." Alexis watched his lips move. Thought about how close they were to hers, albeit higher from the ground.

"It's August in Vegas. I'm not cold." And she shut the bathroom door in his face before she leapt on him.

His bathroom was large and luxurious, white on white, with nickel faucets. A peek in the shower showed a wide variety of gels and shampoos, and there were bath beads sitting beside his Jacuzzi tub. "The softer side of vampires," she mused, as she unzipped the dress and let it drop to the floor.

Alexis wasn't wearing a bra, which was potentially dangerous, but there wasn't much she could do about that at the moment. Standing in her panties, she reached for the T-shirt Ethan had set on the marble countertop for her. But first, she spotted a scale tucked under the vanity. Never one to be able to resist the temptation to horrify herself, she pulled it out and stepped on.

And went blind. "Holy crap, I'm a cow." She sucked in her gut, glared at the digital readout, shifted her feet, and then out of sheer desperation shucked her underwear off, too. They might weigh half a pound. Better to be completely accurate.

This time when she stepped on, it was a gratifying pound less. "Ha. See, I knew it. Damn lace is heavy."

The knock on the door had her jumping and falling off the side of the scale onto the floor, making a loud metal-on-tile scraping sound in the process.

"Alexis? Can I get you anything else?"

Hello. Naked here. With Ethan two feet away on the other side of a thin wood door. Just the thought had her inner thighs humming. Nudity was for bathing or sex, and her body seemed to be ready for the second option. And she'd forgotten to lock the door.

"I'm good, thanks." She tugged on the kelly green T-shirt and reached for her panties. Once they were covering all the important parts as best as a black lace thong could, she felt marginally better. She debated locking the door, but figured he would hear the click and get offended.

"Okay. I spoke with the security advisor a half an hour ago, but I'm going to ask him to bring the tapes up now from the reception area."

"Good idea. You need to find this guy. And can you ask him to bring my shoes, too? I left one in the elevator and one by your bleeding body. In the trauma of the whole experience, I forgot them."

"Sure."

"Hey, Ethan?" Alexis pulled the jogging pants on and was mortified to find that they actually fit her in the waist. Shouldn't a woman be smaller than a man? "How's your vision? Do you have, like, x-ray eyes or anything?" Better to know what she was dealing with.

She could practically hear his grin. "I'm not superman, beautiful. I can't see your naked body through this door, no matter how much I want to."

"Oh." She rolled the bottom of the pants and flipped off the door with her middle finger, just because he'd aggravated her.

"I saw that."

Alexis lost the ability to breathe. If he had seen her falling off that scale naked, she was going to croak. "You said you couldn't see me!"

Now he laughed. Loudly. "I can't. But I know you did something rude. I could just feel it."

Oh, she hated it when someone got the best of her. "You're going to feel me busting your ass in a minute."

"I can hardly wait."

Nine

Ethan opened the door to his security advisor a minute later, still wearing a grin. Alexis made him laugh, in a way he hadn't in a long time. A hundred years or more. He'd been serious lately, trying really hard to keep a lid on his emotions, urges, instincts, temper.

In the process it seemed he'd forgotten how to laugh, and that was rather a shame.

"I brought the disc for you to view, Mr. Carrick, sir."

"Thank you, William. Is he on it?"

"Yes." William stepped into the room, a cardboard box in his hands. "And I wasn't sure which shoes belonged to Ms. Baldizzi so I brought them all."

"What do you mean, you brought them all?" Alexis came up behind Ethan and stared into the box. "How many pairs of shoes are left lying in the elevator?"

"About three a day, miss," William said with a completely straight face, his little electronic earpiece tucked in place, his goatee trim and tidy.

Ethan liked the way Alexis was hovering behind him, sort of leaning around him. Like she was with him. Comfortable being behind his protection. It may have been an illusion or wishful thinking on his part, but she did actually touch his arm to shift him out of the way as she reached into the box. A red bra flew out of her hand and across the room.

"Geez! That's definitely not mine." Keeping her hand tucked behind her back this time, she leaned farther over the box. "There's three more bras in here and a thong. From six elevators? What the hell goes on in these elevators?"

Neither he nor William spoke.

"How long did it take to accumulate all this?"

The corner of William's mouth twitched. "This is since yesterday, miss."

Alexis grabbed her throat and curled her lip back. "Is everyone in the world depraved except for me?"

"Oh, come now, Alexis, I'm sure you're capable of as much depravity as the next person."

She glared at Ethan.

"Are any of these yours?" William looked ready to be on his way.

"I see my shoes, but they're underneath a pair of boxers that I am not touching. I think I'll just get a new pair next payday. Thanks."

Ethan wanted to offer her a new pair, but was pretty sure she'd tell him to stick them in an uncomfortable place.

William retrieved the flung bra from the sofa and tossed it back into the box. "Sorry, Miss Baldizzi."

"Hey, it's not your fault. Thanks for trying." She turned and tapped the disc Ethan was holding. "Does this show us who shot you?"

"We shall see." Ethan dismissed William. "I'll be in contact. Let me know when you've IDed him."

"Absolutely, sir."

William left and Alexis turned to him, crossing her arms over her chest, which prevented him from seeing her nipples. "Just one question . . . vampire or mortal?"

"William? Vampire. Most of the guards are mortal, but as head of security, he needs access to certain information."

"Well, I hope he figures out who that guy is . . . I mean you can't just walk into casinos and shoot people. If you have it on tape, my office can prosecute. I don't normally do homicides, but I can assist the senior prosecutor. I have a ninety-five percent conviction rate, by the way."

Even though she seemed to be handling all of this quite well, there were obviously some issues she hadn't thought through. "Alexis, you can't prosecute. There is no police report, and no victim. I cannot be medically examined by mortals, which is why I had Seamus intercept the EMTs. There is no crime here, according to the mortal world. We want to discover his identity so we can find out if I was a direct target, or if it was an accident. Either way, we'll erase his memory to avoid suspicion."

"Well, that sucks. I wanted to send the bastard to jail." She took the disc out of his hand and headed for the TV. "Will this play in your DVD player or just the computer?"

"The DVD player is fine. And why do I have the feeling you enjoy putting men in prison?" There was true disappointment on her face, which didn't really blend with her cute blond hair, perky nose, and pink lips. Wearing his sweatpants and a T-shirt, she looked more like an escapee from a local high school gym class, not an attorney.

But that gleam in her eye was all prosecutor.

Alexis pushed Play on his remote control. He liked the way she just made herself at home in his suite. Most women were intimidated by him, and waited for his initiative. Maybe not sexually, but to be involved in his life in any way, yes. He hadn't had a woman assume she could take charge in his home since his mother.

Maybe there was something to be said for modern aggressive women.

He kind of liked Alexis's attitude.

Or maybe that was blood loss talking.

"Okay, what the hell are we looking at?" Alexis frowned at the TV screen.

Ethan studied the image in front of him. A man, in his early thirties, lean, well dressed in an expensive but discreet suit, was walking off the elevator. He leaned to the side, whispering, his hand dangling in midair.

Alexis tilted her head. "He's talking to himself or something."

"Actually, he's talking to Kelsey. She took him upstairs, remember?" For which he really should fire her. But Kelsey was not the brightest bulb in the vampire pack, and he had always thought it was better to keep her reasonably contained than to let her loose on her own. She was only thirty years a vampire, and still driven by blood lust. And she had warned him about the attacker, even if she had inadvertently led the guy right to Ethan.

"Oh, my God, I can't see her. She's there, but can't be recorded? That's so bizarre." Alexis sank down into an easy chair a foot in front of his flat screen.

It was odd watching the man talk to nothing. But Ethan was more interested in his face, not his marionette hands moving up and down in thin air. The image wasn't perfect, and the room was dim, with just the overnight lights on, but Ethan was certain he'd never seen him before.

So why did this man want him dead? He obviously thought a bullet would do the trick, so he either didn't know Ethan was a vampire, or didn't understand what would kill one of his kind. This man, the way he turned his head, the way he smiled with a healthy dose of disdain, the way he gripped what Ethan guessed was Kelsey's backside, didn't point to him being insane, or a self-proclaimed vampire slayer. It wasn't fire that burned in his eyes. It was despair. Coldness.

This man was a professional killer, Ethan was sure of it.

They heard heavy breathing from the TV as presumably the pair kissed, grinding against each other. Kelsey must have hit the reception desk because there was a thump as the furniture shifted and the phone was shoved.

"This is really disturbing. I think I'm being scarred as we speak. It's like paranormal porn."

Alexis did look a little pale. "Do you want me to turn it off?"

"No, are you kidding? I have to see what happens. It's like a car accident, but with tongue. You don't want to look, but you have to."

Personally, Ethan was finding the combination of heavy breathing from the TV and Alexis next to him wearing his clothes a bit arousing. Her chest heaved as she stared, head tilted, one eye closed. Ethan watched her watching the recording.

"He's going up her skirt! Oh, man, maybe we should fast-forward."

"How can you tell if you can't see her?" Ethan redirected his attention to the TV. Okay, so he could see it, too. With a little mental imagery, he had no trouble reconstructing the scene.

"His hand is like jerking upward, like he's pulling up her skirt." Alexis fell back against the chair arm. "Aahh! No, no, please don't do that. Just stop!" She yelled at the screen, throwing her hands up. "Don't get out the . . . oh, no, yuck, yuck, yuck, did they have to do that?"

The man, whoever he was, now had unzipped trousers, and a decent-sized erection pointed directly at them. Ethan grimaced. The man gave a tight moan, his hips pumping toward what body part on Kelsey Ethan really didn't want to know. "Jesus, where's the remote? I don't want to see this either."

While he started looking around, a little desperate, Alexis covered her face with a throw pillow and started laughing. Her little snorts were muffled by the plaid fabric, but her shoulders shook.

"What's so funny?" Ethan found the remote, but somehow managed to freeze the screen, instead of fast-forward. Right in mid-thrust. "Damn it." Seamus was the electronics whiz, not him. He was old, for chrissake, they'd barely had the wheel when he was a kid. He couldn't be expected to keep up with all this technology.

Alexis peeled the pillow back, watched him pushing every button on the remote frantically, and started laughing again. "I'm sorry, it's just so weird and gross, you have to laugh. I'm going to die every time I see Kelsey now."

Ethan finally hit the right button and the man's head snapped back, and eyes rolled upward. Yeah, he was going to have a hard time seeing his receptionist in the same way, too, after catching this little glimpse into her sex life. Especially since he was seeing her feed now.

Even without Kelsey's image, he knew that's what was happening. The man's head tilted, neck elongated, ecstasy over his features. Tiny droplets of blood appeared on his flesh, then immediately disappeared. Then suddenly he was moaning in distress, eyes still closed, body suspended, hovering over the desk.

This was where Kelsey had run out on him, leaving him under a weak glamour on the goddamn reception desk.

The elevator dinged.

"Oh, God," Alexis said in a somber voice. "She left him there, didn't she?"

"Yes." Ethan was embarrassed. What they were watching . . . it wasn't how he wanted to introduce Alexis to his world. It shouldn't matter, but it did, that she know it didn't have to be crude like this. "Alexis . . ."

She glanced at him. "Are you going to say something totally embarrassing to both of us, like that it isn't always like this . . . that a feeding can be an exchange of souls, as pure and sweet and sensual as making love with the right person?"

Well, he wouldn't have used those moronic words, but the sentiment, yes. But obviously, she got it and didn't want him to say it.

"No, I was just going to say that you sound like a tortured crow when you laugh."

A laugh burst out of her, half-amusement, half-relief, it looked to him. She hit him in the arm with the throw pillow. "You're a schmuck."

He was a smart schmuck. He knew when to retreat from a woman. Ethan fast-forwarded until the shooter collapsed against the desk.

The man said something, though it was too garbled to distinguish the words. He looked around, pleasure replaced by confusion, which disintegrated into anger. Wiping his hands on his pants, he then put everything back inside and zipped. He straightened his jacket, reached inside for thin leather gloves, and pulled them on. He was walking around the backside of the desk when the elevator door opened.

Ethan knew it was himself, coming to investigate, even though he wasn't visible on film.

Fast, smooth, poised, the man reached into his suit, pulled out a piece, drew his arm up, and squeezed the trigger two times.

Alexis jumped. "Did it hurt?" There was concern in her voice.

"Yes, there was pain when I was hit. Then I blacked out."

The shooter stepped forward, avoiding a puddle of blood forming on the tiled floor. Ethan had forgotten to ask William to send housekeeping to clean the mess up, but his head of security was smart enough to handle all those details on his own.

"He's making the sign of the cross over your body . . . with his gun. I told you there were sickos in this world."

It was an odd last thing to do before the man calmly put his gun in his pocket, removed one glove, punched the elevator button with the other, and disappeared. But to Ethan it still read like a professional hit. When the man had been caught off guard by Ethan's sudden appearance, there had been no hesitation. No panicking.

The question was, who wanted him dead?

"Now that I've seen you lying on the floor in a pool of blood, and then seen your invisible self get shot on camera, I feel like I have the right to ask this." Alexis tucked her feet under her legs.

"What?" He couldn't even imagine what she was going to ask.

"What the hell were you thinking going up there by yourself?"

That he'd been feeling stodgy and white-collar and had wanted to handle the situation himself to prove that he could. That he was so attracted to Alexis that he was distracted and acting on impulse. That he hadn't been thinking at all.

"Hello! I remember what Kelsey said. She said he was going to kill you, that he was empty inside, and that lipstick I thought was bleeding outside of her lip liner really was bleeding, you know what I'm saying. You knew she had fed off of someone, knew she thought he was after you, and like a hugely arrogant 'I can handle anything' man, you just ran off and got yourself shot." Alexis's cheeks were pink, her hands flying all over as she gesticulated wildly. "Do you want to die? What if he'd had a stake or a sword or a sunlamp or whatever it is that can kill vampires?"

Ethan hit the Eject button on the DVD. "A sunlamp is not going to kill me, and it would hurt less than a bullet, that's for sure." The very thought made him scoff, though he found her concern appealing.

"You know what I mean! It's a good thing I went up after you."

"And why exactly did you do that? It was no smarter than me

going up in the first place. What if the shooter was still there? You'd be lying dead on my office floor right now."

Her face paled. But she stubbornly stuck her chin out. "So you're just going to erase his memory and that's it? That doesn't seem like much punishment for shooting someone."

"Now who's the bloodthirsty one here? Look, we have rules, Alexis. We don't kill people. We'll contain him. If he doesn't know how to kill me, it will be nothing more than a nuisance until we find him. Then like I said, we'll contain him, and remove the parts of his memory relating to me."

Alexis didn't look satisfied with his answer. She worked her lip with her teeth and picked at the pillow in her lap. "How many of you are there? Obviously enough that you have some sort of governmental system."

Ethan hesitated only a fraction of a second. He wasn't supposed to tell a mortal about his kind, but he didn't feel much like following the rules when he was with Alexis. "Ten thousand."

"Whoa. That's a hell of a lot more than I thought. You must be sucking blood everywhere."

Ethan sat down next to her and plucked the pillow out of her lap, amused by her lack of fear. "Ten thousand is not a lot. There are two billion Chinese alone in the world."

"Well, that's true."

"We're vastly outnumbered and are able to successfully blend in with society, while still being organized. The Nation exists to ensure we aren't discovered, and can live quality lives." It was a system that worked, kept order and prevented chaos among the ranks of the undead, and provided mentoring for young vampires. Ethan had seen the world before the Vampire Nation, and he didn't want to return to those dark days of rogue vampires and needless human slaughter.

But sometimes being a responsible vampire leader was a heavy burden.

And lately it had really cut into his sex life.

It was definitely time to change that.

Alexis had never given vampires much thought, but when she had, she had always envisioned brooding men living in isolation, snagging a random human victim here or there, and more often than not, lunching on animals while their houses crumbled around them.

Ethan wasn't exactly falling in line with that image.

And never once had it even occurred to her that vampires were democratic.

"So what is your platform? What differentiates you from your opponent?" She couldn't even begin to guess what the issues facing the modern vampire were. Security, financial planning, airport retina scans? Okay, maybe she could guess, but that didn't mean she was going to be right.

He cleared his throat as he set his foot on the coffee table. That shirt of his still wasn't buttoned, and Alexis was in touching distance of his chest. It was very distracting to her, considering that she hadn't been sexually active in six years. If you didn't count battery-operated self-service, which she didn't. That was stress management, not sex.

"Well, we encourage population management, whereas our opponent advocates population growth. He also is pushing a return to direct contact feeding, where we consider blood banks safer. More laws and policies, not less. Essentially, I stand for keeping things status quo, but with improvements in certain policies regarding identity creation and social security."

"Hmm." That was the sound of her brain atrophying. Maybe she was too tired to grasp vamp politics at the moment. "Do you think you're going to win?"

Ethan shrugged. "Seamus and his endless statistics say yes, but by a small margin. These things are unpredictable and Donatelli is a minority."

"He's Italian? That makes him a minority?" What the heck were the rest of them? Eskimo?

Mr. President laughed at her question and ran his thumb over his very sexy bottom lip. Not that she had noticed.

"Being Italian doesn't make him a minority. He's an Impure. Which means he was born half-vampire, half-mortal and was turned later in life. He is the voice of this rapidly growing group."

"Impure? Wow, that's really PC. *Not.* In a thousand years you couldn't come up with a better name than that? No wonder they're crabby and demanding rights. I would be, too. So is there like a vampire civil liberties union? VACLU? No, that's no good. VACLU sounds like a construction adhesive. Hey, how old do you have to be to vote? Two hundred?"

"At moments like this, I find it very distressing that I cannot access your thoughts. I am powerless to understand or predict what is going to come out of your mouth next."

She kind of liked the way that sounded. "That's sexy, isn't it? It drives you nuts that you can't dig in my head, I bet, but it turns you on, too, doesn't it?"

And fatigue must be making her punch-drunk. Baiting the vampire was not a good plan.

He took the bait. "Yes, it turns me on. You most definitely arouse me."

Whoa. When did his hand get on her thigh? She hadn't even seen him move. But now she certainly could feel him, sliding inward, upward, stroking over the soft cotton of the sweatpants she was wearing. His pants. Where she had a little bitty thong underneath just a few inches higher.

Alexis stood up, just this side of panicked. "You know, I think I should get some sleep. I'm feeling a little . . . overwhelmed."

Ethan smiled a knowing little smirk. "Sure. Let me walk you to your room."

What, was she stupid? "Oh, that's okay, I'll be fine." Really. Just fine, away from him and his hot bod and blue eyes. She'd always had a thing for blue eyes.

Alexis booked it toward the door, scooping her purse off the end table. Before she could blink, Ethan was in front of her, opening the door with a charming half-bow.

"Geez!" Alexis pulled up short. "Don't do that. You'll give me a heart attack."

"My apologies." He moved his arm out to indicate she should pass.

Skirting him so there was no skin-on-skin contact, Alexis made it into the hall and rushed her own door. Digging in her purse, she tried to find the key card before he followed her.

Too late. "Let me help you," he said, and before she could even draw a breath to protest, he had his hand in and out of her purse, and the key swiped through the lock.

His speed was really starting to freak her out. He could have sex with her before she could even realize he was in the room. And what would be the fun in that?

"Can you slow it down a little for Miss Mortal over here? You're making me dizzy."

Ethan pushed her door open and brushed her hair back from her forehead. "Sorry. And thank you for calling 911 when you thought I was dying. I appreciate your concern."

She should swat his hand away, but couldn't work up the disdain she should be feeling. In fact, she felt a lot like sighing. "No problem. I couldn't let you bleed to death."

He was touching her shoulders now, leaning over from his foot height advantage. His eyes were serious, searching. "If you want to leave, Alexis . . . I understand. This isn't what you expected. It's not a game."

That made her smile as she stood in the doorway. "I guess I'm not much of a vampire slayer, am I? I tried to save you instead of killing you."

"I find you much more appealing than that skinny Buffy, for one thing. And life isn't always black and white, Alexis, with the good guys and bad guys clearly marked."

That had been obvious many times to her in her career. Which was why she wasn't in a hurry to leave The Ava and Ethan Carrick. She was fascinated by him, and the concept of a whole secret vampire government existing right there in Vegas, of all places, had her curiosity on high.

She didn't want to leave. She wasn't finished getting her answers yet, and while part of her questioned that she would act so impulsively, the other part acknowledged it was actually very logical to want to understand Ethan's world.

Which was why she said, "I gave my word I'd stay and be your bitchy girlfriend. I'd be a wimp and a liar if I backed out now. Besides, I'm not done grilling you yet."

His eyebrow rose. "That sounds appealing. In a kinky, rather sexual kind of way."

She smacked his arm. "Watch it. I know karate, remember? And I'm not afraid to use it."

"I remember." But he didn't look worried. He looked like he was leaning closer to her, like was going to . . .

Damn. He was kissing her. And it felt good, just a perfect slow, sensual meeting of his mouth to hers, his lips warm and soft, commanding, confident. His hand was in her hair, but otherwise they weren't touching, and it was pleasant, powerful, with no fumbling, no doubt, no hesitation.

While he only touched her mouth, she felt the kiss everywhere, undulating through her body in slow, lazy waves. Desire sparked, stoked, grew into a blaze within seconds, and she was opening her mouth, ready for more, when he ended the kiss.

"Good night, Alexis," he said, voice raspy, thick with want.

Afraid she might whimper, she just nodded. Embarrassed to hear her breath ripping in and out in the quiet hallway, she clamped her mouth shut and backed up. His hands were in fists and he looked fierce, like he might grab her and take her against the wall if she didn't move immediately.

She only hesitated for a second, ready to haul him back over to her. A quick progression to naked had its merits.

But then he drew in a ragged breath of his own, even as his hands reached for her, and she caught a glimpse of some really long-ass canines. Fangs.

Fudge, he had fangs. Those hadn't been there before. Alexis blurted, "Night!" then moved back, and slammed the door shut in his face.

She just wasn't ready to take their relationship to the biting level yet.

Ten

"I just got confirmation from our contact, Mr. Donatelli. It's done."

Roberto didn't bother to open his eyes as he soaked in a Jacuzzi tub in his suite at the Venetian. It amused him to stay in a hotel that emulated his homeland in plush, inaccurate opulence. And when he spoke Italian to the women here, they always giggled.

"Thank you, Smith," he told his right-hand man. "That's good to hear. How long do you think until we'll get the official news?"

"Twenty minutes, tops."

"Perfect." Roberto allowed himself a smile, the hot water sluicing over his chest as he shifted a little.

Step one, completed. Excellent.

Time for step two.

Corbin felt guilty for leaving the girl on the roof, but surely she would be smart enough simply to take the stairs down one floor to the elevator bank.

He had found he could not stay there with her one moment longer. Something about her childlike enthusiasm, her guileless expressions, and her cheerful encouragement had set off a swell of emotions surprising in their intensity. Anger, annoyance, attraction had all risen in him, choking him into confusion.

Banished he was, and banished he would stay, and that silly girl would only distract him with her ridiculous Auntie Brittany talk.

Leaning against the wall, Corbin shifted his feet. The window ledge one floor down was not particularly comfortable, being only a dozen centimeters in width. He was certain a bird of some sort had roosted there recently, as suspicious-looking spots lingered near his elbow. He grimaced. The world was such a dirty place.

But from this position, he could listen for the girl, to make sure she found the stairwell. She did not look like the panicking sort, but then again, she didn't seem beset with survival instincts either. Look at how she had stayed with him so calmly, without fear, spouting all that nonsense about helping him.

"Bah," he said out loud, because it made him feel better.

A hundred years ago Corbin could not have imagined he would wind up in the desert surrounded by blazing electronic lights, clinging to a decorative faux window. This was his punishment for breaking the rules of his kind, and it was no less than he deserved.

His keen hearing picked up the sound of Brittany moving around on the roof. She had only called out for him the one time, then had resorted to muttering about the rudeness of men in general, him in particular.

It had been ill-mannered to abandon her like that. But she had spoken about orgasms as if he were her maid, and contemplated kissing his forehead as if he were a boy in short pants. There were boundaries, and she had overstepped them.

"Alex? It's Brit."

Corbin frowned. Who was she talking to?

"I know it's late, but I thought you'd call me after your little soiree with Ethan. I want all the dets, and I'm not waiting until tomorrow, so spill."

Corbin didn't know who Alex was, or what dets were, but he was curious how Brittany was carrying on a one-sided conversation with someone on the roof of the casino.

He jumped up the side of the building, grabbed the edge, and hovered where he could see her, just the top of his head clearing the roof. Brittany was chatting on her cell phone.

That should have occurred to him, but sometimes his brain still worked in a nineteenth-century fashion.

"You suck!" she said into her tiny pink phone. Brittany was lying on her back on the asphalt, staring up at the sky as she talked.

Her body was long, lean, her breasts obvious in a tight, molded T-shirt, her hips shapely. A ribbon of flesh showed above her waistband, and her thick, black hair hung down away from her face, a raven waterfall over her shoulders.

She was a beautiful woman, and full of life, laughter. Even now she giggled, rolled on her side a little, and smiled for whomever she was talking to. The smell of her blood was enticing, rich, and her pulse beat strong and sure. There was vampire in her, on her, yet she seemed to know nothing about it.

This woman was why he had done what he did. For those like her, who flowed with human life.

For the ache inside him when he watched her.

It occurred to him Brittany would be perfect for his experiment.

"Would you care to tell me just what the fuck you're thinking?"

Ethan winced as Seamus railed at him. They were in Ethan's office, a large sumptuous room with thick faux suede easy chairs. He was settled comfortably in one, a glass of Diabetic '87 in one hand to give him a sugar boost.

Seamus was pacing back and forth in front of the floor-to-ceiling window, still wearing a tux from the dinner party, though his tie was dangling loose. They had been friends for a long time, he had actually been the one to turn Seamus, and he was sorry he had angered him.

But he didn't regret his actions. Not really. Not when he felt excited and reinvigorated for the first time in fifty years.

"I don't think this is the disaster you seem to think it is, Seamus. Brittany was not interested in me."

"You weren't even trying with her! And the sister doesn't work as a substitute, Ethan. She doesn't have vampire blood. That is the sole reason for you to be involved with a woman right now."

Ethan could think of a lot better reasons to be involved with a woman. "So Alexis isn't an Impure. Does it really matter? She is a mortal. I look good simply by having her next to me."

Seamus didn't look appeased. He waved his Sidekick at Ethan.

"The polls say they want you to be a reasonable, nonviolent president, that's true. But the Impures are restless and want to know you stand for them. That you care about their concerns. Making it with a mortal doesn't fix that very large problem. It's you, the old school, versus Donatelli, the new order. The Impure population is growing, as more and more are discovered and turned, and if they decide not to vote for you, the presidency is gone."

"I understand that." And he cared. He did. "But I cannot seduce a woman because it is a good political maneuver. I can't make myself use a woman that way."

"You have a new woman every decade or so. Why is this such a hardship to play court to a beautiful woman? She's sweet, thoughtful, a little naive, but charming. How hard can it be?"

Ethan frowned, tilting his glass to stare at the blood as it rolled across the inside of the flute. "But I wanted those women. I was attracted to them. I am not attracted to Brittany, and that makes me uncomfortable. I can't fake that interest, I can't sleep with a woman when I am being dishonest in my feelings for her."

"Well, aren't you the noble vampire?" Seamus had short dark hair, trimmed neatly, but he managed to muss it up by raking a hand through it.

"Hey, you wouldn't do it either. Admit it. It's wrong. If I were attracted to Brittany, it would be different, but I'm not. I'm attracted to Alexis."

Seamus made a face. "Damn it, you're right. I wouldn't do it either. But I suspect Alexis will be more detriment than asset. She is a bit . . . vocal."

Ethan laughed. That was a polite understatement. "It's that very thing that I find so incredibly arousing about her."

"I don't need any details about your arousal, thank you very much." Seamus threw his hand up in the air. "But if Alexis already knows what we are, then that is a plus. Having a mortal wife is better than no wife at all, and her sister is an Impure. You need to tell Alexis about Brittany, you know, or she'll be angry with you when she finds out."

"I need to tell her a lot of things. But I'm easing her into everything." And that night he had come perilously close to easing *himself* into her. It was too soon for that, and he knew it intellectually, even if his body disagreed. He should be grateful Alexis had slammed the door in his face.

"Sit down, Seamus, and have a drink. You're much too tense, it's starting to grate on my nerves." He sipped and reflected on his friend's words. Even when he had discussed the strategy with Seamus regarding Brittany, he had never really believed he could marry her, even before he'd realized they wouldn't suit.

In more than nine hundred years he had not taken a wife, not even as a mortal man, and the thought of taking a mortal wife now did not appeal to him any more than it ever had. Some vampires did marry mortals for short periods of time—ten or twenty years—then left them or divorced when their spouses aged and became uncomfortable with their differences. Ethan had always thought it seemed so temporary, so unfulfilling. That at the end, it would leave you lonelier than when you started.

But vampire marriages were rarer still, because it was a bond that could not be broken. Once mated, the marriage lasted for eternity, and most of their kind were unwilling to risk getting stuck in a relationship for six hundred years after the bloom had worn off the rose. Those who did spoke of a knowledge, a love, that told them this was their chosen one. Their destiny. Their love.

Ethan wanted that or nothing at all. Not a tepid, tomato juice marriage with a mortal when he could someday have a hot, satisfying pure blood passion for the rest of his undead life.

"Let's not get ahead of ourselves, Seamus. I'm not ready to talk marriage to anyone. At this moment, I am fascinated by Alexis Baldizzi, that is all." And suspicious. He'd felt something when he'd kissed her, something he never had before. Something that confused him. He'd felt . . . knowledge. A sense of rightness.

Like he had met *his* chosen one.

Hands in his tuxedo pants pockets, Seamus studied him. "You could turn her."

Ethan couldn't deny the excitement that leaped in him at the thought. Or the fact that it had already occurred to him. That he had embraced it, dissected it, rejected it. "Perhaps. But it would be wrong and you know it."

"This isn't about you, Ethan, this is about all of us. Our way of life. Our future."

That made him snort. "Don't be melodramatic. The end of the world as we know it does not rest on my love life. If it does, then we deserve to go extinct as a species."

Seamus didn't laugh, which made Ethan realize between the two of them, they had become very uptight vampires. Until Alexis had karate kicked her way into his life.

"So let's talk about something else then. Like who tried to kill you."

"That sounds like fun. Give me the report, I'm just dying to hear it."

"Cute, Carrick." Though Seamus didn't really look like he thought it was cute at all.

Ethan shook his head, amused. It seemed everything, every thought, circled him back to Alexis. "You're the second person to call me that today." And he had really liked it when Alexis had said it.

Astonished at himself, he rubbed his chin.

Good God, it was worse than a midlife crisis. He was falling in *love*.

If he wasn't careful, he'd be buying flowers and going down on one knee, making an ass of himself. He'd be spouting poetry and begging her for a lock of her hair. He'd trail after her like a faithful hunter and obsess over getting her into his bed.

It sounded like hell.

He wasn't doing any of that crap. He'd gone nine hundred years without falling in love, he could damn well go another nine hundred unscathed.

Unless Alexis really was his chosen one. Then he might not have a choice in the matter.

He remembered the way his head had spun and his heart had swelled when his lips had touched hers. The beautiful way she had sighed into him, and the way his body had pulled taut in anticipation. How much she fascinated him . . .

Shit. It looked like making an ass out of himself was in his future.

"There's nothing to tell," Alexis told Brittany for the third time as she paced her hotel suite, still wearing Ethan's sweatpants and shirt. "It was a reception kind of thing with a bunch of stuffed-shirt types running around in tuxedos."

Then Ethan had been shot, confessed his vampirism, and kissed Alexis, but nothing *major* had happened that Brittany needed to know about.

"And where are you, Brit? It sounds like you're on the runway at the airport and a jumbo jet is flying over your head."

"I'm on my patio and a jumbo jet is flying over my head."

"Oh. Well, go to bed. Don't you have to work tomorrow?" Alexis was eternally grateful she didn't have to. There was no way she could wrap her brain around a molestation case that was on her desk when her head was full of the fantastical. Vampires up for reelection. Jesus.

"Tomorrow's Sunday, so no. And are you sure nothing interesting happened? I got the feeling that Ethan was attracted to you. He didn't even try to kiss you or anything?"

"Just once." She didn't want to admit to that little lip-touching episode, but she couldn't bring herself to lie straight out to her sister either. Their relationship was the most important one in Alexis's life, and she had always played it straight with Brittany, even when their mother had overdosed.

The excited scream that ripped through her cell phone almost shattered her eardrum. "Alex! So help me . . ."

There was a shuffling sound, and Alexis waited, rubbing her temples. This was so embarrassing. She had kissed a vampire. Celibacy did strange things to a woman. "Brit? Did you drop the phone?"

"No, I don't need help, it's my sister. But thank you, that's so sweet."

"Who the hell are you talking to?" It must be one of Brittany's neighbors in her apartment complex. Probably wondering why she was screaming into her cell phone on her patio at one in the morning.

"Hmm? Oh, I'm so glad you and Ethan are getting along. I think he really needs someone like you."

According to Ethan, he needed a wife, and she wasn't going that route. Had always known she wasn't ever going to get married. Not that he had suggested anything of the kind, but if she ever lost her mind enough to think she wanted marriage, it wouldn't be with a dead guy.

"Yeah, he's okay. Now let me go to bed, please."

"Sure thing, Alex. I'll see you tomorrow?" There was a rustling sound as Brittany shifted the phone and said, "Don't go. I'm hanging up now."

"Who are you talking to?" She'd forcibly removed Brittany from the company of vampires. If her sister now took up with some yahoo, Alexis was going to be seriously annoyed.

"I'm talking to you." Brittany giggled. "No, not you. Her."

Alexis groaned. "You know what? This conversation is beyond me right now. I love you, good night, lock your doors, see you tomorrow."

"Bye, Alex. I love you, too."

Hanging up the phone, Alexis went into the bathroom and brushed her teeth.

Her mind still racing, she wasn't sure she could sleep just yet, so she decided to check her e-mail on her cell phone. "Only seventeen messages, a light night."

Nothing but crap. Irritating e-mails from coworkers who

couldn't think without someone holding their hands, an advertisement from Ticketmaster for "Yanni Live," and an invitation to join something.

"What is this?" Alexis hovered the cursor over the invitation. "From The Redeemer? Doesn't sound like porn." Against her better judgment, but curious enough to risk it, she clicked on the e-mail.

Hello! You've been invited to join VampireSlayers@yahoogroups .com. We are a group dedicated to the destruction of the unholy undead. Join us for lively discussion and strategy planning on this private list. Your invitation will expire in seven days.

Okay. Alexis read it again. "That's freaking weird." She double-clicked on the sender—The Redeemer—and saw the e-mail address was theredeemer@yahoo.com, which told her nothing except the sender was grandiose in his view of himself.

Without conscious thought, her eyes drifted over to the open drapes at the hotel window. She yanked them shut. Granted she was twenty-some floors up in the air but it made her feel better. The e-mail gave her the creepy feeling of being watched.

"How could someone know who I am? Or my e-mail, or who and what Ethan is." Grabbing her room key and still holding her cell phone, she went into the hallway and pounded on Ethan's door. He needed to see this.

There was no answer, even when she hit the door with the butt of her hand six times in a row. It occurred to her that as a vampire he probably slept during the day and worked at night. There was no guessing where he was.

"Argh." She stomped back to her room, went to the minibar, and grabbed herself a Coke. After popping the top, and taking a huge sip that made her eyes water, she sat down on the couch in her little sitting area.

And clicked on the JOIN THIS GROUP! button.

Four hours later she lost the fight to keep her eyes open, and fell asleep on the couch, cell phone clutched in her hand.

Eleven

Ethan jerked straight out of sleep. He sat up, scanning the dark room, and assessed what he had sensed. He had been born the son of a warrior, he himself had fought in battle, and his undead instincts had averted him from many a danger. No longer needing a weapon, since he could kill any mortal or young vampire with his bare hands if necessary, he still had the habit of reaching behind his head for his dagger.

Naked, arm stretched up, and feeling like he'd been doused in freezing lake water, he heard violent knocking on his door. "Ethan! Get up, damn it."

Relaxing his tense body, he sighed and rubbed his eyes. No threat there—just Alexis, having no respect for the sanctity of his sleep and privacy. Maybe if he was quiet, she'd go away. Sleep was a luxury he'd discovered later in his life, when he had time, money, and better security. It was a gift he'd taken to really well, and he liked his eight hours uninterrupted.

From the way his head felt, he'd only gotten about four.

Sitting still, he held his breath when the silence continued. Maybe she'd gone back to her room. He hoped. That was the downside to involvement with a mortal. They were awake during the day, something he was decidedly out of habit doing.

Probing with his mind, he tried to find his way into her thoughts since she couldn't see him and might not be guarding against him. There was nothing. No feelings, no snatches of thought, no real sense even of her temperament, mood, or posture.

It was frustrating to feel so merely mortal around her. To not have the benefit of one of his greatest vampire gifts.

Then again, maybe she had left and that was why there was only silence.

"Ethan! Come on, I want to talk to you."

So much for hope. With a groan, he got out of bed and stretched. He felt sluggish and tired, perhaps residual effects of losing so much blood the night before. Or getting ripped out of sleep by a persistent, loud, short woman.

Not bothering to put clothes on, he went to the door. If she was going to force him out of bed, she was going to get him as he was. In the flesh.

It gave him a sick sort of anticipation to know he was going to shock her. Nine hundred years didn't necessarily bring profound maturity when dealing with women.

Ethan pulled the door open, knowing he was probably smirking.

Alexis paused with her hand in the air. She was wearing jeans and a tank top, which did nice things to her breasts. Tight, snuggly things that gave him the sudden urgent need to suck and bite her nipples until she moaned.

"Oh, there you are. Were you sleeping?" Alexis blinked innocently, like she hadn't just been making direct contact with her fist on his door.

"Yes, I was. Is there something I can help you with, my dear?" He leaned on the doorframe, crossing his arms and ankles.

She glanced down. Where he had expected blushes and squeamishness, he got a bold, direct stare. Her head tilted a little, her eyes widened. Maybe with a little surprise, yes, but mostly with interest.

Which had him reacting to her interest.

Her tongue slipped out and licked her lower lip, while she tucked her loose, wavy hair behind her ear. He may not have been able to read her thoughts, but he could see the desire on her face. Or at least, the very real sexual curiosity.

"Morning woody?" she asked, eyes still trained on his erection.

"I imagine so."

"Hmm." She made a little sound in the back of her throat. "Well, I can admit it. I'm impressed."

Cabinet members had complimented his political speeches, men had praised his bravery on the battlefield, and ancient vampires had told him he was their leader, and yet nothing had sounded quite as ego-satisfying as Alexis acknowledging he had a nice package.

"Get in the room, Alexis." He took her arm to tug her forward.

She gave him one of those karate maneuvers and sent his hand sailing up in the air. "No pulling."

"I wasn't pulling," he said in exasperation. "I was encouraging you to move forward."

An extensive eye roll was her response.

"What time is it?" he complained, giving his door a satisfying slam shut when she finally moved forward enough for clearance.

"It's like three in the afternoon." She went over to his minifridge and opened the door. With a muffled scream, she slammed it back shut. "Geez, there are bags of blood in there. I was hoping for a diet soft drink."

Ethan scratched his chest and sat down on the sofa, spreading his legs apart for full effect. "To what do I owe the pleasure of your company? I didn't expect you back until this evening."

But he really liked that she'd shown up early. So much so, he had to wonder why.

"You're not going to get dressed, are you?" Alexis stood with her hand on her hip.

"No, I am not. Once you leave, I am going back to bed."

"So you don't have a coffin?"

"Not since the seventeenth century, and I don't miss it in the slightest. Wood does not make a comfortable bed."

"I read online that vampires can't stay awake during the day. They fall into a coma-like sleep. Does that happen to you?"

Now he was tempted to roll his eyes. "Do I look like I'm in a coma to you?"

"No, you look raring to go."

"Then there is your answer. Perhaps we should go over some vampire basics."

"Okay. But first I have to know if you heard anything about the guy who shot you."

"No. Not yet. But I expect we'll have some answers tonight."

"Does that happen a lot? People trying to kill you?"

"Hardly ever," he assured her. "Maybe once a century or so."

She frowned, a delicious little pout that had him considering sucking her lip into his mouth.

"Ethan, who knows about you? Vampires, I mean. That there are vampires in Vegas."

"No one." Sin City made a perfect cover for their kind. In a city of fluorescent lights and twenty-four-hour-a-day gambling, shopping, eating, and banking, no one thought a thing about him entering his casino every night instead of during the day.

Alexis didn't seem to like his answer. She tugged on the hem of her tank top, flipping it up, then down, up, then down. "Do all of you live here?"

"No. We're all over the world, scattered to make us less noticeable, but also because we are of different backgrounds, speak different languages. Most want to stay near where they were born and lived their mortal lives."

She was pacing back and forth, clearly agitated. Ethan knew she needed answers, but he also knew too much information too soon might overwhelm her, turn her from him. That he most definitely did not want.

"Alexis, would you like to see the casino? I could give you a tour and we can talk."

"I don't gamble. I don't drink. I hate burlesque shows. And I'm not real crazy about smoking or the sound of slot machines."

"Then why do you live in Vegas?"

That stopped her pacing. She looked startled. "I don't know." Tugging on her shirt again, she said, "Because I was raised here, I guess. I've never lived anywhere else. And because of Brittany."

He wondered if it was time to bring up the sticky issue of

Brittany being a half-vampire. Alexis seemed to have forgotten that he'd mentioned that little tidbit when she had thought they were still playing a game. Deciding to let it go for the time being, he asked, "Are your mother and father still here?"

She snorted. "No. My father left when my mother told him his newborn baby girl, Brittany, was not his child. Never to be seen or heard of again, I might add. And I *was* legitimately his kid."

Ethan stood up, suddenly sorry he was naked. He had the urge to pull her into his arms. She was so tough, so determined, so hurt deep down inside. He wasn't a man who carried past hurts around with him, but he understood loneliness.

"My mother died of a drug overdose. She was a stripper." The look she shot at him was defiant, proud.

He stopped where he was. Alexis wasn't a woman who would appreciate his pity. That would send her running from him. "I hear there's good money dancing," he said, forcing nonchalance into his voice. "Good way to raise a couple kids when you're a single parent."

It was the right thing to say, even if it rubbed against his every instinct of protectiveness.

Alexis let out a sharp burst of laughter. "Shut up and put some pants on, Carrick."

But he caught the smile that crossed her face before she turned, and Ethan had the sudden frightening feeling that something had just happened to him that would have far-reaching consequences.

Time to pull out the poetry.

He had met his match.

As Alexis watched Ethan's fine-looking butt head into the bedroom, she gave a construction worker whistle, fingers between her lips, just to rattle him. And it was a damn sexy behind. Tight and muscular.

Ethan paused. "You know," he said over his shoulder, "for a woman who claimed she didn't find me attractive, you're a voracious ogler."

Sometimes he sounded a bit too British. "A voracious ogler? Is that like a vicious ka-nid? Can that be my title?" She gave a stately stroll across the room. "Hello, I'm a voracious ogler." With a queen's wave, she nodded her head. "Yes, yes, thank you so much. I know. Yes, good to see you, yes, quite so. We *are* pleased with the results of the election. Here's to four more years of prosperity and progress."

"Forty."

"Forty what?" She dropped the accent.

"Years. The term of the presidency is forty years."

That was a little reminder of what she was dealing with here. It still seemed so incredibly make-believe. Except she'd seen Ethan bleed out, and twenty hours later he was healthy and standing, without a single scratch on his naked, hard body. It was real.

"Well, aren't you guys thinking ahead? That makes total sense." She resumed her regal persona. "Here's to forty more years of prosperity and progress in the Vampire Nation."

The words were barely out of her mouth before she suddenly found herself hauled up against Ethan's naked body. "Wha—"

He cut her off with a kiss—a long, juicy, hello Mr. Tongue kiss—that had her swallowing her question and clinging like shrink wrap to his chest.

"You're turning me on, you know," he said, even as his lips trailed down her neck.

Alexis dropped her head back, the crotch of her jeans erupting with volcanic heat, her breath shallow and excited. Damn, he knew what he was doing. Years of experience, she imagined. "Was it the queen voice? That can be a turn-on."

"It wasn't the queen voice." His tongue moved into her ear then out again, leaving her feeling warm, wet, and invaded. "I'm just having a hard time resisting you."

"It doesn't feel like you're being very successful at resisting me." Alexis took advantage of the moment and slapped her hands onto his buns. Oh, yeah. Hot and hard.

"I don't suppose I am." He yanked the top of her tank down practically to her belly button. And sucked the swell of her breast.

"Mmm," she said eloquently as her knees went weak, her nipples sprung up, and her doo-dah rolled out the welcome mat. Oh, yeah, this was working. Hot vampire kisses.

What a difference a day made, twenty-four little hours . . . as her brain sang, so did her body, and when Ethan reached her nipple with his mouth and plucked it through her bra, she came dangerously close to levitation.

Right as his tongue made wet swirls over her sensitive nipple, his erection managed to slide right between her thighs. Perfect fit. Denim was no barrier against the hot heat of him nudging along her clitoris, and as Alexis dug her fingers into the bare flesh of his upper arms, Ethan stroked.

Once, twice, while she sucked in massive amounts of air and gave an agonizing groan of abandon. She wasn't sure when she had suddenly morphed into go-with-the-flow girl, but he was going and she was flowing.

Until he yanked back so fast she almost landed in a heap on the floor. "Sorry," he said, running his hands through his hair.

Alexis just stared at him, her body cursing and whining and screaming for more. "Excuse me?"

"I didn't mean to do that. I apologize for moving too quickly."

Said the man who was naked. There was a red flush to his skin. Everywhere. And he looked a bit sheepish.

Men obviously never changed. "I would think that after all these years of living, you would have figured out that no woman on earth, or any other planet for that matter, wants a man who has just kissed her to apologize. If she didn't slap you, say no, or knee you in the nuts, and she kissed you right back, chances are she wanted it. And she doesn't appreciate the 'gee, sorry my hormones overtook me and made me suck face with the first available female, but now I wish it hadn't happened' response."

"I beg your pardon?"

"Go get dressed and take me on your damn tour," she snapped at him, annoyed that he looked genuinely puzzled.

"Brilliant idea." He did that vampire trick. There one minute, gone the next.

Lips still wet and swollen, she stuck her hands in her pockets. "Brilliant idea," she mocked in a low voice, glaring at the empty room. "It'd be a brilliant idea to stick my foot in your ass."

"I heard that," he called from the bedroom down the hall.

"What?" she asked, playing the innocent. Then whispered, "Sorry? Shit. I'll give you sorry."

"Will you now?" Ethan murmured from behind her, his mouth right next to her ear. She could hear the rustle of his clothes as he leaned forward, gripping her upper arms from behind. "That sounds promising."

"Quit doing that whole faster than the speed of light thing. It irritates me." Then she gave real punch to her words by leaning right back against him, her backside bumping his front side in a fun, cheap thrill collision.

Ethan ran his lips over her temple. "Sorry for saying sorry."

"Fine. It's all good. And maybe I'm sorry for waking you up."

"No, you're not."

Alexis had a George Washington moment. She could not tell a lie. "You're right. I'm not sorry in the least."

Because if she hadn't woken him up, she wouldn't have discovered that vampires don't need Viagra. She had to admit that had been worrying her a bit after all those messages she had read in the vampire slayers e-mail loop.

Not that she was going to sleep with him.

But it was good to know he was fully functional, in case she did decide to sleep with him, undersexed single woman that she was.

Time to call a spade a spade. There was a reason she hadn't alerted the vampire slayer group to her presence, or to the fact that there were hundreds of vamps in Vegas at the moment. There was also a reason she'd changed her mind and decided not to tell Ethan about the group, though her rationale behind that was much murkier. It kind of felt like she was protecting him, or somebody anyway, and she and Ethan were clipping along nicely. She selfishly did not want to interrupt that.

The reason she didn't date was because the men she met were shallow, patronizing, and intellectually narrow.

Ethan Carrick was the first man in almost a decade to arouse interest in her. To arouse anything in her.

His hands dropped to her waist as he nipped her earlobe.

Yep, he was really good at the arousing thing.

And she did want to sleep with him.

Ringo strode through the lobby of the Venetian. He didn't like being summoned by anyone. Donatelli was no different.

He had been hired. He'd completed the job. There was no reason for further contact aside from a cash payment, but he knew that wasn't the purpose of this meeting. He had been commanded to get himself down to Donatelli's hotel room for a reassessment of the contract's terms, according to the businessman's whipping boy.

Ringo was prepared to tell Donatelli to go fuck himself. He worked alone for the very reason that he didn't want to answer to anyone. He had left that behind when he was discharged from the service and he had no intention of being forced into bootlicking.

Fortunately, the hotel had zero security, because he was packing his piece.

The hit hadn't gone the way he had planned it, but he was smart enough to take advantage of an opportunity. What he didn't understand was what had happened in the few minutes prior to that. One minute he'd been getting it on with Kelsey the giggler, the next he'd been standing there with his dick hanging out and a big-ass crick in his neck. Alone.

He didn't black out for no reason. Which meant she'd slipped something into his drink. Yet she hadn't stolen his wallet, so he had no idea what she'd been after. And he wanted to know.

But first he had to resolve this little paperwork problem.

The door to Donatelli's room swung open before he could knock. "Mr. Donatelli is waiting on the veranda."

Ringo ignored the doorman and walked right past him to the sliding glass doors. The rush of heat hit him as he opened the door and stepped onto the patio. Donatelli was lounging in a wrought iron chaise in the shade, a glass of red wine in his hand, black Italian sunglasses covering his eyes.

"Columbia."

"Donatelli."

The man didn't look at him, but stared out across the Strip, and lifted his cigarette to his mouth. "There will be no payment. You didn't do what I asked you to."

Though Ringo was not an emotional man, the patronizing nonchalance of the Italian irritated him. But he just shrugged and leaned over the balcony, the sun hitting him in the face once he cleared the overhang of the balcony above. "I did what you asked. I killed him."

"I asked for specific requirements and they were not met. You neither killed him nor removed his head."

"I hit him. He was dead." But suddenly Ringo wasn't sure that he had. If Kelsey had drugged him, maybe the shooting of Carrick hadn't been successful. He'd thought it had gone off. That he'd plugged his mark straight in the heart twice, but maybe his perceptions were off.

If he had demanded payment from Donatelli without completing the hit, then his reputation was going to be damaged. Which wouldn't be good for business.

"Let us not argue over this. Go to The Ava and see if you killed him or didn't kill him. I'll give you until tomorrow morning to do the job, then I'm hiring someone else."

Ringo ground his teeth together, but managed to say, "Fine."

And this time, he'd stay the hell away from leggy brunettes and keep his mind on work.

Women were career suicide, and Ringo didn't want to wind up dead.

Twelve

"So how rich are you?" Alexis asked him as they entered the main gaming room on the first floor.

Ethan glanced down at her, amused. "I don't believe that is any of your damn business."

"Oh, come on. If I'm going to be your campaign girlfriend, I need all the facts." She looked up at him with bald curiosity.

"Here are the facts. This hotel and casino opened in the year two thousand to replace a venture I'd had in the early nineties when Vegas decided it wanted to go clean and cater to families. That replaced a smaller-scale hotel I'd had in the seventies. The Ava matches the pomp and grandeur of any other luxury hotel on the Strip. We have over two thousand guest suites, eight bars, six restaurants, a full service spa, three pools, two fitness rooms, and an indoor shopping complex that is designed to look like a Hollywood movie lot in the thirties and forties. We have a three-screen movie theater that plays two current releases and one black-and-white classic. It's a very successful establishment."

Arms crossed as she surveyed the room, Alexis glanced up at him. "You're proud of this hotel."

"I am." He liked the challenges it presented and the over-the-top grandeur. And the longer his immortal life lasted, the more he wanted to connect himself to the earth, to the feeling that people knew him, that he wasn't just a shadow shifting through life unknown.

"How the hell do you find time to run such a huge business and be president?"

"Being president really isn't a full-time job. Maybe twenty hours a week when I'm actually in office. Campaigning can be time-consuming, but Seamus organizes my schedule. He tells me where to go and I do it."

"And what to say?"

He heard the insult. "Not always. I do think for myself."

She snorted.

Which couldn't go unchallenged. "For example, Seamus doesn't approve of you as my choice for a mortal girlfriend. But I told him I didn't give a damn. I want you."

Alexis caught his innuendo, which was just as he'd intended. Her eyes narrowed as she stared up at him. Even with rather impressive pointy-toed heels on, she was still much shorter than he was. She licked her plump bottom lip, which made him want to direct this tour right back up to his suite, when she broke eye contact and started walking.

The way she went boldly into the room, charging ahead of him, attracted attention. The floor manager looked flustered to see him, and Ethan realized he wasn't usually around at four in the afternoon. He was never with a woman. Not on his casino floor anyway. Normally, he kept his affairs private, and in recent months there had been no affairs at all because of the election. He'd been a good little vampire.

It was absolutely killing him. Celibacy was for monks and ugly people.

"Mr. Carrick, what a surprise. Is there anything I can do for you, sir?"

"No, thank you, Jason. I'm just giving a tour to a friend."

"I'm his girlfriend," Alexis said and stuck her hand out. "Alexis Baldizzi, Clark County prosecutor." She pumped Jason's hand while he murmured a startled greeting.

Alexis smacked Ethan on the wrist. "I'll just introduce myself since you're too rude to do it."

Now Jason was wide-eyed.

Ethan was annoyed, but refused to show it. "Sorry, my dear. How inexcusable of me."

"See what I have to put up with?" Alexis asked Jason, hands going into the pockets of her jeans. "Now he's mocking me."

"I am not." He couldn't quite keep the edge of irritation out of his voice.

"Don't start with me, Ethan. I am so not in the mood." She gave him a glare. "Now get me a drink."

He hadn't expected Alexis capable of flouncing, but she did an admirable job. Clearing his throat, he said, "Excuse me, Jason, I need to, uh, get her a drink."

"No problem, sir."

Fuming, Ethan caught up with her. "You're not supposed to

make me look like an idiot. You're supposed to make me look considerate. And just with vampires, I might add," he said in a low undertone.

"Jason isn't one?"

"No."

"Well, how the hell am I supposed to know? How do you know if you meet someone for the first time?"

Ethan steered her past the bar. "I can sense it. Smell it."

Her lip curled. "Eew. What do mortals smell like?"

"Blood, among other things. Vampires smell like cool water, and their strength is like an aura surrounding them."

"Seriously?" She ground to a halt. "I smell like blood to you? That is so incredibly disturbing."

Oh, wonderful, he'd curled her stomach. "I can smell it, yes, but it's only part of the overall sense of you. I smell vanilla, clean flesh, mango shampoo." He leaned closer, whispered, "I smell your desire for me."

Her breath hitched. "Oh. So how am I supposed to tell who's mortal and who's not?"

"I'll tell you who is."

She moved away from him. "Brilliant. *Not.* How do I know how to act then? I should just be bossy all the time with you to be safe."

He bet she would love that. "I don't want you to be nasty to me. I'm trying to project the image of a kinder, gentler Vampire Nation, yes, but not a 'walk all over me' Vampire Nation."

"You really don't know what you want, do you?"

Oh, yes, he did. With a charming smile, he said, "I want you."

"Bite me, Carrick."

"That can be arranged." He loved the way her eyes told him everything, the way they lightened and darkened with her emotions. Maybe he couldn't read her thoughts, but he could see her feelings on her face, and while her words were tough, her eyes were starting to melt.

"Don't be a pervert."

He laughed. "Have you eaten dinner? Let me get you something."

"It's four in the afternoon, Ethan."

"Is that a no? Then walk the Strip with me and we'll have dinner." It had been months since he had been outside before sunset. He wouldn't mind revisiting the day with Alexis.

"Won't the sun fry you to a crisp and leave you in ashes on the sidewalk? Because I don't think I want to see that."

"No. And I wouldn't suggest a stroll if it would." They were standing right smack in the middle of the main floor, three feet from the bar. People were walking in every direction, and the constant ring of the machines vibrated the room around him. There was a low hum of voices, dealers and gamblers, and soft, piped-in music, but none of that was really registering with Ethan.

He saw only Alexis and the desire on her face that mirrored his.

"If I go for a walk and to dinner with you, will you let me practice my Soo Bahk Do on you later?"

That had the potential to be entertaining and sexual. "Sure."

"No campaign stuff tonight?"

"No. Tomorrow is the debate between myself and Donatelli. But tonight the main attraction in my casino is an appearance in the lounge by Tom Jones."

Seamus was going to burst a blood vessel when he found out

he was planning a night out with Alexis, but Ethan couldn't work up the regret. He did not need to go over another endless round of questions and note cards to prepare. He was as ready as he'd ever be to face his opponent.

Alexis grabbed his arm. "Tom Jones? Wow, I totally love Tom Jones. He's like quintessential Vegas—over the top and indecent fun. Let me just go grab a pair of underwear to throw at him and we'll be all set."

Over his undead body. If anyone was getting her underwear tossed in his face, it was going to be him.

"I don't think so, Ball Buster. You're not giving your panties to an old man."

"Oh, and you're so young, Garlic?"

"Garlic?" What the hell was that?

"Yep. Now we have pet names for each other, isn't that adorable? You're Garlic and I'm Ball Buster. Now everyone will believe we're a real couple."

Oh, God. Ethan would not laugh. He would not laugh.

He laughed. And Alexis laughed with him.

Normally on a Sunday, her only full day completely free of work, Brittany liked to go swimming in her apartment complex pool, do a little laundry, and cook dinner for her sister. This Sunday she was trolling around the shopping complex at The Ava, trying to run vampires to ground.

Or *a* vampire.

She wanted to see Corbin again. When she had screamed on the phone the night before, he had suddenly appeared beside her, full of concern. When she had reassured him she was okay, he had left her, but not before he gave her a ride down from the roof. And not before she'd seen the compassion in his eyes.

It had convinced her what she had thought all along about Seamus and Ethan. Vampires weren't soulless. They were lost souls. They just needed to give up the whole bloodsucking thing and they could be perfectly happy and productive people, with just an incredibly long life span.

She wasn't sure how long that life span would last if they did give up putting the bite on people, but it seemed worth investigating. It was sort of like with children. Parents didn't like their kids' actions at times but they still loved their offspring. Biting was bad, but vampires weren't.

It all made sense to her, except she didn't know where to find Corbin. He wasn't registered at the front desk, at least not under the name he'd given her, and Ethan didn't seem to be in his room. Hopefully, he was with Alexis being saved from eternal damnation. Brittany thought that would be ideal. Ethan saved, Alexis laid. Everyone benefited.

Wandering through the lobby for the fourth time, wondering if she should just go home, she ran into Seamus.

"Hey, Brittany. Have you seen Ethan?"

"No, I haven't. Have you seen Corbin?"

"Who?" Seamus looked at her in confusion. He was wearing a suit, as usual, and he had dark circles under his eyes like there hadn't been a whole lot of sleep for him lately.

"Corbin. The French guy."

He stiffened just a little. "I'm sorry. I don't know who that is."

How obvious was it that he was lying?

"No? I thought he was a friend of yours."

How does she know the banished one?

Seamus's thoughts floated over to her, and Brittany was just itching to know why Corbin had been ejected from the vampire coven, or whatever it was called.

"No, sorry, Brittany. If you'll excuse me?"

"Sure, Seamus." If he wasn't going to tell her, there wasn't much she could do about it. But Brittany had an idea. If she could hear vamp thoughts, maybe she could make them. Maybe she could locate Corbin by calling him.

Moving down the hall, her heels sinking into the soft gray carpet, she absently adjusted the strap of her orange sundress and clutched her purse. Maybe there was somewhere a bit more private, so she didn't look like an idiot mentally screaming for Corbin.

A hand touched her arm. "Kelsey."

She turned, startled, and looked at a man wearing a black silk shirt and dark glasses. Like the prescription sunglasses that take a few minutes to ease up after you've gone inside.

He realized immediately she wasn't the woman he was looking for. "Oh, I'm sorry, I thought you were someone else."

"That's okay." She smiled.

There was no responding smile. He just nodded, and Brittany felt the anguish from him roll over her like a rising tide. The emotion swelled and crashed over her, and she gave a little gasp as he walked away.

Swallowing hard, she shuddered as he turned the corner at the end of the hall.

Moving behind a large potted plant and screwing her eyes shut, she mentally screamed for Corbin. *Corbin! Corbin Jean Michel*

Atelier, where are you? I need you! That was a bit of an exaggeration but it never hurt to gain the jury's sympathy. Alex had taught her that.

Brittany? What ez wrong? Where are you?

The lobby at The Ava.

I am coming.

"Cool." She fluffed her hair and touched up her lipstick. No reason to look like a wreck. Less than sixty seconds later, he suddenly was right next to her.

Not there one minute, very much there the next.

Corbin grabbed her hand and raked his eyes over her, clearly looking for injury. "What ez the matter? Are you ill?"

She smiled. "No, I just wanted to see you."

"What?" He dropped his hand from hers. "Are you serious? You cannot do zat. You cannot call me, letting me think you are bleeding and dying and it ez nothing."

"Oh, lighten up. I didn't know how else to find you." Corbin was wearing another one of those perfectly put together man out-fits, heavy on the black. "Now that you're here, let's go play."

"Play? Play what?" He gave her a look of distress.

"Just play. I want to get to know you. I want you to tell me all about yourself. You can unburden to me . . . I'll be your confidant."

"I do not ask for a confidant. I do not want to share ze things with you." He waved his hand in the air. "Zat is for your Dr. Phil, not for Corbin Atelier."

Alexis pouted. She really thought he was just adorable, but very melodramatic. Memories of him caressing the woman on the chaise lounge rose in her mind. She wondered what it had felt like to be that woman . . . what his mouth would feel like on her neck, his hand on her thigh.

"Stop zat, with the lip, and ze thoughts," he said, looking appalled. "You do not understand who and what I am. You do not even understand who you are."

Hello, this was not news. "Well, I'm trying to understand you. I keep asking you what's up, but you won't tell me."

He crossed his arms, and glanced down the hall. He had thin lips, and an inch-long white scar at the base of his chin, which kept his elegant bone structure and proportioned face from looking too pretty boy.

"Just tell me . . . why are you banished? It can't be that bad. I mean, you're not like in jail or anything. Did you sleep with someone's wife? Or insult a bigwig?"

"Nothing so ridiculous." Corbin swung his gaze back to hers. His jaw locked. "I killed a woman. Zat is why I am no longer part of the group. Carrick allows me to live here if I do not cause trouble, but I am not welcome at anything vampire."

Brittany heard the words, but couldn't quite register their meaning. "You killed a woman? What do you mean?"

"I mean, our kind is not allowed to kill mortals. Zat is the law. I broke it."

She shook her head. "But . . ." She didn't sense those feelings from him at all. He felt sad, lonely, lost, but not angry. Not murderous, or malevolent, or violent. There must be more to the situation, because she just didn't believe him.

"You will get us both in trouble if you persist in contacting me. I must bid you adieu, before we are seen. And before I find myself tempted to do something with you zat I should not."

"Corbin." Brittany knew, as sure as she knew her upper left molar had a cavity, that he wasn't telling her the whole story. She could not believe he was a ruthless, coldhearted killer.

He leaned closer, like he would touch her, but he only whispered, "Guard yourself, *ma chérie*. Eventually they will come for you."

Then he was gone.

But Brittany felt his hand on her cheek as if he were still in the room, and she closed her eyes against the confusion, embracing the melancholy feeling of longing instead.

The longing that echoed within her, surprising the heck out of her.

Clearly she was meant to help Corbin, whether he liked it or not.

Ethan wasn't so bad now that he was trying to seduce her instead of her sister.

She just might actually let him. He was working pretty hard. Dinner at a luxurious buffet, where he'd sipped wine while watching her tuck back about nine plates of food. Touring his casino and hotel, strolling down the Strip, and now sitting in a private garden on the roof of the first-floor restaurant on the backside of his building. The little alfresco patio's purpose seemed to be to camouflage several large air-conditioning units with indigenous desert plants, but it also made a nice secluded seating area.

The units created a soft hum, drowning out the traffic noise from the street, and there were several seating groups of teak chairs and love seats, with thick aqua cushions. It was a little hot, but not too bad since the heat of the day was over, and Alexis had ditched her shoes.

Normally it was a matter of pride to keep them on, so she could feign height, but Ethan already knew she was the size of a nine-year-old, so she figured it wasn't necessary to keep up appearances. She was stretched out lengthwise on one of the love seats, her legs draped over the opposite arm, and she was feeling content with the company she was keeping.

Ethan was talking about his childhood in England as he sat on the love seat opposite her, his feet crossed at the ankles. He was telling her about his mother. "She was blond, like you, with very fair skin. Petite, with a delicate appearance, and a soft voice. At sixteen she was given to my father to help establish Norman control amongst the Anglo-Saxons. My father was older, in his thirties, and a brisk, dominating sort of man. Yet it's my understanding that she was the only person on earth who could make my father feel fear."

"My kind of woman."

"No doubt." Ethan placed his hands behind his head and closed his eyes. "It has been over nine hundred years since my mother died, yet I can still see her face. Hear her sweet voice as she sang to me. She was a good woman and I loved her dearly. Love her."

Alexis felt something stirring inside her. A sympathy for him, a compassion for the difficulty of losing everyone in his mortal life nearly a millennium ago. And she felt her own loneliness reflected in him.

"She sounds wonderful." Alexis swung her feet and sighed. She didn't talk about her mother. Ever. Not even with Brittany, unless it was to make a snide comment. She knew that she should be over it, but she wasn't, and so she didn't talk about it. But with Ethan, somehow she felt he would understand. He had seen a lot of life, known a lot of people, and it wouldn't shock him to hear the story of a woman who'd had four husbands and never been happy.

The woman who had convinced Alexis that marriage wasn't in her future, sparing herself from the torment and drama her mother had gone through.

"My mom . . . well, she was just someone who shouldn't have had children. She wasn't a bad mom, she just wasn't all that great either. She was selfish, you know? Always running around with this or that guy who was the love of her life, or the one who was going to give her a big break in show business. She forgot birthdays, she forgot parent-teacher conferences . . . and she would give my friends coupons for her strip club to pass on to their fathers."

"That sounds very difficult."

She shrugged. "Yeah, but I know a lot of kids have it worse. I've seen those kids. I've seen horrific abuse cases . . . I've talked to those children and had to put them on the witness stand. I don't have anything to complain about so why am I such a baby?"

"Maybe because you love your sister and would do anything to protect her, even become a vampire slayer, and you don't understand why other people—including your mother—don't feel the same way about their families."

Alexis closed her eyes against the last fading sunlight and sighed again. Ethan made a lot of sense, and his words made her feel a thousand times better. That scared her a little, at the same time it thrilled and pleased.

She could like him. She could even sleep with him.

But she could not fall for Ethan Carrick, for about four hundred reasons.

Like . . . there was no family health insurance for mortal-vampire unions.

And she would eventually be a saggy, wrinkly, incontinent old woman and he would still be sexy.

Plus she was sure her boss would not like her hooking up with a guy who drank blood. It would be really lousy publicity for the office.

But just talking? Just hanging with him for a week was a temptation she couldn't pass up.

"You might be on to something, Ethan." She studied him sitting in the shade of the building. "So how come sun doesn't kill you?"

"I don't know. It's very draining but it certainly doesn't kill me. We are night dwellers, but not unholy demons who will explode in an agonizing death when a cross is shoved at us. I suspect we have mutated genes, but I leave that to the scientists, not politicians."

"*Mutant* doesn't sound any better than *vampire*."

"I'm over it," he said.

Alexis laughed. "So have you been married like thirty times?" She was sure this was going to lead in unpleasant directions, but she couldn't let him kiss her again, with tongue, until she heard that he wasn't a total dog.

Life longevity didn't mean he was exempt from morality, in her opinion.

"I've never been married."

She wasn't sure if that was good or bad. At first, it sounded good, like he was holding out for Miss Vampire Right, but then maybe he was just a selfish, confirmed bachelor.

"Have you been married?"

The question startled her. She hadn't thought that maybe he would wonder about her past, too, short as it was compared to his. "No. I've been building my career. And the men I meet on the job are either attorneys or criminals and neither really appeals to me. Besides, not every man sees the charm in a short, extremely independent woman who has a peach butt."

Ethan played with the leaf of the oleander bush growing in a pot next to him. "I confess I've never really spent a lot of time with independent women. I was always drawn to the sweet, feminine, simple types, but since meeting you I've come to realize I've denied myself a great deal of pleasure. While sweet women can be soothing, it seems in my old age I crave intelligent conversation as much as pretty smiles. You give me both, Alexis."

It was so sexy and romantic, she didn't believe it for a second, and treated him to a heavy eye roll.

"And your backside looks nothing like a peach, though I haven't seen you without clothes. Perhaps it's fuzzy?" He shot her a grin.

Whenever he turned her words around on her, she had to struggle not to give in to the juvenile urge to stick her tongue out at him. "No, it's not, and if that's some kind of psychological maneuver to get me to take my clothes off and prove it, you're going to be disappointed. I'm stubborn and competitive, but my butt is none of your business."

"You're the one who brought up that particular body part in the first place."

"I hate it when you're right." She forced herself to sit up. "So, no wife, huh? You like playing the field?"

"Yes. And no. Had I found the right woman, my chosen one, I would have married. But I didn't."

Chosen one. Like a soul mate. Alexis figured if she'd ever stumbled across one of those for herself, she would take the plunge, too, despite her lack of successful role models. Yet she was pretty sure such an idealistic thing didn't exist. "Can you have children?"

"Only with a mortal woman, and that is frowned upon. Vampire women can't have children at all."

Oh, that figured. The guys were a thousand years old and still making sperm, and the women got nothing.

"So . . . if you have a kid with a mortal, what is the kid? Vortal? Mampire? Do you give them blood in a bottle or what?" It sounded a little creepy, actually. It was one thing to know intellectually that Ethan had to drink blood, from a blood bank, to survive. It was another thing to picture a little five-year-old whipping his fangs out on the playground and biting into a blood bag for an afternoon snack before his nap.

"No. No blood bottles." Ethan shook his head, like she was being outrageous.

"What? It's a legitimate question."

"Impures are raised mortal, some never even knowing they are half-vampire. But they are strong, free from many common ailments, and have a very long natural lifespan. All those hundred-and-ten-year-olds you see on the news? Impures."

"Really." Alexis thought that wasn't such a bad bargain. You didn't have to suck blood but you got to live a long time in good health. Sign her up.

"They also tend to sunburn easily and excel at sports.

Occasionally, they have the unique vampire trait of crying blood tears, which is usually chalked up to sinus infections."

"Hey, Brittany used to have that. It was totally gross. She hardly ever got colds, but when she did, her eyes would swell up and this nasty, bloody, pus-like stuff would come out. Freaked my mom out every time." Alexis gave a laugh remembering the way her mother used to make gagging noises when she'd hand Brittany a tissue.

Ethan didn't say anything.

Alexis glanced over at him. "What? It was funny. Brittany was such a girly-girl, even though she was always really good at sports, and to see her all puffed up like that, it had its element of humor."

He just stared at her expectantly. "What? Why are you looking at me like that, Ethan?"

Suddenly she remembered what he had told her the first night she'd met him. That Brittany was an Impure, half-vampire. She wasn't, of course, Alexis was sure of that, but here she was spouting all these similarities.

"Oh no, I know what you're thinking," Alexis said, her face going hot. Her baby sister was not a vampire, and she wouldn't accept anyone saying otherwise. Brittany loved garlic—it just wasn't possible. "Don't even go there. It's just a coincidence. Brittany's my sister, and while my mother was impulsive, I don't think she would have fallen for a vampire."

"Why not?" Ethan asked sensibly. "We seem like regular mortal men, don't we? We blend into society for the most part, and we are strong, some of us are attractive and charming . . . and some have stronger moral fiber than others, just like mortals. There is no reason to believe your mother would have known the truth if she were seduced by a vampire."

Alexis wasn't sure why she was so upset, but she was. Choosing to be with Ethan for a few days was one thing, but accepting that Brittany was vampire was more than she could handle. It was scary and unbelievable, disturbing and shocking. And if Brittany were an Impure, then she had a whole community that Alexis could never be a part of.

She was pretty sure that's what scared her the most.

"Given what you've said about your mother, it doesn't sound like she would have asked a lot of questions."

That made shame, pride, and anger all spark within Alexis. "Hey, that is still my mother you're talking about. She was a lot of things, but indiscriminate slut wasn't one of them."

Ethan sat back hard on the bench. "Alexis, I apologize. I didn't mean to sound insulting. I just meant she seemed impulsive and carefree."

Anger dissipated as quickly as it had formed. "Shit, I know. I'm sorry. And you're right. My mother was perfectly capable of meeting a man at her club and having an affair, thinking she was in love, without really asking a lot of questions. It's just . . ."

"If Brittany is Impure, where does that leave you?"

Tears rose in her eyes. It amazed her that Ethan cut so quickly to the heart of what was bothering her. That he understood her. "Yes."

He stood up and came over to her. He went down on his haunches in front of her, taking her hands gently. "You're still her sister, the most important person in the world to her, and that will never change. You're still Ball Buster, the best prosecutor this county has seen."

Yeah, yeah. She tried to choke out a retort, but she couldn't manage it.

His thumbs stroked across her palms. "And you're a very attractive woman. I hope you'll consider dating the president of the Vampire Nation for real."

Feeling vulnerable and needy were not emotions Alexis aspired to. But Ethan didn't make her feel small or melodramatic. He looked sincere, and strong, and unbelievably good-looking with his sharp bone structure and changeling blue eyes. They were light now, a sky blue on a sunny day. It seemed he wanted her, for now anyway.

And she didn't have any desire to protest or play hard to get.

Maybe there was more of her mother in her than she cared to admit.

She sniffled. "I have control issues, you know. It kills me that I might not be part of something important to Brittany. Not that I'm convinced she is half-vamp. She's not exactly fond of blood. She gets her steak and burgers well-done and flips out over getting her blood drawn."

Ethan tucked her hair behind her ear. It always amused Alexis when he did that. Despite her stature, Alexis had never really inspired nurturing from anyone. Not her mother, not teachers, not boyfriends.

Yet Ethan, the bloodsucking vampire, seemed determined to cuddle and comfort her, and treat her like she was delicate.

She liked it. She liked him.

"As for me and the president . . . well, as long as he knows what he's getting himself into."

Ethan smiled, his touch on her hands turning from soothing to seductive, sliding up her wrists. "He knows."

"Then tell the president that he should consider us dating for real."

"The president is pleased." Ethan moved into the space between them, head tilted, mouth open.

Alexis closed her eyes in anticipation. His lips covered hers softly, gently, with respect and kindness. She wasn't sure she'd ever been kissed quite like that, with a confidence, but also a reverence, and it awakened all sorts of emotions in her. Made her want more with him.

Lots more. With tongue more.

With a quick shift, she brought her arms around his neck, and moved forward so that her thighs slid between his chest and his biceps. Ethan had a hard, muscular body. He didn't even strain with his legs bent the way they were, or lose his balance as she wedged herself into him.

The kiss shifted quickly, gained speed and heat, and careened into erotic as he urged her mouth open with his tongue and invaded her with wet, darting strokes. Alexis groaned, her nipples budding painfully, her inner thighs restless and aching. She was close to him, brushing here, touching there, but it wasn't a full body slam, and it was enough to tease, but not to satisfy. She couldn't see or feel his erection, but she knew he was as aroused as she was.

His breathing was hard, urgent, and his technique became less exact, more grasping. Their lips were slick, colliding, and when he plucked at her nipple with two fingers, she jerked on the seat at the sharp bite of ecstasy. If he didn't stop, they were going to wind up naked on this teak outdoor furniture, and while that had its pluses, Alexis figured they'd be visible to people in approximately twenty thousand hotel rooms in Vegas.

"Ethan."

"Yes, BB?"

"BB?" she asked, distracted by his words and his wandering hand. Somehow he'd made his way up her T-shirt. "What the hell does that mean?"

Ethan's mouth moved over her neck. "Ball Buster is too long to keep saying. And BB can double as bold and beautiful."

"I see. Very charming." Alexis dodged the kiss he was about to press on her, and scooted her legs around his. It was time to get a grip on her control—she was not going to have sex outside. "But now you need to take me to Tom. It's time for the concert to start, Garlic."

He groaned, toying with the clasp on her bra. "Ah, come on, Alexis. Let's just skip it and go upstairs straightaway."

She wriggled out of his arms and headed for the door, despite the ache in her body. Walking away would hurt, but she'd thank herself for it later. She was too vulnerable to do this with Ethan right then—too raw and too willing to fall for him.

Forcing a sassy smile, she said, "You may have forever to live, but Tom and I don't. This may be my only chance to see him."

Thirteen

Of all nights for Carrick to break his fucking routine, it had to be this one. Ringo sat at the blackjack table and glanced at his watch for the third time. Every night Carrick came onto the floor at 8 P.M., except for tonight. It had been a risk to come to the casino in the first place since it was likely they had Ringo on tape, or had security on high alert because of the shooting.

There had been a shooting. Ringo knew he had definitely pulled the trigger on his gun since there were two shots missing. But whether he had actually hit Carrick or not was a mystery. And with the guy not showing tonight, it meant Ringo still didn't have answers. Carrick was either late, dead, or wounded. The news hadn't mentioned anything about Carrick or The Ava, and there wasn't a hint of any shooting, so Ringo didn't know what the hell to think.

The whole situation was starting to piss him off. His specialty was quick, clean kills with high-caliber weapons. He'd been a sniper in the Marines, and in a manner of speaking, he had continued with the same work.

He didn't kill with his hands, or with messy, convoluted sick shit like rope or a blunt object. He didn't want to beat anyone with anything, exert any sort of energy, or have to resort to violence. There was no blood on Ringo's hands, clothes, or shoes when he did his job, and half the time his victims never knew what had hit them.

If he had known Donatelli wanted something weird, he'd have said no thanks right from jump. But he'd thought an Italian businessman would appreciate a quick shooting, not go in for this mutilation crap. Ringo didn't even know how to cut someone's head off. He'd looked into it, and the bottom line was, it was messy as hell.

The Italian was going to have to settle for a slit to the throat, and even that didn't thrill him. He just wasn't comfortable putting his hands on anyone. Not that it mattered since Carrick was a no-show and come morning Ringo was either going to have to beg for another chance, run for his life, or plug Donatelli to end the situation.

Not happy choices.

"Hi!"

Fuckin' A. Ringo studiously ignored Kelsey, even as she popped her skinny little ass into the seat next to him. He did not need this shit right now.

"Don't you remember me?" She sounded hurt, as she tugged on his jacket sleeve.

Sitting very still, he turned his head and just looked at her. She was wearing a red dress this time, with crisscrosses under her breasts. She wasn't giggling, but pouting.

"I remember you with regret."

"That's not very nice."

If she was looking for nice, she needed a better strategy than hitting on guys hugging the gambling table. "I also remember you leaving me right when things were getting interesting."

"I got scared when things went so fast," she told him with a perfectly straight face. Her fingernail was trapped between her teeth and she slouched in the seat, looking worried. "I'm really, really sorry. Do you forgive me? I shouldn't have run out on you like that."

What was he, fucking stupid? "Yeah, let me guess. You're a virgin and you've never done anything like that before." He moved his money over to the dealer to go in for the next round, and scoffed at her. "I don't know what game you're playing, but find another fool. I don't make the same mistake twice."

"Me either, I promise. This time I won't get scared, because I know what to expect."

That made no sense to him. Expect what? It wasn't like he had a defect or a double-wide dick or anything. He wasn't a nature show, and there weren't that many ways to have sex standing up.

Kelsey smiled and leaned a little closer. "Tell me your name."

He blew cigarette smoke in her face. "I don't have a name."

"Oh, come on. Pretty please, with sugar on top?"

Ringo wanted to tell her to go fuck herself, since she had left him sixty seconds from sexual completion, feeling like he'd swallowed a shot glass of Demerol. Yet there was something about her . . . the way she was so perky and naive and flat-out stupid that he found he couldn't do it. He felt sorry for her.

Which shocked him, right down to his Italian leather sandals. It had been a helluva long time since he'd felt any emotion for anyone.

"No. Now here's a twenty." He put a chip in her hand. "Run along like a good little girl and find someone else to talk to."

She made a distressed noise, but he turned back to the table. He noticed she didn't set down the money he'd given her when she stood up.

But instead of leaving, she draped herself over his shoulder. Ringo stiffened. He didn't want her touching him. And under his jacket he carried his gun.

Ready to shove her off, or leave the table, he was shifting when she whispered in his ear, in an urgent voice, "You can't kill him, you know."

That stopped him cold. Abandoning his money and the game, he stood up and clamped a hand onto her wrist. She sucked in an exclamation of shock and pain.

But he just held her and said quietly, "We're going for a little walk."

Fear flashed in her eyes, but she didn't call for help.

And when he pulled her, she came along with him, giving zero resistance, like a skinny lamb with lipstick straight to slaughter.

Ethan couldn't believe he'd let Alexis throw her panties at Tom Jones on the stage.

But she had said she was repressed, and never did anything

fun, and this was necessary to prevent her from becoming an angry, shriveled-up cat woman.

Ethan couldn't follow the leap in logic, so he had just nodded. But now that they were heading upstairs in the elevator, he was very much aware of the fact that under her tight, low-rise jeans, she was panty-free.

He wasn't a big fan of denim, finding the seams uncomfortable, and jeans awkward as hell to get off a woman. There was something much more satisfying about a dress dropping to the ground in a pool of satin or muslin than yanking and jerking at tight pants, but he was resigned to modern fashion.

And the thought that Alexis wasn't wearing a stitch under that denim did things to his own jeans.

Like creating a pop-up tent.

"That was so much fun."

"I'm glad you enjoyed it."

"I'm sorry you were the only man there besides Tom and the bouncers." Alexis turned and put her hand on his chest. "But at least you're the owner of the casino so it didn't look too weird."

"I can handle looking weird." Ethan gripped her waist, determined to end the night buried deep inside Alexis. After enduring that screaming estrogen fest, he wasn't going to settle for anything less.

"And I'm sorry I hit you in the face with my panties when I wound up to throw." She smirked as she walked her fingers up his chest.

"I didn't mind, trust me." Though he would have liked to have kept the scrap of satin himself, not watch it arc through the air and wind up at the feet of a geriatric sex symbol. He hadn't been thrilled when she'd rushed into the bathroom to strip them off in the first place, but he was trying to focus on the end result, not the why.

She was naked under there, and that was the important thing.

Especially now that his hands were on her tight backside, running over those curves and dipping down between her legs. Her breath hitched and Ethan leaned down, intent on claiming those plump pink lips, when the elevator door dinged and slid open.

"Bloody hell," he said, as she darted away from him.

Alexis ran down the hall to her room, shoving the key card into the door slot. Half the time Alexis didn't carry a purse, she just stuffed her keys and driver's license in her pants pocket, and Ethan found that an interesting trait in a woman. Most he knew carried an entire drugstore in their handbag.

He strolled casually after her as she stepped into her room, his still present erection discouraging speed. With a quick burst of energy, he could catch her, pick her up, and have her clothes off before she could even take a breath to protest. But he didn't feel like doing that now. He wanted to let Alexis lead. She craved control and he would give it to her.

It was hard to remember why that was an intelligent idea when he walked through her door and got a foot right in the chest. A whoosh came out of his mouth as a sharp pain vibrated through him.

"What the hell was that for?" he asked as she dropped her leg back down, her fists up and ready.

"You said I could practice," she said, bouncing on the heels of her tiny feet. "But I guess I shouldn't have nailed you right where you got shot. I wasn't thinking. Sorry."

Ethan realized Alexis was still thinking of him as a mortal man, with all the inherent vulnerabilities and weaknesses. That was inaccurate, and the one thing he could not tolerate was pity. Concern was well and good, and showed she cared about him, but Alexis didn't seem to understand the full scope of his powers.

Ethan got a little irritated.

"I am a Master Vampire, nearly one thousand years old. I battled the Turkish in the First Crusade, the French in the Hundred Years' War—which I fought for all one hundred years, by the way—and the Germans in both World Wars. One little foot in my chest from a pint-size prosecutor is not going to take me down, bullet or not."

Her mouth dropped. He realized that perhaps his words were more incendiary than informative, right as the butt of her hand shot out toward him. This time he saw it coming and blocked her.

But while he was busy preventing her hand from ramming into him, without actually using any sort of force that could hurt her, she pivoted and kicked him right below the knee.

A wince slipped out before he could prevent it. It had been a long time since he'd seen a battle. Maybe he was getting soft if a blow to the shin hurt.

"Pint-size? I'll give you pint-size."

Once again Ethan wished he could read Alexis's mind so he could anticipate what she had in store for him. He was hoping this was the point where she stripped and seduced him, but somehow he didn't think that was where she was going with it.

Just in case things got ugly, he closed the door and moved away from the mirrored closet doors, and into the open living area, backing up slowly so he could keep his eye on her.

"I didn't mean it as an insult. I was merely pointing out that I am not the wimp you seem to think I am. And you're not a wimp either, as you have demonstrated on several occasions."

Instead of replying, she threw a series of kicks, punches, and jabs that had him scrambling to block her. With his reflexes, it should have been a breeze, but since he couldn't read her thoughts or anticipate her moves, and was very conscious of holding back his strength so he didn't hurt her, she managed to land a few shots.

Most he blocked, but she got a foot to his shoulder, a hand to his gut, and an elbow in a place that was just going to hurt both of them if she wasn't careful.

"Alright, BB, you put Buffy to shame." He held up his hands in mock surrender. "You kick vampire ass." Now he wanted her ass in his bed.

Alexis grinned. That scared him. And he had agreed to this. In her mind, he had no doubt she was simply practicing. She wasn't going to let it go yet, not until she was finished.

Ethan felt himself smiling back. Alexis got his blood flowing, aroused his competitive nature. He could hear her blood pumping faster than normal, her heart rate increasing as she lightly danced on the balls of her feet.

"What, you're not finished? Got something else for me?"

"You know it. I'm just getting warmed up." She gave one of those karate yells that impaled his eardrums like a steel rod.

Then she came at him with a flying front kick. Afraid he'd knock her to the ground if he thrust her leg aside, he stepped back out of her reach.

"Ooohh, vampire speed," she said as she landed with a soft thump on the carpet. "That's cool." Her hands unclenched, and she looked finished. Satisfied.

Ethan relaxed his own shoulders and fists. In time to take a blow to the chin, one that sent his teeth slamming into his tongue, drawing blood, and rattling his skull. For such a little foot, which had to reach so far in the air, it packed a wicked punch. Shaking his vision back into focus, he gave her an assessing stare.

"All right, my dear, I'm done holding back. That annoyed me."

"Holding back? Please. You weren't holding back. You just can't handle me."

But this time when she went at him, he was ready and didn't temper his response. She went right with a knife hand, and he blocked. Left, he grabbed her wrist. He dodged out of the way of her palm, and stopped the right, right, left combo she threw at him. She pivoted, he ducked the kick, she threw a fake kick, then went with the opposite foot, only to find her toes jammed into the palm of his hand.

Sweat dampened her forehead and her eyes narrowed in concentration. They circled each other, Alexis poised for attack, Ethan on the defensive. His enjoyment of her grew with each blow she threw, his respect for the warrior in her higher than he'd ever felt for a woman before, and he found himself aroused. Excited.

Physical exertion mixed with the competitiveness between them. When tossed in with the attraction he had for her, which had been hovering close to the surface all night, like a pile of kindling ready to be lit, their sparring took on a sexual tone to Ethan.

Aggressive foreplay, but foreplay nonetheless. He was turned on, fully hard, and breathing in quick, shallow bursts. His fangs wanted to let down, both from blood lust and from sexual want, though he resisted that. He'd save the first bite for when Alexis was writhing in passion beneath him.

After several long seconds of circling each other, she darted forward. He blocked, but she rained strikes on him one right after the other until they were both a blur of arms and legs, sweaty and bruised from the smack of skin and bone colliding, neither the clear winner. Alexis was relentless, and her determination and skill gave her enough of an edge to sneak in a punch or a jab here and there, which annoyed him and thrilled her.

Especially when she pulled that leg swipe move on him, and he tripped. Taking advantage, she thumped him in the chest and he lost his balance. Knocking his knee on the coffee table, he stumbled back. Alexis threw a punch with a loud "Ki-Hap!" but when she touched him, Ethan clamped his hand around her wrist.

When he fell, she went with him, landing on his body with a grunt. Not giving her time to react, Ethan flipped her onto her back. But she kicked him in the ass and skidded herself out from under him. They were rolling, bumping the coffee table, locked together, squeezing thighs and calves, and both trying to get the best of each other. Neither willing to give up.

"You know, this can only end in sex," he told her as she flattened her palm on his forehead in an attempt to hold him down on his back.

"That's what I'm hoping," she said, breathing hard, breasts brushing his chest.

If he wanted to, he could send her thirty feet across the room with one push, but he wanted to fight fair, and on her terms. That didn't mean he couldn't take it to the next level, though. On his back, Alexis on his lap, he reached forward and grabbed the fabric of her tight T-shirt. With just a little yank on his part, it split into two pieces, resisting only a bit at the neckline before completely giving way.

"What the . . ." Alexis exclaimed, then moaned when he cupped both breasts, flicked open the front latch of her bra, and kneaded the firm, warm flesh.

Eyes glazed, pupils dilated, a thin sheen of moisture on her upper lip, she leaned down and kissed him with hard, eager movements. She nipped his lip with her teeth, which shot desire through every inch of his body, while she ground her spread thighs on his erection.

They kissed with hot, tangled tongues, her nipples beading under his thumbs, and the air was filled with their excited breathing, the rapid race of their hearts, and the seductive flow of Alexis's blood through her plump veins. He rolled her onto her back, and she kicked him in the thigh.

"No, I want on top."

"Then take it," he told her, desire thick in his mouth, and arousal reaching a fevered pitch. It had been hundreds of years since he had wanted with this desperate level of intensity, this slam-and-take instinct.

When she got turned on, her eyes went the most amazing shade of aqua. They were that color now, cloudy with passion, and sparking with sensual confidence.

"Okay." She tried to turn him, but he kept himself stiff, hovering over her. Dropping his head, he flickered his tongue over her nipple.

There was a tiny shudder from her, a pause as her eyes fluttered shut, but then she gathered herself and yanked at his shoulder, trying to roll him. Legs clamped around his thighs, she tugged and swore while he laughed.

"Nice try."

"Bite me." Then she stopped struggling. "Shit, I've got to stop using that expression." Letting go of him, she wiggled out of the remains of her shirt and slid her bra off her shoulders.

Ethan ripped off his shirt. "I'll take that as an invitation."

Alexis clapped her hand over his mouth. "To bite? I don't think so."

He nipped her finger, then sucked it in between his lips. She jerked beneath him, her eyes rolling back as he drew her into the hot moisture of his mouth.

"That's not so bad," she admitted.

"That wasn't a bite. That was a nip and a suck." He took the tip of her wet finger and swirled it over her nipple. "When I bite, you'll know it. You'll feel it everywhere, like a thousand tongues caressing all over your body, and you'll beg me not to stop."

A moan ripped from her. Then she was unzipping her jeans and trying to shove them down one-handed. "If you bite me, I won't become a vampire, will I?"

"No." Ethan gave her some assistance, pulling her pants down inside out. He didn't even stop to regret the passing of dresses and pantaloons when her bare body was revealed to him. He swallowed the excess saliva in his mouth.

Alexis was incredible. Curvy and feminine, that wonderful modern combination of physically fit, with defined muscle tone, but all woman, rounded and contrasting. A woman who made him feel like a man.

She was kicking violently at her jeans, still trapped on her ankles, and the jerks did interesting things to her breasts. He took one into his mouth, stilling her. Oh, yes. She was sweet and salty, her tight nipple tantalizing and teasing his teeth.

Too soon. It was too soon. Yanking back, Ethan bent down, disposed of her pants, and ran his hands up the length of her soft, supple body. "You are beautiful, you know." Brushing over the curls at the apex of her thighs, he added, "Golden. I want to eat you." He pressed a kiss right on the dewy mound.

Alexis was surprised she didn't climax right then and there, and all thoughts of waiting to have sex were banished. They were doing this now, hard and fast. She groaned and pulled him by the hair back up to her mouth. Ethan brought out the violent in her. But between the talking, and the show, and the electric sparring, she was feeling inhaled by an intensity of feelings for him. Swallowed, urgent, desperate, like she would do anything to get him inside her. Like nothing would be enough until he was.

Between hot kisses, she murmured, "Get your pants off." Groping at his waist, she tried to find the snap on his pants, but it eluded her. So she settled for a killer squeeze on his tight butt.

His taste was tangy, like salsa, and his tongue did delicious circles around hers. But then he pulled back, forcing her hand to fall off his backside. Alexis gave a groan of disappointment, and he settled back down against her.

With no jeans on.

Holy vampire erection. It was nudging right against her, big and thick, and oh, my. "Where did your pants go? Did you vaporize them or something?"

Ethan rocked his hips, grinding their bodies together. "No. You blinked. And while you were blinking, I took them off."

That was kind of scary. "Show-off." But she wasn't all that up-set when she resumed her previous position and got to stroke all over his bare butt.

"No, just desperate for you."

That was a good thought. "Condom on, too?"

He paused. "No."

"Well, get to it, speedy." She didn't want to think about the re-ality of it, but she had to face it. Lord only knew some of the places his stake had been buried in the past nine hundred years, and she didn't want to find out anytime soon.

Ethan stood up, completely and gloriously naked.

"Where are you going?" she asked, panicking that he didn't have condoms. She certainly didn't.

"I have one in the pocket of my jeans, but I threw my jeans a little farther than I meant to."

One? Like that was going to be enough. And where the hell were his jeans, the hallway?

Almost. They were dangling off the minibar, clear on the op-posite side of the room. Considering Alexis had never even seen him take the pants off, there was an element of freak-out to that, but she decided to ignore it.

Especially when he retrieved a condom from his wallet—which made Alexis briefly wonder what else was in a vampire's wallet—and sheathed himself. When he turned, she decided any and all questions could wait until the end of the session, because that thing was coming at her.

"Hail to the chief," she said with enthusiasm, moving her legs restlessly on the thick carpet.

Ethan laughed. He had a nice laugh, rich and full, like a good beer sliding down your throat on a hot day. "You aren't going to start humming, are you?"

"No, but I do feel like I should honor you in some way. Wow." She didn't even mind that her words might go straight to Ethan's head. Both heads, and she'd be in business.

"You do realize that by saying things like that, you've eliminated my ability to make love to you slowly and tenderly." He dropped to the floor in front of her and spread her legs with a quick jerk on her calves.

"I didn't think we were going for slow and tender. Maybe next time." Alexis closed her eyes when he kissed her, licking along her bottom lip. He moved, nuzzling into her neck, while his finger worked its way inside her, sinking deep, then stroking her clitoris.

"Yeah, definitely next time. Fast and hard is good," she panted as he petted and kissed, his tongue doing a delicious little swirl over her flesh. Then she felt his teeth sink into her neck, a quick sharp invasion that startled her.

"Oh!" Alexis tried to shift away from him, but Ethan held her firmly, and as he drew on her with erotic tension, she felt an answering ache between her legs. When he pulled harder, she went wet, her body aching with want, as the room tilted dizzily behind Ethan's head. Closing her eyes, her startled gasp drew out into a moan of ecstasy.

"*Oooohhhh*, yes," she breathed, raising her hips into his finger, her breasts crushing into his hard, warm chest.

It was like the ultimate tease, like he was stimulating her everywhere, over every inch of her body, dipping into and tasting every crevice, drawing her passion right out of her, except the one place that so desperately wanted him.

"More," she said, wiggling and squirming beneath him, pinned on the hard carpet.

Ethan broke the embrace, removed his finger, placed his mouth over hers. His tongue thrust between her lips right as he entered her body with a hard slap.

Alexis came, rocking and shuddering with her violent climax, unable even to reach up to grab hold of Ethan. She heard the yelps that ripped from her mouth, couldn't believe them, even as she rode the wave of pleasure on and on, squeezing herself around him as he thrust.

He moved through her aftershocks as she murmured, "Damn, I'm easy." She sucked in a gulp and tried to shake her hair out of her eyes, woozy and drowning in endorphins.

But he didn't stop thrusting in her, not even when he rolled onto his back, landing her on his chest and lap. "Move on me," he demanded. "Make me come."

There was a challenge. Alexis propped herself up with her hands, still wet, still aroused, but feeling limp and done in. She looked down at him, his fierce expression, which had more of the warrior he'd been than the angel his mother had called him. Ethan was a complex man, of many shades and sides, and he obviously knew just how to push her buttons.

Without hesitation, she dug her nails into the carpet, sat half up, and rode him. Slowly at first, then faster, then with total abandon, until they were both moaning in tandem, the slick sound of their bodies joining driving her like a whip. When Ethan gritted his teeth, she knew he was there, and she rocked down hard, letting go with her own orgasm right as he catapulted into his.

Hands on her arms, he squeezed harder than was comfortable as he convulsed inside her, but Alexis didn't care. Vampire sex rocked.

After an eternity in which nations could have fallen, and whole new species discovered, Alexis collapsed on his chest. She needed water, but first she needed to rest for about a decade.

His fingers raked through her hair as he continued to pant. "Now I'm the one wowed. That was absolutely incredible."

She smiled against his chest. Considering how much experience he probably had, she was thinking that was quite a compliment. "You know it."

When he kissed the top of her head, she felt a weird lump rise out of nowhere and lodge itself in her throat. Embarrassed, she stayed draped over him, but pinched him lightly on the arm. "So what was that bite all about? You got hungry and had to take the edge off?"

Not that she had minded. She should, but Ethan hadn't lied when he'd said she would like it, and there was no pain now, just a sore satisfaction over her whole body.

"That wasn't a bite to feed. I only tasted your blood, I didn't drink it."

"So what was it for then?" It was nice to know that he saw her as more than a snack.

"That was a bite to mark you. To claim you as mine." His hand landed on her butt and he held her tightly against him.

It wasn't PC, but Alexis liked the way his words sounded. Elemental. Raw. When man wants woman. "Like a 'keep away' sign for other vampires?"

" 'Keep away.' 'No trespassing.' 'Touch her and you die.' And it's just for me, too, the desire to touch you, to invade you everywhere I can."

Hello. That was sexy. But he didn't need to know that. "Well, I let you this time, but don't expect to do that whenever you feel like it."

Alexis shifted, adjusting her sticky body on his. He really made a nice contoured mattress.

"Yes, dear." He bit her ear.

She lifted her head to give him a glare.

"Whatever you say, dear." He reached out and nipped her bottom lip.

"Stop that." Because she was getting aroused and it really seemed like she should play hard to get at some point.

"Make me."

Oh, yeah, Ethan liked to play it rough and tumble. And she was just the girl to give it to him.

Fourteen

Kelsey pursed her lips at him and avoided his eyes as Ringo pressed her back against the wall with his body, one leg wedged between her skinny thighs.

To anyone walking down the hall, they looked like a couple getting it on. But all he felt was a cold, unpleasant fear that his carefully constructed, unemotional life might be collapsing in on him. "What did you mean by that? And don't think you can play me, because I can snap your neck right now and get away with it."

He was lying. He wouldn't kill her. He didn't even like the way he had to threaten her, but he had no choice, and no time to feel sorry for the dark-haired ditz.

Kelsey licked her already glossy lips. Her breath panted in his face, quick and distressed. It had a sickly sweet scent to it, like she'd been drinking one of those girl drinks with fruit in them.

"You have to stop what you're trying to do . . . you won't be successful. I can't see who wants you to do it, but you'll only get caught, and he still won't die."

Ringo stared at her, his heart pounding, his grip on the waist of her red dress tightening. She had to know the Italian, there was no other way any of this made sense. But how and why, that was the question. And was he being set up? Had Kelsey purposely been a distraction?

Damn Donatelli for pulling him into his games.

"Are you his girlfriend?"

"Mr. Carrick?" Her dark brown eyes widened. "No. He hasn't been dating anyone at all. Not until now, with Brittany's sister."

"Not Carrick. The other one. The one who sent you to me." Frustration made his voice hoarse as he tried to keep it low.

"I don't know what you mean." Her shoulders scrunched up, like she was trying to protect herself from him. "I know you wanted to kill him because I heard your thoughts in your head."

Oh, my God. He fucking could not believe he'd had the idiocy to even speak to this girl the night before. He should have pretended he didn't speak English. Been Italian himself for the night.

"I speak Italian," she said. "My mother was Italian."

"What?" Ringo dropped his hands from her waist. He hadn't said any of that out loud.

"You couldn't have pretended to be Italian and not able to speak English because I speak Italian. That's what I mean."

"How are you doing that?" And how had she left him in a confused stupor with his pants unzipped the night before? He didn't even remember having a drink when she sat down next to him.

"You didn't have a drink."

"I didn't say that out loud." Ringo narrowed his eyes at her.

Some of her nervousness was disappearing and she stared at him expectantly. He didn't believe in this kind of psychic crap, hadn't believed in much of anything since the service.

"What's the service?" Kelsey blinked. "Oh, the Army or something?"

His hands went cold and his throat closed. A sweat ran down between his shoulder blades. "You can read my thoughts?"

She nodded. "I've never been that great at it, but with you, it's like one of those things . . . what are they called? The thingy they use to have the news guy read the, you know, things he's supposed to read?"

Ringo pressed his temple, brushed his hair off his forehead, his brain understanding what she was saying yet at the same time unable to accept it. "A TelePrompTer?"

"Yes! That's it." She reached out and touched his chest.

Ringo stiffened, but she only stroked him with an odd sort of tenderness. "Don't worry. I won't tell, but you have to promise not to try anymore. It won't work."

"Why not?" Thoughts raced and tumbled in his head and he was unable to get a solid grip on anything. None of this made sense. Since the minute he'd said yes to this hit, things had been off. Out of balance. "I can get around security."

"It just won't work. Mr. Carrick is untouchable. Trust me." She moved her hand to rest on his shoulder and gave him a smile, her fear clearly gone. "I wish I knew your name."

Ringo tried to close his thoughts down, panicked that she would know who he was. Kyle, Kyle, Kyle ran through his head. It was the first name to pop to the front of his consciousness—his kid brother's name.

"Kyle? You don't look like a Kyle." Kelsey giggled. "More like a Mario. Something that ends in 'o' anyway."

Ringo felt a cold pit settle down into his stomach. The silly bitch could actually read his thoughts.

He didn't even like to be in his own head. He sure in the hell didn't want anyone else in there.

Ethan ignored the first three voicemail messages from Seamus and drank two bags of blood in rapid succession. He was thirsty from all the physical exertion of the last hour. The thought tripped a memory of being inside Alexis, the way she'd clamped her legs around him and yelled her pleasure.

He'd known she would be aggressive, and she hadn't disappointed him. But now he wanted his turn, to set the stage and the seduction. He'd left Alexis sleeping in her room next to his, so he could come back and feed. She wasn't used to being awake during the night, but Ethan was, and he couldn't change a pattern nearly a millennium old, despite the fact that in his casino he could move about during the day without ever encountering the sun.

Not that the sun bothered him that much anymore anyway, now that he was older and stronger. If he had lived in a northern or eastern city, he could probably have even spent an entire day out in the sunlight. In Vegas it would be a little tough, but he could do it on occasion for an hour or two as he had that day. And despite Alexis waking him earlier than usual, he wasn't feeling sleepy.

What he felt was reenergized. He'd been sleepwalking lately, letting his job prod and push him through his nights. He knew in his gut that it was essential he win this election, remembered all the reasons why, but at the same time realized that he had become a workaholic. The job and nothing more. It was time to find better balance in his life before he suffered burnout.

Before he became a dried-up old crank of a vampire, with no sense of humor and zero sex life. That was a horrific view of the future—Ethan would do anything to avoid that, even incur Seamus's wrath.

"You're starting to piss me off," was Seamus's fourth message. It made Ethan laugh as he held his room phone up to his ear. Seamus was halfway to old crank already, and he was only a few hundred years old.

Leaving his dirty glass in the kitchenette, Ethan went back into his living room. Since this was home about eighty percent of the time, it was designed for his comfort and convenience. He had a bedroom with luxury bath, an office, a living area, and a kitchenette with a Sub-Zero minifridge and a dishwasher for his glasses. Alexis had noticed that the décor was a little out of the ordinary for the desert, but he liked the stately, dark colors that reminded him of England.

It wasn't easy to remain obscure in the English countryside these days, and he found Vegas was a perfect cover-up for a vampire.

Bloody hot and lacking in trees, but a man couldn't have everything. There was a certain charm to the constant ebb and flow of humanity in Sin City—a sort of perpetual defiance of reality.

A knock pounded on his door. It didn't sound like a Seamus knock, which would be polite but firm. This was a ragtag, pay attention to me kind of knock.

Alexis.

"Ethan?" she called.

Barefoot, he walked to the door, vampire speed. He had it open before she even finished speaking his name. "Hey, come on in. I thought you'd be asleep for hours still. It's the middle of the night."

She looked adorably rumpled and grouchy, wearing his sweat-pants and a T-shirt that said MY GIVE A DAMN IS BROKEN. "You're not blowing me off? When I woke up and you were gone, I thought maybe you're one of those guys who won't spend the night and I just wanted to clear up right now that that irritates me. If you can stay long enough to have sex with me, you can damn well stay a little longer. This isn't a drive-through service."

It was a struggle to keep a straight face. "Trust me, I'm not one of those guys. It's just I can't sleep at night, and I didn't want to disturb you, so I came home to eat and do some work. I had every intention of waking you up at the crack of dawn so I could make love to you again before I sleep for the day."

Her nose wrinkled. "Well, this sucks. It's like we're on swing shifts. I either have to stay up half the night or you have to force yourself awake during the day."

Ethan didn't like that any more than she did. "If I start getting up a little earlier, say five or six o'clock, and you stay up a little later, like one or two in the morning, we'd have plenty of time for dating and other *activities*. No less than other couples who both work."

She leaned on the living room wall. "Are we a couple?"

"You agreed that we're dating, and we are now sexually intimate, so I believe that makes us a couple, yes."

"Wow. And look at how well we compromise already. We've got this couple thing in the bag." That was capped off with a yawn.

"You can go back to bed if you'd like, gorgeous. Or we can go flying, get some fresh air."

"Flying? Whattaya mean?" Her words started to slur together as her shoulders and eyelids drooped. "You're not going to turn into a bat, are you? I really think that would freak me out."

"Not a bat. It's more like a Superman maneuver. I can go for a mile or two at a time. It's sort of like running in the air for me."

She stood straight up, tugging at her shirt. "No kidding? Can all vampires do that?"

"Just ancient ones like myself." A hint of braggart entered his voice, which surprised him. He'd thought he was past the pride of youth.

"Well, aren't you the shit?"

That stripped away any feelings of grandeur. Alexis had an honest way of putting everything into perspective. "Younger vampires can go up and down and hover, but not laterally."

"Cool. Do I need my purse?"

"Just some shoes." He had his wallet in his pants pocket. Not that anyone would see them. They'd be going too fast.

A minute later, she was back with gym shoes on, and they stepped out onto his balcony. Being in the penthouse, he had one of only four balconies in his hotel.

Alexis leaned over the edge and took a deep breath of the cool night air. "So what do we do? Do I need to have a Wendy moment? Think happy thoughts? Or do you have fairy dust or something."

"Think happy thoughts if you want. But I resent being compared to Peter Pan."

She laughed. "You're definitely more man than boy."

At least she'd noticed. "Stand in front of me, facing me, and wrap your arms around my chest with your legs around mine."

Alexis sort of jumped up onto him, legs way up around his waist. "No, not like that, gorgeous. Keep your feet on the ground for now. If you're up too high, you push out from me and wind will get between us, which will tug you away from me, making it harder to hold on. I don't want you to slip off."

"That's reassuring." She slid her waist and legs down his.

"That's it. Nice and snug against me."

The little minx took his words to heart and did a sultry rub all up and down on him, which was incredibly distracting. "You'd better stop that. My erection will create wind resistance."

She laughed. "Nobody's that big, Garlic."

Ethan didn't answer, but just bent his knees and jumped off the balcony, arms locked around her.

With a squawk, she clung tighter to him. "Geez! We're in the air!"

"That's kind of the point." Then he got going faster, and concentrated fully on the feeling of heading through the night air. The times when he allowed himself full use of the powers of his body he felt amazing, like he was free and at peace with who and what he was.

And with the weight of Alexis in his arms, for once he was not alone on his strange journey.

That was the unexpected gift of finding his chosen one. And he just might stick that in a poem.

Alexis had feared for her bladder for a split second, but now that they were winging across the sky, like they were on a motorcycle at seventy-five miles per hour, her fear had given over to exhilaration. Ethan had her securely in his arms, and she was half on her back, her hair straight across her face from the force of their forward motion.

Jack and Rose from *Titanic* had nothing on them, baby. They were flying.

She held on to the cotton of his shirt with a fierce grip and locked her feet behind his ankles. Eyes closed, she felt the wind, smelled the desert, heard the low hum of the Strip below them, still alive at three in the morning. Moving like this—it was a roller coaster, a convertible with the top down, a bungee jump.

They went higher, then lower, and Alexis laughed in delight. She'd wanted new experiences, wanted to loosen up. This was certainly that.

And she was falling for Ethan. Absolutely falling for him head over ass, bullet-train speed.

He was everything she could ask for in a man, except human.

Which could be a problem.

They slowed to a hovering stop, in a vertical position. Her back bumped into something. Alexis looked around, trying to get her bearings, shoving the wild windblown hair off her face. She was pressed against a wall, slightly angled, held up by Ethan.

"Where are we?"

His arm went under her butt and made a seat for her. "This is the Sphinx on the front of the Luxor. We're on its neck."

Alarmed, Alexis tried to turn. She flung her arms out and tried to find purchase with her gym shoes.

"Careful." Ethan gripped her harder, pinning her to the wall.

He kissed her, but she couldn't get into it. They were hanging out in the air, with nothing but Ethan's arms keeping her from swift and painful death.

She wasn't sure why that was different from flying, but it was, and she was sure she was going to die.

"Relax. I didn't expect you to be such a wimp," he whispered in her ear, before invading her eardrum with his tongue.

Her body reacted predictably. Nipples up, panties damp, legs spread. Head lolled back and breath went shallow.

"I'm not a wimp." A hussy maybe, but not a wimp. But his words relaxed her, staved off the panic. He seemed to be holding her without any strain, and the building was helping take some of her weight off him.

"No, you're not." In the dark, with his lips nearly flush with hers, his face was shadowy, eyes black as the night behind them. "You're amazing."

This kiss she enjoyed, the force of his tongue felt all through her body and clear down to her toes. Ethan had a wonderful mouth, which he moved on hers with just enough pressure to excite and entice and give thought to getting back to either of their rooms.

"You taste delicious," he murmured, "fresh and sweet."

"You make me sound like fruit."

"I barely remember what fruit tastes like. Right now, there is only you."

Damn, he was good at this. Alexis closed her eyes—suspended in the air, in time and space, and desire, as Ethan suckled her neck, the top of her breast.

Through the T-shirt she was wearing, he plucked at her nipple with his teeth. And when his hand slipped beneath the loose waistband of her sweatpants, she groaned.

"You're not wearing any panties," he said, sounding scandalized.

"I haven't been wearing any all night. Why start now?" Alexis arched into his touch, gripping his shoulders.

"It certainly makes this easier." His finger pressed inside her, stroking up and down.

"Oh, shit, that feels good." She was who the hell knew how many feet in the air, suspended by nothing more than the strength of Ethan's vampire arms, and he was getting her off. This had to be the most unusual date she'd ever been on, by far, and that included the time a guy in college had taken her pig wrestling.

"Are you sure this is safe?" she asked between moans as her hips thrust forward onto him.

"Absolutely." He sucked her nipple through her shirt again, sending a jolt vibrating around her inner thighs. "Just whatever you do, don't come."

"No?" She was about three seconds away from doing just that. The way he was sucking and stroking, plucking and pressing, she was spiraling quickly to the point of no return. With supreme willpower, she tried to scoot back away from him and his talented invasion, but there was nowhere to go. Her back was against the wall, literally.

His touch was relentless, a second finger sliding in with the first, and she pushed her feet against the steel wall, desperate to get away. Gravity kept pulling her down, settling his fingers deeper inside her, the base of his hand bumping against her vulva.

"Ethan, stop. I can't . . ."

"Can't what?" he asked in a harsh whisper, pulling his fingers apart and stretching the swollen flesh. He was deep, just buried so far in there, his breath blasting across her cheek, her neck, his teeth plucking at her nipple.

"Oh!" This wasn't going to work. Alexis bit her lip and knew she was about done. "You can't . . . and expect me not to . . ."

Talking was too much effort. All her lung capacity was going to moaning, and her brain power was focused on keeping her eyes uncrossed.

"Don't do it, Alexis," he said, even as he pinched her clitoris.

"Too late." Her head snapped back, and her whole body stilled for a split second, before she succumbed to a massive orgasm. It ripped through her, wracking her with shudders, convulsive waves of pleasure, and forcing a violent cry from her.

Feet scraping on the Sphinx, she rode it to the end, gripping the straining muscles of his forearms. When she was limp against him and panting, he finally removed his fingers from her with a triumphant smile.

"You wanted me to do that, didn't you?" she asked, kissing the corners of his mouth.

"Yes, I really, really did." And he looked about as satisfied as she felt.

And as aroused.

Arms tight around her, he pulled them away from the building. "Now let's move before we're spotted."

Though Alexis couldn't imagine anyone would guess the truth—floating vampire gives killer orgasm—if they saw a spot high on the Sphinx, she sure didn't want any investigating.

"You're a man with a plan. Take me wherever you want." Slack and satiated, she held weakly on to Ethan and let him fly her through the night.

Brittany couldn't sleep. She had the prickling sensation that someone was watching her, and it was unsettling. Never one to be paranoid, she didn't have trouble sleeping, not even after scary movies. And Alexis was the occasional insomniac, never Brittany. She had always fallen asleep practically before her head even hit the pillow.

Sunday night, she was lying on her bed beneath a gauzy thin white sheet, staring at the ceiling, her heart beating a little too fast. It was a safe apartment building in Summerlin, with bright floodlights, new windows, and a security entrance. All her doors and windows were locked. There was no reason to be feeling this sense of disquiet, this weird negative anticipation.

Maybe it was guilt. She shouldn't have left The Ava. She shouldn't have let Corbin walk away from her. She really needed to figure out a way to help him—surely he didn't deserve banishment, no matter what he had done. Maybe she could talk to Ethan, discuss it with him, and see if there could be a better solution.

Corbin was a tortured soul.

That stressed Brittany out, stirred her compassion.

Brittany had never been tortured, in any sense of the word, and it broke her heart to see other people struggle. Her mother had been tortured. Alexis didn't see that—maybe had been too hurt to realize it—but it was true. Their mother put her faith in all the wrong people and was burned over and over again, and the whole time she had desperately tried to grab on to happiness, seeking a higher thrill, through men, sex, drinking, dancing.

Her eyes would light with that feverish desperation, and Brittany had felt sorry for her. Even at six years old, Brittany had seen her pain.

Punching her pillow, she turned on her side. Why hadn't she drawn the drapes? The linen sheers didn't block out the moonlight, and it was fanning out across her legs. That was probably what was keeping her awake. She scissored her legs, kicking off the sheet. Either it was the moon, her shorty pajamas riding up, or she had just way too much on her mind.

Her sister Alexis was tortured, too, but in a different way. She had been hurt, felt rejected by their mother, and she marched through life ready to smack down anyone who dared to try to get close to her. Alexis couldn't get intimate because she didn't want to get hurt.

If Alexis had an affair with Ethan Carrick, it would be temporary, because at a certain point she would resist it going any further. Which was a shame, because Brittany liked Ethan, thought he was a good foil for her sister. Then again, he was a vampire, and that had the potential to be a bad thing.

Eyes wide open, Brittany hugged her shabby chic floral heart-shaped pillow, and wondered if she should just get up, get dressed, and drive back to The Ava. That tremor, like fingers walking up her spine, rippled through her again.

She wasn't sure whether to take that as a yes or a no.

Corbin sat on the garage roof across from Brittany's bedroom window and wrestled with himself. It was ridiculous, his behavior. Why was he hanging out in the shadows again, watching this woman? Why did he not just take what he wanted?

Some blood, that was all he wanted.

He was very close to the cure, he was certain.

Brittany could be the key.

Go inside, he commanded himself.

His body stayed exactly where it was.

He reminded himself he was possibly running out of time. If Donatelli won the election, Corbin would not be allowed to remain in Las Vegas. More likely, he would be sent to Alaska or someplace equally horrible, where he would have to draw blood from moose or bears or something else with fur.

The very idea offended his sensibilities. He did not even enjoy Vegas all that much, with all its glitz and bright lights, but it was civilization, with conveniences and decent tailors. Not nineteenth-century Paris, that was true, but it was accommodating and full of seductive women.

Taking blood from a showgirl or a moose. There was really no comparison.

Corbin sighed. Climbed down off the garage roof.

And went to break into Brittany's bedroom window.

Fifteen

Alexis should have been tired. She'd only slept about three hours in the last twenty-four. But she couldn't sleep, and after a fruitless effort to force it, she'd given up and had flicked on the TV and raided the minibar for M&M's. The problem with dating a vampire was he was never hungry.

She, on the other hand, never went more than five minutes without thinking about food. Popping a blue into her mouth, she crunched and reached for her Sidekick. Ethan had wanted her to sleep in his room while he had some kind of meeting with Seamus. But she preferred her own space. This side-by-side suite thing was perfect for her—convenient to Ethan, but still a locked door away if she needed time to herself.

There were a slew of new messages on the vampire slayers loop when she went to check the private message board. She was lurking, and hadn't announced her presence to the group at large, but the moderator knew she was there, and probably anyone else who wanted to pick through the member roster. She'd used her free social e-mail address, not her work one, and had registered under the name *shorty1994*. Still, anyone with any savvy could trace it back to her.

Probably not a good thing. But she'd had to see what this group was all about, and if they were loons or actually had info about Ethan and the other Vegas vampires.

Her attorney brain urged her not to draw any conclusions, while her natural skepticism had her leaning toward loons. Then again, they had known about her, which meant they had some level of organization, and someone knew where she was.

Message 16532 . . . What kind of stake do you recommend using to kill the undead? Thanx, Vampvixen.

Alexis put three M&M's in her mouth. "Do stakes really even kill vampires? Note to self: Ask Ethan for details on this whole dead thing."

The man she was dating was a vampire. It wasn't a fantasy, or a movie, or the result of an aneurysm to the brain. Ethan was older than dirt and she was sleeping with him. Alexis poured half the bag of candy onto her tongue. This was why she was never getting married.

All the great men were either taken, gay, a foot and a half taller than her, or were vampires. It sucked.

Not that she'd ever really pictured herself married. That was more Brittany's style. But a nice, long-term boyfriend, companionship, and some stellar sex, sure, she wanted that. All she was going to get was this one week with Ethan. Then he'd go off to do presidential things, and she would go back to her job. He would live another thousand years while she got weak and saggy and forgetful.

Fun.

Reply to Vamp on stakes . . . I use stakes hand carved from Transylvanian oak, twenty-four inches in length and two in diameter. They're expensive, but highly effective and can be purchased online with free shipping.

Ooo-kay. Thanks, Rock, duly noted.

"Next we have Kitty . . . Kitty?" Alexis rolled her eyes. "Kitty and vampire slaying just don't go together."

I just buy dowels from Home Depot, Vix. They're like fifty cents apiece and work just as good. Take care, hugs and love, Kitty.

The idea that someone might attempt this whole staking thing with Ethan or any of the other vampires she had met really bugged her. Whether these slayers knew what the hell they were doing or not, Alexis didn't want to see the man she l . . . liked a whole lot get a piece of wood shoved in his chest.

Her role in the game, which was no longer a game, was not vampire slayer at all, but vampire protector. Well, maybe not protector. But watchdog. No, she didn't want to be compared in any way to a dog. Special vampire friend. Which sounded like a paranormal episode of *Barney*, the purple dinosaur.

So there was no title for what she was. Fine. But she wanted

Ethan alive and well, and the reason behind that didn't require close scrutiny.

A noise had her turning to her right. That wasn't the TV. It was her door. Someone was swiping a key card through it. Jumping up, she tossed the Sidekick on the couch and moved into the shadows, wondering where she'd left her purse and her cell phone. Damn, she really hoped this wasn't a vampire slayer coming in person to recruit her. That could be awkward.

Figuring it was better to catch the person off guard, when the door opened and someone stepped into her room, she threw a kick.

When she met air instead of body mass, the doorway suddenly empty, she realized it was Ethan.

"You know, most women greet their lovers with a kiss, not a kick."

He was behind her, the smart-ass. Whirling, she tried to retrieve her heart from her throat. "Yeah, well, most women aren't dating vampires either. Why the hell are you coming into my room, with a key, in the middle of the night?"

That was seriously going to cramp her feelings of independence. And hadn't that been a contingency of her stay in the contract he had signed? Of course, was a contract signed by a vampire valid in civil court?

"I thought you were a serial killer, rapist, stalker, burglar type, Ethan. I was defending myself."

"Of course you were. And I can't tell you how pleased I am that you can defend yourself if need be. But next time, I truly would prefer the kiss."

He sat down on her couch like he owned it. Wait a minute. He did own it. How annoying.

"And I thought you were asleep, so I didn't wish to disturb you by knocking."

Alexis crossed her arms and just stared at him. There were so many things wrong with what he had just said. "If you thought I was asleep, then why the hell were you coming into my room? Were you going to bite me in my sleep or something? Because that is a serious no-no. There will be only consensual biting in this relationship." And she wasn't even sure how often she was going to let him do that. It was the same way with sex toys. Once you let a guy have them, he couldn't do without.

Ethan crossed his feet on the coffee table and looked unperturbed. "I wasn't going to bite you. Or wake you up with kinky sex acts, though that does have a certain appeal. I just wanted to check on you, assure myself you're all right, sleeping peacefully. I planned to gaze a bit on your angelic beauty, and sigh with contentment, fortified to go back to a long, boring round of questions and answers with Seamus."

He smiled, baby blues swimming with innocence and sincerity.

Alexis made a gagging motion with her finger. "I hope you have a speechwriter, Mr. President. Because that was lame."

"Poorly expressed, but true. And I had another reason for coming in here."

Big surprise. "Oh, now the truth comes out." Trying to be discreet, Alexis sauntered over and picked up her Sidekick, so Ethan wouldn't glance at it. She was truly embarrassed to be surfing the vampire slayers message loop. And she wouldn't want him to get the wrong idea. Like she was some kind of double agent who would stab him in his sleep.

Ethan snaked a hand out and tugged her down onto his lap. "I'm still waiting for that kiss."

While he had a pleasantly muscular lap, and her bare legs rubbed against the denim of his jeans in a sensual comfort, she wanted to know the real reason he was there. They had agreed to meet at 5 P.M. Monday night before the presidential debate. Her arms somehow wound around his neck without any command from her.

"I couldn't sleep. That's why I'm awake. Now why are *you* here, Ethan? Seriously."

He sighed. "Actually, it's probably nothing. But you know how I can't get in your head?"

"Yes, thank God for small favors."

A little frown wrinkled his forehead. "I don't have that problem with any other mortal. Vampires close their thoughts to me, but mortals don't. And I heard Brittany. And I was wondering if you had talked to her today."

Ethan looked casual. His voice strained for casual. But it was almost overly so. Casual to the point that alarms went off in Alexis. "No. I talked to her last night . . . after midnight. Why? What did you hear?"

If anything was wrong with Brittany, she'd . . . well, hell, she was pretty sure she would dry up, turn to dust, and blow off in a thousand directions.

"I heard surprise. Loud surprise." Ethan rubbed his forehead. "I'm not sure why it even came to me . . . Brittany's not here, and I don't usually focus in on an individual like that anyway." He shook his head. "But it was there, right in the middle of a strategy session with Seamus, and I just wanted to check with you. See what you thought. If you wanted to call Brittany and check on her. It's probably nothing . . ."

The vampire slayers . . . they knew who Alexis was. And Brittany was half-vampire, according to Ethan, but she didn't know it. Couldn't defend herself. From a fifty-cent dowel from Home Depot.

Alexis picked up the hotel phone and dialed as fast as her fingers could move.

"Why are you in my bedroom?" Brittany clutched her sheet and blinked at Corbin. After she'd screamed loud enough to be heard in Reno, she had realized who the man was climbing in her window.

"Why are you not sleeping?" he asked, brushing off the knees of his designer pants and sounding annoyed.

She wondered how a man who was banished got the cash to buy such fancy clothes. Propping herself up with her elbow, she let her heart rate return to normal. She wasn't afraid of Corbin. Not in the least. "I couldn't sleep because it felt like someone was watching me."

His mouth fell open before he recovered and slapped it shut, though a faint blush tinted his cheeks.

"You were watching me, weren't you?" The thought should freak her out, but it kind of pleased her instead. He really was a cute and sweet vampire. She grinned. "Do you have a crush on me, Corbin?"

"Do not be ridiculous. I am a research physician . . . I am banished. I do not have crushes on skinny women." He was pacing back and forth, stopping only to grab a pink fuzzy pen off her desk, frown at it, then put it back.

"Then why did you climb in my window?" she asked reasonably, lying on her side with her head resting on her hand. She was glad she was awake for this, though she was going to have a word or two with the building manager about the security of her building. These windows were clearly crap.

"Because my research demands zat I ignore ethics. I am zis close to a breakthrough." He held up his two fingers, an inch between them. "Discovering you ez a rare opportunity to find ze gaps and links between vampire and mortal."

Wow. She was a rare research opportunity. That wasn't as sexy as she would have liked, but it was still flattering. "What are you researching, Corbin?"

Crossing his hands over his chest, he pursed his lips together. He seemed to struggle with himself, his green eyes going opaque right as she was watching them.

All her amusement vanished. She could sense his turmoil. "What? What is it?"

"Ze cure," he said in a hoarse whisper. "For ze curse."

"What curse?" Brittany sat up, feeling too vulnerable lying down.

"Ze curse of vampirism. I am very close to discovering how to reverse ze effects of a turning, and restore a vampire to mortal life." He glared at her defiantly, like he expected her to protest.

"Corbin," Brittany whispered, overwhelmed. This was what she had been hoping for. What she had been hanging around The Ava endlessly for. To save Ethan and the others. To rid them of their bloodsucking existence.

They were good people, all of them, and she didn't want them to spend eternity condemned to a liquid diet. And she didn't think it was all that healthy for the soul to feed off other people.

"Is that really possible?"

"I am certain of it." He scratched his chin. "Ez this where you tell me any sane person craves immortality and zat no one will willingly return to ze weakness of mortality? Ez this where you beg me to give you ze Gift, which ez in fact a curse?"

"No." Brittany swung her legs around so she was fully sitting up. "Corbin, no. I think you are right. I think what you're doing is courageous and honorable, and I bet most people would agree with me."

He sighed. Sat down on the bed next to her. "I can hear ze sincerity of your thoughts. But Brittany, you are rare among mortals. Many people hunger for more, always more—more power, more beauty, more love, more life. They embrace what the Dark Gift promises. But ze Gift is a curse because it brings great loneliness . . . at some point, there is no one left walking zis earth who was connected to you in any way, no one who shares your past, your memories, your understanding of a time, a people."

His pain was palpable, like a throbbing thumb after a hammer hit, and Brittany touched his hand. Squeezed gently. "I do understand that. That when faced with eternity, you might lose your grounding with the past, lose your purpose for the future."

"Yes. Zat ez very true." He tried to remove her hand from his, but Brittany held it tight.

"I could remove my hand if I wanted to," he said, with French arrogance.

"I know that." Brittany nudged his shoulder with hers. "But obviously you don't really want to. I want to help you find the cure . . . What is it you need from me?"

She already suspected. Blood. A shiver went through her.

"Yes, it ez what you are thinking." He turned toward her, studied her. "I need your blood."

Brittany swallowed hard, and pulled up the neckline of her shorty pajamas, which only brought it to her collarbone. Her neck was still exposed, as was a lot of the rest of her. "Did you bring your little kit thing?"

A needle in the arm wouldn't be so bad. No different than going to the Red Cross to donate blood. Which she never did, because she was afraid of needles and tended to pass out.

"Yes, but I left it in the car."

"Where is your car? Because I can't stay up all night . . . I have to go to work tomorrow, you know. I'm a dentist," she said pointlessly.

"And you're afraid of needles?"

"Well, not when I'm the one using them." She took several deep breaths and gave herself a mental pep talk. No big deal, this was for the good of vampirekind. Only a total selfish wimp would refuse to give blood because of a teeny-weeny needle prick.

"You are terrified." Corbin returned the pressure on her hand. "You are shaking, and your skin has gotten clammy. Besides, I can sense your fear, it ez like a pulsing electrical charge. And your thoughts are wild and scattered."

"I really wish you wouldn't listen to my thoughts. It's just not nice, Corbin." Brittany cleared her throat and hoped her heart wouldn't leave her chest like a cartoon character's. "And maybe you can just throw one of those glamours on me before you do anything with a needle."

"I can't put a glamour on you. I have tried and it does not work."

"Why not?" This whole experience would be much less nerve-wracking if she were in some kind of pleasure coma. Sort of like her twenty-first birthday when she had consumed three cosmopolitans in rapid succession.

"No alcohol." Corbin gave her a stern look. "Zat would alter my test results. And I don't know why I can't put a glamour on you. I have tried many times."

"Why were you trying to do that?" she asked in shock. What exactly had he been planning to do to her? And she was sure blood removal would be easier if she were drunk. Not that she was a partyer—that had been her mother—but while she wanted to help the cause, she really couldn't do the needle thing.

"Do not be alarmed. I just meant there are times when you've seen things, said things, called to me, and I would have liked to, uh, soothe you."

"Soothe me? That's very sweet." Brittany took a deep breath, calmed herself down. "I want to soothe you, too, you know. I look at you and I can feel your anxiety, your desire to do what's right." Stomach jumping just a little, she added, "You can draw my blood. I promise. But please do it quickly, okay? I don't think I can sit still for you to fill up whole pint bags."

Decision made, she screwed her eyes shut and shoved her arm at him, turning her head away. If pain forced her eyes open, she didn't want to see any needles, veins, blood flowing, or skin pulling.

"I have to get ze kit still."

She let out the breath she'd been holding in a gigantic whoosh. "Oh, shit, that's right. Well, go get it, and hurry. If you give me too much time to think, I might just pass out. Of course, that might make the whole thing easier for you." Brittany glanced over at him. "Corbin?" The room was empty.

Barely a blink later, he was climbing back in her window, a black leather attaché case in his hand. Eek. That looked scary. Serial killer–like.

"What ez this obsession with serial killers?" he asked, opening the case on the nightstand.

"I don't know." Brittany peered around his back, trying to see in the bag. "I'm American. That probably explains the whole thing."

He turned to her, wearing latex gloves, needle with vial attached in his hand. She broke out into a sweat in various icky places. Without direction from her, her body leaped off the bed and took two big steps backward.

"Shhh," Corbin said. "It ez not a big thing. I will be very quick and it won't hurt but for a split second."

"That's what my first boyfriend told me. And he was *so* wrong." Brittany's butt hit her wicker dresser. The picture frames on it shook, and she didn't even care. She could not let Corbin near her with that thing.

The needle went down by his side. "I can distract you if you'd like. Zat is what I normally do."

"What do you mean?" Even as the words left her mouth, Brittany remembered his lips on that woman's mouth, her throaty moans of pleasure. "Oh! Like that?"

He nodded, eliminating the space between them with sure, steady, sensual steps. The look on his face had turned from compassionate to intense, determined. The hunter assessing his prey.

And how completely embarrassing that she felt sexual interest rouse itself in her body. Her hand fluttered over her breasts, a ridiculous gesture of protection.

"Yes. Like that. But only if you want me to." He leaned over her, arm brushing her bare shoulder, took in her scent with flared nostrils, and whispered in her ear. "Do you want me to?"

Brittany shivered. No, of course she didn't. That was crazy. Impulsive.

Fun and sensual, and much more pleasant than a needle. And Corbin was French. Surely he knew how to distract a woman. "Yes, I want you to."

A faint smile crossed his face. "Ah, zat ez a wonderful answer, Brittany, because I desire you."

Without using his hands to touch her, he kissed her, with more urgency, more fire, than she was expecting. An ache started low in her belly when his tongue demanded entrance to her mouth. Gripping the dresser behind her, she hung on under his assault, fear disappearing, hot, wet, need building with NASCAR speed.

A moan ripped through the room and she realized it came from her when Corbin lifted his mouth from hers. She didn't want the kiss to end, ever, and certainly not after a few seconds. But he only left long enough to maneuver himself between her legs, forcing her thighs wider apart.

The move, the intimacy so much more suggestive than a simple kiss, had her panting in anticipation. "Corbin . . ."

"Yes, *ma chérie*?" He kissed along her neck, over the swell of her breasts, back up, and took her mouth with ferocity.

Brittany had been kissed many times, by many men. More than she cared to consider, and way more than she would ever admit to her much more sexually conservative sister. But Corbin's kisses were potent, like the first bite of double chocolate ice cream, the last dregs of coffee at the bottom of the cup, or a shot of vodka straight down in one gulp.

"Don't stop," she murmured.

There was movement on her arm, him brushing against her, pressure, but with his mouth on hers and his erection—hey, which was Eiffel Tower in proportion—pressing against her, she couldn't think, didn't care what he did to her as long as it felt good. The room was dim, but the moonlight passed over his face, showing the intensity of his pale eyes.

"Never," he assured her. "I will never stop until you say so."

There was a thump onto her dresser, and a shuffling by her hips, then suddenly both his hands were on her waist, her breasts, tweaking her nipples into hard, sensitive peaks. It came to her that he had taken her blood already, must have, because he wasn't wearing gloves any longer.

"Yes, I did," he whispered in her ear, nipping the lobe. "I did not lie, did I? I distracted you."

And then some. "Yes." Brittany panted when his hands changed tactics and went up and under her PJ top, cupping and stroking her. "But if you're finished, shouldn't you stop?"

"You told me not to."

"Oh." Brittany let her head fall back. "Then I guess you should listen to me."

Help, his hands were in her shorts, and when his fingers spread her apart and sank into her wet, willing flesh, they both groaned. There was a sharp sting in her shoulder, and she realized with amazement that Corbin had bitten her, and was running his tongue over the puncture marks, the thick beads of blood disappearing.

She should tell him to stop, because this was getting a little kinkier than she was usually up for, but she didn't tell him to stop. In fact, she begged for more, as the touch of his tongue set off a thousand pinpricks of pleasure all over her body.

Desire spiked, shifted to demanding.

"Do that again," she said, excited, hot, and eager, thrusting her hips against his fingers.

With his free hand, he pulled off her shirt. Laved across her nipples, then sank his teeth into the plumpness of her breasts. Brittany's head snapped back and she grabbed his hand, held it deep inside her as an unexpected climax whipped through her.

"Oh, oh, oh," she groaned, with a hysterical cadence of shock and ecstasy. Holy cow.

Corbin lifted her, tossed her on her bed two feet away. Pulled down her shorts, while she tried to remember her name and why being a vampire's sex slave would be a bad thing. His mouth closed over her hipbone, sucking on her flesh. Legs shifting restlessly, she grabbed at his hair, her quick orgasm a minute before only driving her desire harder, desperate for total satisfaction.

Teeth sank into the curve of her hip, and she shuddered. When he pulled like that, sucked and drew her into him, it was a pure sexual joining, like he was touching all of her body at the same time, with tongue, fingers, lips. He released, mouth tinted a wet crimson, which he licked away as if he were tasting her sex juices and found them absolutely delicious.

Brittany hovered on the edge of another climax, wet with want, titillated by what she was feeling. Shocked at herself and him, but thrilled with the wild, edgy desire that shoved aside her inhibitions and sank her in bliss.

When his tongue touched her clitoris, she screamed, "Corbin! Please, more, please . . ."

When he bit the soft, tender flesh between her legs, and again on her inner thigh, when he sank his erection into her, and his teeth into her neck, she scratched and clawed at him in approval.

And when he came inside her with a hot, deep rush that had her clamping down on him in triumph, she careened into another orgasm with a cry hoarse from yelling, and a feeling that she had never known or understood her body until that moment.

Never known that two people could blend together with such wild, animal intensity.

That heady sensation lasted the length of her orgasm.

Then when her body settled back onto the sheet, and Corbin licked her torn flesh, she blinked up at him, every feeling sucked right out of her, leaving nothing except a vague embarrassment. As fast as she'd shot up, she crashed down even quicker. Crap, crap, crap, what the hell had just happened?

She'd had unprotected sex with a vampire, that's what.

Her phone rang. Immediately pulling out of her, Corbin turned his back to her, fixing his pants. Brittany felt a fierce blush burning her cheeks. Oh, my God, she was a total, shameless slut who had begged a vampire to give it to her.

A glance over at her nightstand showed Alexis's cell phone on her caller ID. It was nearly four in the morning. Why would her sister be calling?

She grabbed the phone, a sick panic in her mouth. "Hello? What's the matter, Alex?"

"Nothing, I was going to ask you that. Ethan thought maybe you were in some kind of trouble."

"Why would he think that?" Relieved, Brittany grabbed the sheet and covered herself, determined not to look at Corbin, who was packing his case back up.

"He thought he heard . . . shock from you. Yelling."

Alex sounded worried, but Brittany wanted to laugh in total horror. Ethan had heard her orgasm over at The Ava? That was so completely mortifying she wasn't even sure she could speak.

"Well, I'm fine," she managed to choke out. "Thanks for checking on me, but I need to get back to sleep." As if she'd been sleeping. "Call me tomorrow?"

"You're sure you're okay?"

No. "Positive. Love you, Alex."

"You, too, sweetie."

Brittany hung up the phone, shimmied under the sheet, and pulled the pillow over her face. She could never look at Corbin again.

Maybe if she ignored him, he would just leave.

Corbin checked the zipper on his pants for the fourth time and stared at Brittany, currently hiding under her pillow. He was very embarrassed and ashamed of himself. He never, ever turned a test subject into a vessel for his own pleasure. He had lost complete and total control of himself.

But Brittany was such an amazing woman, compassionate and honest, with a sensuality that was made even more appealing by the fact that she wasn't aware of it. She had pranced around in nightclothes that practically left her naked, yet never even seemed to notice. He had been lying to himself when he'd sworn he wasn't attracted to her.

Using passion to ease her discomfort over the needle had been a stupid, stupid idea. One taste of her and he'd been unable to stop from taking more. A lot more.

Moving out of her bedroom, he let his eyes adjust to the dark. He had much better than mortal vision in the dark and he wanted to find her kitchen.

"Are you leaving?" she called, her voice muffled, but hopeful.

"I am getting you something to drink." He found her refrigerator, which was neat and tidy, with lots of little bottles, some of which he wasn't even sure what they contained. He recognized orange juice, knew that was a good source of sugar to replenish the blood she'd lost.

Lost? No—the blood that he'd taken. He had bitten her eight times. Eight. Taking blood each time, though not a lot. And it had been fantastic, the best sexual joining he'd had in centuries. Perhaps ever. Even now his manhood hardened in memory.

Corbin clenched his fists. "Ugh, stupid, stupid, idiot."

"What?"

"Nothing." He went back to her room, found her lying exactly the way he'd left her. "Drink this. You will feel better." He set the tumbler of juice on her nightstand next to the phone.

"I feel fine."

The pillow didn't move and she was nothing but a white bedding lump, a few strands of her black hair visible on either side, her knuckles taut as she clutched.

"I guess I should be going." Corbin stood there feeling ridiculous. He should kiss her *au revoir*, say something nice about their lovemaking. But he felt like a young boy who takes a girl in a barn and then is unsure what comes next.

"Bye." Her fingers wiggled out from under the sheet and waved.

It had been many, many years since he had felt this kind of embarrassment and uncertainty. He did not like it.

So he left, understanding there is no bigger fool than an old fool.

Sixteen

"You're still worried about her, aren't you?"

Alexis picked at the eggs on her plate with her fork. "Yes." She abandoned the food and rubbed her eyes. They were eating— well, she was eating—room service in Ethan's suite before she left for work.

"She said she was fine." Ethan took a sip of his drink, which looked remarkably like a strawberry daiquiri, minus the cherry.

"I know." Alexis leaned back and unbuttoned the jacket of the suit she was wearing. "But I have something to tell you, Ethan." She felt like hell, running on zero sleep, and worrying about Brittany. While showering and slapping some makeup on, she had realized that not only did she feel like hell, she looked like it, too.

But she trusted Ethan, which kind of blew her mind, but she did, and she needed his advice.

He was looking at her, a touch of wariness in his eyes, his glass hovering in front of his mouth. "Yes?"

"The other night I got an e-mail inviting me to join a vampire slayers message list. I don't know who they are, or how they got my name. But what if they know about Brittany? Do you think we should tell her? Is she safe out there in Summerlin by herself? Maybe she should come stay here." Just the thought of telling her baby sister, hey, your dad was a vampire, made her sick, but she'd do whatever she had to do to keep Brittany safe.

"Vampire slayers?" Ethan looked amused. "It's a minor annoyance to be so popular these days. We have to deal with these enthusiasts. I can't imagine that Brittany is in any danger from them. But certainly, she is more than welcome here."

"Cool. Thanks, Ethan. I'll make her stay here for a while."

"Make her?" His eyebrow rose.

What? Like she was going to feel guilty? "Hey, it's for her safety! And maybe you should tell me everything there is to know about this undead thing, so I have all the facts before I decide whether to tell Brittany or not."

"What would you like to know?" He sat back in his chair, the perfect English gentleman. Who was very intense, rough around the edges, and drank blood.

"How did you become a vampire?" Alexis went back to her eggs, turning her plate a little on the white linen tablecloth of Ethan's round dining table.

"I was ambushed on the way home during the First Crusade. I was made a Turkish prisoner, starved, and beaten before they slit my throat. The guard turned me to vampire and helped me escape by tossing my body out with the dead."

Lovely. "Why did he save you? He must have seen hundreds of prisoners die."

Ethan smirked. "Not he. She. Let's just say during my captivity she was impressed with my show of strength."

Alexis rolled her eyes. "So you're saying she had the hots for you? So what happened to her?"

His smile fell. "She was a young vampire. I never saw her again. I expect she got the guillotine when the guards determined she was a woman."

"Oh. I'm sorry," she said, reaching across the table to touch him. She meant the words. She couldn't imagine being suddenly thrust into vampire-hood without anyone to guide you. In movies and books they always had mentors, even if it was just a jerk like Lestat. "Damn, I can't even believe how many people you've known in your life. It must be millions."

Ethan met her halfway, enclosed her hand with his. "Why do you think we've banded together in a governmental body? Yes, for law and order, but also because there is something inherently lonely about being a vampire. We experience so many relationships, acquaintances, people coming and going, yet we exist in perpetual solitude, locked within our unique world. Together, we can bridge that gap between mortal and vampire, Impure and fledgling, and thrive as a healthy, prosperous people."

Alexis stared at him, checked the earnestness on his face, and raised an eyebrow. "Did Seamus write that for you?" Because it was a total load of crap.

"Yeah, for my speech tonight. What do you think?" Ethan sat back in his Irish farmhouse ladder-back chair.

"I think you're overreaching with that last bit," she said honestly.

"That's what I told Seamus, but he's like a terrier with a bone about this kind of stuff. Sometimes I think he should be president, not me."

"He's wound pretty tight, isn't he?" A little round of golf would probably do him a world of good. "But if you want to get people's attention, you need to stand strong, confident. You need to tell them what you've done right, and if most people, vampires, I mean, are happy, don't fix what isn't broken. And I don't think you're going to recruit Impures—I really do hate that name, by the way—with some 'why don't we all just love each other' kind of BS."

"No?"

Alexis liked how Ethan pretty much always looked relaxed. Intense, but relaxed. He was wearing navy blue lounging pants and a white skin-tight T-shirt since he was on his way to bed for the day, and he was sexy hot.

She stuck her feet up onto his chair, between his legs. Even when her toes brushed his crotch, he didn't flinch. Damn, she liked that. Especially since she could feel him getting hard. But she'd never admit it out loud.

"No, you're not a touchy-feely guy. Let Seamus pass out hugs if he wants to. You need to tell these people straight up whether you'll give them what they want or not. No dancing around the issues— just hey, Impures, you can have national health insurance—or whatever it is they want."

Ethan nodded. "That's the way I would like to approach it."

"So do it." She curled her toes over his erection, grinning at him.

Strong, cool fingers gripped her bare toes, shifted them off him. Ethan sat slowly up, leaning forward, lips parted. Eyes deepened to a rich cobalt and Alexis sucked her breath in.

Sexual energy radiated off him and he was coming to get her. She licked her lips.

Ethan said, "Move in with me, Alexis. Permanently."

Huh? Her feet fell to the floor. "What? Can you run that by me again?"

"Move in with me. Not for the election, but because you are my chosen one. My mate."

Hello. Alexis almost swallowed her tongue. "What? Where did this come from?" And why did it suddenly make her feel inflated, giddy, euphoric?

But he didn't back down and he didn't let go of her hand. "From the first moment I touched you, I knew you were different. I have known many women—"

"Thanks for reminding me," she sniped. They were probably all taller and darker than she was, too.

"And none have given me the sense of completion you have. I've fallen in love with you."

She gasped, the words like a blow to the chest. "Oh." Tears pricked at her eyes, startling her. She never cried, ever, but she did now because, looking at Ethan, she realized the strange truth was that she might have fallen in love with him, too, at some point. It was possible. But she wasn't ready to commit to it yet.

Concern furrowed his brow. "Alexis?"

Shaking her head, she bit her lip. Tried to speak. Blinked hard to keep the tears behind her lids, where they belonged. "I'm falling for you, too."

Okay, so she'd left off the "l" word, but hey, she'd gotten close.

"You are?" He looked inordinately pleased.

"Yes, Garlic, it's sad, but true. I really kind of have a thing for you." She cleared her throat and squeezed his hand, hoping she could say this right, wishing that she could leap into his arms without the bitterness that seemed to plague her, the understanding that she wasn't a woman who could manage a long-term commitment.

"But I can't live with you . . . I mean, what would we have, ten years? Fifteen tops? And I've seen how people get when they're married, how they make each other miserable with all their personal flaws spilling out onto each other. I don't want to walk away from you in ten years hating you, or you hating me."

He frowned.

"I don't know how . . ." It wasn't coming out coherent at all. She bit her lip. "Ethan, I'm never going to get married . . . Okay, I know you didn't ask me to marry you, but I'm assuming eventually that would happen, or even if it didn't, I mean, living together is committed, it's like marriage in that you're in each other's space and . . ."

Alexis took a deep breath and tried to reorganize her thoughts, clamp down on her panic. "I told you a little bit about my mother, but I didn't tell you about the day I realized I hated her. Brittany didn't hate her, but I did, because her own selfishness, her own personal shit, ruined her relationship with every person she said she loved."

God, she'd never told anyone about any of this stuff. She didn't even talk to Brittany about it. But Ethan had to know, deserved to know why she felt the way she did. Why she felt damaged beyond repair.

"She was married four times, the first time to my father. The second husband was short-lived, which was good, because he used to scare me. He had a motorcycle and all these tattoos and he drank. But when I was nine, my mom married Bill. He was a good man, he worked for an insurance company, and we moved into his house, which was clean and kept up. He treated Brittany and me like we were his, and he loved us, Ethan, he did, you could see it in his eyes. Some men can't love kids that aren't theirs but Bill wasn't one of those guys."

Alexis felt the fat, heavy tears roll down each cheek, but she didn't bother to wipe them off. "I was so happy, because for once everything was so normal, and the way it should be, and I took Bill to the Girl Scout father-daughter dance and I was so proud. I didn't know it at ten years old, but my mom was jealous of that affection he had for us. It took his attention away from her, you know? The more he cared about us, the more she gave him hell for it."

Staring at the glob of yellow putty her eggs had become, Alexis forced the words out. "When I was twelve, she called the cops and told them Bill was molesting us."

"Good God." Ethan's hand jerked in hers. "Alexis, I'm so sorry. What happened? Surely they could tell you weren't being harmed?"

"They said I was protecting him. That since I was almost thirteen, I had created a fantasy that I was in love with him, and he had probably told me that if I kept quiet, he would marry me. It was so sick . . . they were so-called professionals and they were ignoring everything I was saying, ignored the physical evidence that showed I hadn't been sexually assaulted. But I realized I hated my mom when I figured out she was talking to Brittany, telling her things, confusing her, so that when Brittany was interviewed, she said things that the police and my mom led her right into. Yes, Daddy Bill likes to tickle me, yes, he helps me get dressed." She shuddered. "It was just disgusting . . . Brittany was barely six years old and she didn't understand what they were doing. They were taking everyday things a father does in the care of his child—stuff my mother couldn't be bothered to do—and turned it into something vile."

She knew her voice was hoarse, knew she sounded hateful and full of anger, but she didn't care. "That's when I decided to become a lawyer. To wade through all the crap and find the facts. And I decided I would never get married, and that I would never forgive my mother for taking a father away from me twice."

"Did Bill go to prison?"

Ethan's voice was compassionate, though she couldn't bring herself to look at him. "No, thank God. But he was barred from any contact with us ever again." Alexis swiped at her eyes, tears blurring her vision. "When my mom died, I tried to find him. He had died of a heart attack six months before, but his current wife showed me these boxes he had . . . filled with pictures of Brittany and I, cards we'd made him for Father's Day. She said it broke his heart to leave us with our mother."

Her voice shattered into a sob, and she was totally mortified. But Ethan stood up, pulled her over to him, and she let him. She was grateful for the way his arms came around her, the way he sat her down on his lap and tucked her head against his shoulder.

She never cried. And now it felt like nearly thirty years' worth dislodged all at once. Weakness was something she despised, but sometimes it was damn hard to always be the strong one, to fight it and shove it all aside, and be tough.

The prosecutor's office was still mostly male territory, and she worked with male criminals. Being the blond broad, as her boss had once eloquently called her, was something she enjoyed.

Most of the time.

At the moment, she just wanted to curl into Ethan Carrick and let him support her. Let someone take care of her for a change.

Ethan rubbed Alexis's back and murmured words of comfort. He felt bloody helpless. Women crying had always bewildered him, because they cried over everything. Happy tears, sad tears, laughing tears, manipulative, angry, and fake tears. Tears of pain. It was hard to believe just how much pain he had witnessed in his very long lifetime.

Yet only one other woman's tears had moved him the way Alexis's did.

After his turning, he had gone home, to England, and arrived right after his sister's death. His mother had stood over Gwenna's body as a woman who had buried all her children, and assumed her oldest son was lost in the Holy War. Silent, stoic tears had trailed down her pale cheeks. Ethan had felt at that moment that his heart had been torn out of his body and hacked by a sword.

He felt that same way now. He couldn't help Alexis, couldn't make it better for her, and that was a man's pain.

"I'm sorry that the woman who gave birth to you didn't know how to be a mother." He brushed his lips over the soft, silken strands of her hair. "But I would imagine that if someone had asked Bill, he was glad to have been part of your life. I would imagine he wouldn't have changed that, despite the outcome."

Her sobs had quieted down to gulping tears. "I guess I know that."

"And I guess you know that you give the woman who gave birth to you too much control over your life. She doesn't deserve that much attention." She hadn't deserved to be a mother at all, but that was one of life's mysteries Ethan would never understand.

"I guess I know that, too. But it's not all that easy, you know."

"I'm sure it's not. But I have learned through the years that sometimes we make things more complicated than they need to be." He played with the waistband of her skirt and rubbed his thumb over the small of her back, amazed at the depth of what he felt for this woman. "I'm sorry if I moved too fast for you, but I think I'm at the point in my life where I can trust my feelings and instincts. I've lived long enough to know real versus imagined, and what I feel for you is real. You're the first woman I've asked to live with me."

Neither had he ever told a woman he loved her and truly meant it, but he didn't think he could say that without sounding like a cad. *Yes, with you those words have meaning, but all the other women before got exaggeration in the course of seduction.* That wouldn't exactly win his case.

Nor could he really explain why he hadn't asked her to marry him. For all his self-realization, something had made him stop short of that, and he was fairly certain it was because he expected her rejection.

"I didn't mean to rush you, Alexis. It's just that I look at you and I think, damn, she's just perfect for me. Absolutely perfect. I'll never be bored, never stop laughing, never stop desiring her. Do you understand what I mean?" And she'd said he wasn't a touchy-feely kind of guy. He was feeling pretty goddamn poetic at the moment.

Not to mention sweating vampiric bullets. God's teeth, it was painful to lay your heart out on the table for a woman to toss onto the floor.

But he couldn't hide his feelings, didn't want to. He meant what he'd said. When you lived nine hundred years, you knew what you wanted when you found it. Alexis was born to be his mate—the one woman who could lock him out of her thoughts, and the one woman who could drop him to the floor, literally.

"I understand what you mean." She talked to his chest, her voice raspy, but she had definitely stopped crying. "But a decade or so is all we'd have, Ethan, and I just can't give you that much of myself then watch you walk away. I can't."

He sighed, burying his chin in her hair, disbelieving. He couldn't have found her, only to never really have her. That he couldn't accept. He would take whatever she was willing to give. "So what can we have?"

"Now. We can have now. This week. Until the election's over, which is what, six weeks? I can't promise anything beyond that, Ethan, I just can't."

The blood in her veins flowed frantically with the rapid beat of her heart. He could smell her fear, a sickly sweet odor that clung to her skin. He didn't want to be the source of that, but he couldn't bring himself to drop the subject either. It felt too cruel just to accept the crumb of six weeks with her. Six bloody weeks in a life that would last another thousand years. Fifty-two thousand weeks . . . this time with her would be nothing.

It would be everything.

"Let me turn you." The words were barely out before he regretted them. He'd never offered the Dark Gift to anyone before . . . it

231

was a temptation too great for most mortals to refuse and he didn't want to think that the lure of immortality was what brought Alexis to him. That she'd chosen eternal life instead of just him, freely and without doubt.

She moved back away from him and stared. "Are you crazy? Did you drink bad blood? Straight from the psych ward blood? If I became a vampire, I would have to quit my job. I wouldn't be able to play with the kids Brittany's going to have someday. I wouldn't be able to eat chocolate. No, I absolutely do not want to be a vampire."

Pushing on his shoulders, she stood up and wiped her swollen eyes. "You know what, I need to go to work. We can talk about this tonight. I'll be ready at eight, okay?"

Alexis tossed her hair back, blotted her lips and under her eyes with her napkin, then grabbed her purse and rushed out of the room, the door gently gliding shut behind her with a soft snick.

"Smooth, Carrick." He scratched his chin and rubbed his chest. There was a pain there that must be residual aftereffects of the shooting.

No wonder he'd never proposed or professed love to a woman before. He'd completely botched the whole job.

He'd sounded desperate and ridiculous. Impulsive and weird.

And he couldn't even blame it on bad blood.

It was love.

Master Vampire reduced to idiocy by his romantic heart.

How cute. Why didn't he just wear a smiley face button while he was at it.

Ethan threw Alexis's abandoned bowl of fruit across the room, satisfied when it crashed through the glass of his balcony door, juice and shards flying with appropriate drama.

Then he realized that the bowl itself, a white ceramic job, had gone hurtling over the balcony, and would be landing on the Strip—and possibly someone's head—in a second or two.

"Shit." Ethan ran across his room and jumped off the balcony in a swan dive, grabbing the bowl as it flew past about the tenth floor.

Which meant there wasn't time to stop, reverse.

He hit the ground with a splat and a crunch, as his nose and both wrists broke. Pain shot through him and he heard a woman screaming hysterically.

Damn, love hurt.

And he didn't think Alexis was going to appreciate that he'd literally fallen for her.

Seventeen

Ringo thought Kelsey was a lot like herpes. A constant sort of painful itch that reappeared at the worst possible time.

"Hi," she said breathlessly as she stood up, her hair in a ponytail, still wearing the same red dress from the night before.

He ignored her as he stepped past her on the way out of his hotel room. He'd ditched her twice the night before, but somehow she kept managing to find him. Now he strongly suspected she'd spent the night in the hallway here at Caesar's Palace.

If she wanted to get in his head, she could just read this little thought—*Go away*.

"Mr. Carrick dropped to the sidewalk this morning," she called from behind him. "They thought maybe he was pushed off the first-floor overhang."

"Excuse me?" Ringo froze.

"I didn't spend the whole night sitting outside your door. I'm not that lame." She smiled with a shrug. "I just didn't have time to change. But at The Ava, Mr. Carrick was splatted on the sidewalk about seven this morning."

"He's dead?" That could be very good, or very, very bad.

"Nope. And he says he just fell. But you could tell the Italian that you pushed him. Then he won't be mad at you."

Ringo turned around, a little desperate, unable to think through the implications of Carrick's accident when it was so damn disturbing to talk to Kelsey. "Why are you in my head? Why are you helping me?"

She bit her lip, for once lipstick-free. Without the crimson smear across her mouth, she looked younger, more vulnerable. "I don't know why I can hear your thoughts so easily. And I'm helping you because I want you to get out of all this stuff."

Her hand came up and stroked his cheek. Ringo moved away. He didn't want anyone's touch on him. And he despised the way she looked at him, with pity.

"I can feel your pain, Ringo." Her black eyes swam with compassion. "Tell the Italian you quit and walk away. Save yourself."

The laugh came quick and bitter, especially when he realized she might be able to snatch his name right out of his head, but she couldn't see the plainest truth of all. "Kelsey, honey, it's way too late for that."

Alexis had called Brittany three times during the day to reassure herself that her sister was okay. Now before she headed back to the casino, she wanted a quick glance at Brittany in the flesh.

And maybe Alexis also needed to see her sister, talk to her, touch her, after everything she had spilled to Ethan that morning about their childhood.

When he had asked her to move in with him, make a commitment to him, and she'd said no.

But she wasn't reassured that all was well when she met Brittany for dinner at a Mexican restaurant on the Strip and Brittany was pale, with dark circles under her eyes. Even her smile looked tired, which wasn't standard for Brittany at all. She had a genuine power smile, with a hundred-watt brilliance.

"Okay, Brit, what's going on?" Alexis took a sip of her margarita and pressed her temples. She was starting to get a headache. An alcoholic drink probably wasn't the best thing for that, but it sure in the hell tasted good.

"And why is your scarf so tight on your neck? It looks like it's strangling you." The black, teal, and olive scarf was pretty, but Brittany wore it like a noose.

Her fingers went up and fiddled with it. "I didn't want it falling down in my patients' faces. But I get so tired of wearing the same old."

It sounded reasonable, except her sister's eyes were darting all over the restaurant and there was a pink tint to her cheeks.

"How's Ethan?" Brittany asked. "Are you having fun spending time with him?"

Oh, yeah, that she was. Alexis meant to say something flippant, meant to blow it off, as she played with the chili pepper–shaped chip dish. But instead she blurted, "He asked me to live with him."

"What?" That drew Brittany's astonished gaze right to hers. "Are you serious?"

"Yes." Now Alexis was sure she was the one who was blushing.

Her cheeks felt hot and it wasn't the margarita, even though she'd already finished half of it. "Isn't that just insane?"

Her burrito platter was dropped in front of her by the waiter, and Alexis stared at it. No answers in the guacamole.

"That is a little crazy, but it's very cool." Now Brittany gave her a real smile, one that wasn't distracted. "Can I have your house?"

"Brittany!" She should have known her impulsive sister would see nothing wrong with moving in with a man she'd known for all of four days. "I just met Ethan! I'm not going to shack up with him so soon."

"But you love him." Brittany sipped her mojito and delicately reached for a bean with her fork.

"What makes you think that?" Did she? Maybe. Probably. Weird as it sounded, yes. But she didn't want anyone to *know* that. "And he's a vampire."

"That doesn't matter. Seriously. And if it bothers you that he is, maybe someday he'll be able to return to a mortal man. Maybe sooner than you think." Brittany shook her head. "The thing is, if you love him, which you do, and he loves you, which he must if he asked you to live with him, then why throw that away? Go for it, Alex, let yourself be happy."

The thing was, she wasn't sure she knew how. Purposeful, she could do. Happy? Content? That could take some work.

"I have something to tell you, Alex."

"I have something to tell you," she said, almost simultaneously. Then when Brittany laughed, she added, "You go first, Brit."

Instead, her sister took a bite of her food and Alexis's cell phone started ringing. "Damn, let me just answer this. It could be work related." She flipped her phone open. "Alexis Baldizzi."

"Alexis, this is Seamus Fox."

"Seamus," she said in surprise. "How can I help you?" Since she got the distinct impression from Ethan that Seamus was not at all pleased with the amount of time he'd been spending with her, she couldn't imagine why Seamus was calling her. Unless she was going to be treated to a lecture on the proper behavior of a vampire first lady at social engagements.

If so, she'd tell him to stuff it. She could write the manual on political savvy and appearances, and it wouldn't sound asinine like Seamus's speech had.

"I'm calling because Ethan asked me to. He's had a little accident and he would like to see you."

Her heart about stopped and she fumbled with the chip in her hand, letting it fall to her plate. "An accident? Is he okay? Was this another assassination attempt? I told him he needed to take that more seriously."

Seamus made a sound that was impolite, but Alexis wasn't sure if it was directed at her or Ethan. "He's fine. He just, well, uh, fell off his balcony and hit the sidewalk below. It's getting a bit of news coverage because he refused medical treatment, even though he assured them he had a personal physician who could set his wrists. He claimed eccentric rich man and all of that, but anyway, he wants to see you."

"Then why didn't he call me himself?" She wanted to hear he was okay, damn it. Between Brittany and Ethan, she was going to go gray, no doubt about it. "And how the hell did he fall off his balcony? Did he sneeze and lose his balance?"

"He's sleeping right now. But he said to wake him as soon as you got here. And he can explain what happened to you himself.

I'm just the secretary." Seamus spoke with more than a hint of annoyance and impatience.

"What is your problem with me?" she asked him, tired of catching his attitude, when she'd never done a thing to him.

"I don't have a problem," he said coolly.

Yeah, sure, she believed him. "Thank you for the message. I'll be there in half an hour."

Shoveling two bites of food into her mouth, she told Brittany, "Ethan had an accident. He's fine, but he wants me to see him." Then she realized how anxious she appeared and tried to temper her reaction. "You know, it's the least I could do after rejecting him and all."

Brittany raised an eyebrow. "Oh, Alex, just give it up. You are so gone for him."

She gave her sister her haughty courtroom glare. "I object."

Twenty minutes later, they were entering Ethan's room with the key card he'd given Alexis. Brittany had insisted on coming with her, and Alexis was grateful. She kept having mental flashbacks to the night she'd found Ethan bleeding all over the floor. Seamus said he was fine, but that didn't mean it wasn't gross.

Brittany came along behind her as they headed toward his bedroom. The whole suite was hushed and still, and it bugged Alexis that they'd just left him alone. Shouldn't someone be sitting with him at least? Apparently it was every vampire for himself, even the president.

Ethan sat straight up in his mahogany four-poster bed when they walked through the door, his eyes snapping open. "Alexis?"

Then he sniffed the air. "What the hell is that? I smell vampire. I smell . . . the Frenchman. Why do you have another man all over you?" He sounded absolutely outraged.

The fall must have thrown his nose off. "What are you talking about?" She moved closer to the bed, kicking off her high heels and peeling off her suit jacket. He didn't look injured beyond two very faint black eyes, and a pasty tint to his flesh. Nor did he sound like he was in pain.

But she still found herself touching his forehead. Crap, what was she doing? He wasn't going to have a freaking fever. After the scene that morning, she'd expected to feel embarrassed, but instead she was just worried about him.

"What the hell happened, Ethan?" Alexis fought the urge to kiss him.

He didn't look to be struggling with the same amorous feelings. His eyes shifted around her. "Brittany? Come here," he demanded.

"Hey, that's my sister you're bossing around." Alexis glared at him.

Brittany just stepped forward, looking miserable. "Hi, Ethan. I hope you're feeling better." But her voice sounded small and guilty.

Alexis was getting a bad feeling.

"Take off your scarf, Brittany."

Her sister sighed, than undid the knot. When the scarf fell away, two puncture wounds leaped out at them, tiny, but an angry red on Brittany's fair skin.

Alexis gaped in shock.

"And your jacket."

Brittany was wearing a white jacket with a teal sleeveless shell, and white cropped pants with sandals. She peeled her jacket off and there on both shoulders were more puncture wounds.

"Uh . . ." Alexis said, completely stunned.

"You've mated with the Frenchman," Ethan said, looking very stern and foreboding.

Alexis didn't know who the hell the Frenchman was, but he obviously wasn't very popular.

"I'm not sure mating is exactly the right word," Brittany said, folding her jacket over her arm. "And I don't see that it's really any of your business."

Ethan gaped at Brittany. He couldn't believe what he was hearing, seeing. "The Frenchman is banished, you know."

"But you let him stay here, you let him continue his research."

Because Ethan was an idiot, obviously. Jesus, Alexis was going to kill him. He'd let her sister get involved with a radical, eccentric vampire.

And Brittany may not realize what had happened between her and Atelier, but Ethan knew. Corbin had marked her. No other vampire could go near her without recognizing she belonged to Atelier.

Just like he had done with Alexis.

Vampires were territorial about their mortal lovers, especially when they loved them, like he did Alexis. But Brittany was an Impure and that complicated things. Immensely. Ethan wished Seamus's discreet inquiries into who Brittany's father could be would give them an answer, but so far, Seamus hadn't been able to draw any conclusions, and it made Ethan nervous.

Especially if she was involved with Atelier.

"I do let him stay. But his views are not always popular with the majority. He is seen as a threat." Ethan turned to Alexis, who was just staring at them. He could smell alcohol on her breath and wondered what she'd been doing all day, what her mood was. "BB, it's time you told Brittany. Unless Atelier already told her."

He looked at Brittany for confirmation, but she only looked puzzled and annoyed.

"Ethan . . ." Alexis had a pleading to her voice he didn't understand.

"Tell me what? What is going on? What does Corbin have to do with Alexis?"

"Who's Corbin?" Alexis asked, sounding exasperated.

"The Frenchman," Ethan told her, wishing he could read her thoughts and send her his, so he could explain why it was important that Brittany have full knowledge about who she was.

"We sort of, you know . . ." Brittany blushed. "He's a scientist. He's trying to find a way to reverse vampirism."

"You had sex with him?" Alexis yelled.

"So?" Brittany knotted the scarf around and around her finger, before letting it go. "You had sex with Ethan."

"You don't know that!"

Ethan cleared his throat. Alexis whirled and pointed her finger at him. "You don't say a damn word."

"Hey, I'm staying out of that discussion. I just think Brittany needs to know who she is."

"Who am I?"

"Drop it, Carrick."

Ethan knew that Alexis was worried about losing Brittany, that it was safer to keep her sister in the dark, but the truth was, she was putting Brittany in jeopardy.

"Alexis." He willed her to understand. He could leak his thoughts to Brittany, but Alexis would kill him. Never even consider changing her mind about moving in with him. Wouldn't even give him the six weeks she'd promised.

"You're scaring me," Brittany said, her pulse beating rapidly in her neck. The scarf twisted nervously in her hand.

Alexis looked tortured. "Damn it, I'm sorry, don't be scared. It's just that Ethan has wondered about your biological father."

"What about him?"

"Well . . . Ethan thinks he might have been a vampire." Alexis grabbed her sister's hand and squeezed it. "But that's just speculation."

"How could that be possible?" Brittany stared at Alexis, then him. "I didn't think vampires could reproduce."

"Only with a mortal woman. The resulting child is a genetic blend . . . not immortal, but very healthy, and destined to live to a hundred years old or so. They don't need blood to survive, but they exhibit some other vampire traits—burning easily in the sun, athletic, ability to read people's thoughts." Ethan wasn't sure there was a delicate way to relay the news, so he just laid it all out for Brittany to deal with at once. "I can sense your vampire blood. I know you're one of us."

Alexis snorted. "You are only guessing."

But Brittany didn't seem to have Alexis's doubts. She shook her head, looking thoughtful. "It's weird . . . but I believe you. It's like I just know you're right. I always knew there was something different about me. And Corbin . . . Corbin told me that my blood was a link between mortal and vampire, and a way for him to isolate gene mutation in vampires. I didn't know he meant because I had DNA from both . . ." She rubbed her hand over the bottom of her mouth.

Alexis looked tortured. "Brit, I wasn't sure if I should tell you . . . Ethan just told me and I didn't know if it was true or not. But this isn't a big deal, sweetie, I promise. You're still you."

Brittany smiled at Alexis. "I know that, Alex. It's okay, really. I'm fine and I'm glad you told me. It doesn't really change anything, but it explains a lot." She looked back at Ethan. "Do you know who my father is?"

"No." He shook his head. "But Seamus is looking into it. I owe you an apology, Brittany. I encouraged you to come to The Ava because I knew you were an Impure and I wanted political leverage with minority Impures heading into my campaign. It wasn't fair to you, but it was always my intention to tell you when I thought you were ready to hear the news, and I wouldn't have influenced you to do anything you didn't want to."

In fact, just thinking about it, he felt like a first-class cad. Out loud, it sounded much ruder than when he and Seamus had been strategizing.

Just one more reason he was starting to regret he'd agreed to run for reelection. He was getting tired of the entire political process, and the manipulations it required.

But Brittany Baldizzi was a forgiving sort of woman. She patted his hand. "It's okay, Ethan. I stayed because I knew you were vampires and I wanted to save you from hell, you know. I'm not sure anymore if you all really are damned, but I do like that Corbin can offer vampires an alternative. They have a choice to be vampire or mortal."

Ethan agreed to a certain extent. Part of the reason he'd supported Atelier's research was because it kept him close at hand, and also because he hadn't really thought the Frenchman would ever be successful. But if he were successful, Ethan cautiously felt that it could be very positive for vampires who were turned against their will or older vampires who were ready to die. But it would have to be very controlled, very guarded. Hell, it was an ethical nightmare, and despite his thousand years of life, he wasn't even sure where he stood on the issue.

Did a vampire have a right to choose or was he bound to this earth by his Dark Gift? There were rare vampires who were successful in suicide attempts, and Ethan had always sympathized for their depression or despair, but he wasn't sure if he thought he had the right to take his own life.

It was a very complex, emotional issue, and if necessary, Ethan would be prepared to deal with it, but he had hoped they were years from it being relevant.

"Atelier's research is an explosive issue, Brittany. If you associate with him, you will be caught in a huge controversy if he succeeds in finding a way to reverse a turning. There has been talk, too, that Atelier knows how to clone vampires."

"Jesus," Alexis said, her normally golden skin bleached, showing freckles Ethan hadn't realized she'd had.

"If he does, he would never do it. Corbin's research is focused on what he calls the cure to vampirism."

Alexis sat heavily on the bed next to him. "Brit, why the hell didn't you marry an accountant like I told you to? This Corbin sounds a little scary."

"Oh, he's not at all," Brittany said warmly. "He's very sweet, with the cutest little accent, and this sort of proper outrage when he thinks I'm being unladylike."

Uh-oh. That sounded like the serious beginnings of an infatuation. And they'd already been intimate, Ethan was certain. The bites proved it.

Alexis seemed to sense it, too. She looked liked she'd been chewing on nails. Ethan rubbed her back. She turned to him.

"So what happened to you? Did you really fall off the balcony? You don't look hurt." She sounded accusatory, like she'd prefer if he were laid up with casts and IV tubing.

Ethan cleared his throat. "I dropped something over the edge and I didn't want it to land on someone's head and kill them, so I jumped for it. I couldn't stop myself, so I hit the sidewalk with my wrists and nose. No big deal."

"Then why did Seamus call me?" She sounded exasperated, but at the same time, she massaged both his wrists, like she was comforting him and reassuring herself he was okay. Alexis cared way more than she was probably willing to admit.

That thought eradicated the last of his discomfort with the way their discussion had ended that morning. Alexis just needed time. And he had plenty of that.

"Because I didn't want you to see it on the news. Because I was in a bit of pain and wanted to see your beautiful face to ease my suffering."

She rolled her eyes.

Brittany laughed.

Ethan dropped a smacking kiss on her lips and held her tight when she tried to wriggle away. "I love you," he said.

Her cheeks turned crimson. "You're such a freak."

"Alex!" Brittany sounded horrified. "Geez, be nice." She moved over to his dresser and watched herself in the mirror so she could tie her scarf back on.

"Yeah, be nice," he murmured to Alexis, nuzzling along her neck.

She pinched his arm. "I love you, too," she said, before jumping off the bed and joining Brittany at the mirror.

Ethan stared after her in shock. Well, hell. She'd said it.

And it had sounded bloody brilliant.

Eighteen

"You're late." Donatelli glanced at his watch. "By about ten hours. Give me one good reason why I shouldn't just kill you."

Ringo pulled his gun on Donatelli. "Because I'll kill you first." He was going on no sleep, and he was getting himself out of this if he had to waste the man in front of him.

Donatelli merely glanced at his gun, looking unperturbed as he sat on his ivory sofa, stroking an ugly little brown dog. It was such a fucking cliché, Ringo almost laughed.

"This is how we're going to play this. I shot Carrick, then sent him over his balcony. I did my job, but I won't take any money. I'm just going to walk away and you and I are both going to forget we ever met."

"Do you really think I'll agree to that?"

"You don't have a choice."

Donatelli snapped his fingers, which nearly got him shot. Ringo stopped from pulling the trigger at the last possible second. Then he regretted his self-control when Donatelli spoke.

"Maybe your girlfriend will give me some choices back."

Sweat trickled down Ringo's back, sticking to his silk shirt. "What are you talking about?"

But he already knew, because he could hear Kelsey crying from behind him. A quick glance over his shoulder showed her being held by two brawny guys, her shoulders shaking as she sobbed. Her eyes pleaded with him.

Shit. "Do you think you could listen to me?" he yelled at her. "I fucking told you to stay at the hotel."

"I'm sorry . . . I thought that I could help."

"Women are such a hassle, aren't they?" Donatelli clucked with sympathy, the bastard. "You should just hire a mistress like I do. Much lower maintenance, and they know to stay out of your business."

"Thank you, I'll consider that in the future." Ringo stepped closer to Donatelli, marking the heart as his target, watching the other two men with his peripheral vision. "Let her go."

They did, shoving her forward toward him. Kelsey stumbled in her heels and fell to the ground five feet behind Ringo. The ping, ping sound and a scream had him spinning around and firing his own weapon at the bodyguard—who was already pumping Kelsey full of bullets.

Ringo dropped both men with quick shots, but not before a whole round had gone into Kelsey's back and side. Blood spatter was on her dress, her arm, an arcing mist of red dusting the carpet.

Jerking at her arm, he turned her on her side and saw her eyes were open, but empty, her breathing stopped. Her body limp and very much dead.

Donatelli hadn't moved on the couch, just sat with his leg crossed over a knee, stroking, stroking the rat-like dog, who let out a yip as Ringo knelt beside Kelsey.

Checking for a pulse, he felt everything inside him that he'd pushed down, trampled over, hidden, and ignored burst forward. Sorrow, rage, disgust, grief all ripped out of him. He brushed a hand over Kelsey's cool cheek, closed her eyelids.

"You didn't have to kill her," he told Donatelli in a hard, low voice. "She had nothing to do with anything."

And she was dead because of him.

"Oh, on the contrary, she has everything to do with this. Boys, take care of Miss Kelsey, please. She's bleeding on the carpet."

Ringo turned, wondering who the hell Donatelli was talking to. What he saw made fear and disbelief crawl up his spine like an aggressive spider. The two guards he'd shot were sitting up, brushing themselves off.

"Holy shit . . ."

He'd put three bullets through the hearts of each of them. There was no way they could be alive. Cold panic iced his limbs and he positioned himself in front of Kelsey. They weren't going to disrespect her corpse, throw her in some Dumpster. "You're not doing a damn thing with her."

"You don't really have a say in it."

Ringo felt around for his gun. He'd set it down when he'd checked for Kelsey's pulse.

They were on him in a second and Ringo kicked, punched,

clawed, but they pinned his arms behind him. The big one with dark hair, who smelled like mothballs, covered Ringo, blocking out the light. He brought his knee up, making contact, but it didn't stop the man's descent, his body crushing out Ringo's breath, his face leering and grinning as he bent over, closer and closer.

Fangs, long and violent, flashed in the man's mouth, and Ringo felt pure and total terror as the creature, person, whatever the hell he was, cut off his air, light, sound. A sharp pain sliced into his neck.

Ringo heard himself moan, felt the shock, the pain, the cold as a violent tugging consumed him. He hurt everywhere, frozen in place, his body shuddering and panicking, his cells collapsing in, his teeth sinking down into his tongue. From across the room, he heard Donatelli's voice floating over to him.

"I knew you couldn't kill Carrick, you know. Not because you wouldn't try, but because you cannot kill the undead unless you cut their heads off, and I strongly suspected you would think that too messy. All I really wanted was to rattle Carrick, throw him off his game as we head into the homestretch of our campaigns. It was a psychological tactic, but I didn't expect you to get involved with Carrick's secretary."

Ringo tried to open his eyes, tried to focus, but the room was spinning and exploding behind his eyelids. He must have been injected with a drug, something that was paralyzing him, threatening to send him unconscious.

"A little more, Smith."

Ringo gave a silent scream in his head as his insides felt scored and raked, trussed and sliced.

"That's it. Good. Now go take care of the girl, give her your excess. I'll finish here."

Ringo fell back on a soft heap as hands let go of him. Then he hit the carpet with a hard thud that jarred his skull when Kelsey's body was pulled from beneath him. He wanted to move, wanted to protest, but he was a fly caught in the spider's web, and Donatelli was playing with him.

Warmth smothered his mouth, a sharp, tinny kind of liquid that moistened his dried, cracking lips, and lifted his tongue off the roof of his mouth.

"I appreciate your qualities. And I find it rather quaint that you thought to protect the girl—I didn't expect that of you."

Ringo sucked eagerly on the source of liquid dribbling into his mouth. It tasted exotic, necessary, easing the pain and cramping in his body with each swallow. He managed to open his eyes, but was too close to the man that knelt over him—he could only see shirt fabric, flesh hovering in front of his face.

He drank with a thirst he'd never experienced before, greedy and gulping, taking it in, refilling his dehydrated body, arms and feet going warm again.

"That's it. Just a little more." Donatelli stroked his forehead.

The sensation repulsed Ringo, made him suddenly realize that he was sucking on the Italian's arm . . . and his blood. His mind screamed for him to pull away, to get up, to run, but his mouth, his body begged for more, and he whimpered when Donatelli pulled away.

"You shouldn't overdo it."

Ringo stared up at him, confused, full, hot, yet frozen, and followed the pattern of the crow's-feet trailing out from Donatelli's eyes. Hard eyes. Obsidian black, and full of deep, ugly secrets.

"You see it, don't you? Yes, I am a vampire. Now you are one, too, and in my service."

Ringo had thought he'd seen hell in Grenada in the Marines. But when he stared into Donatelli's empty soul, he saw it all over again tenfold.

🦇

Alexis ran a brush through her hair and frowned at her reflection. She didn't look stately. She looked like a twelve-year-old playing dress-up in her mother's evening dress. And why was it that she couldn't fill the cups up in the bodice, but the butt was straining?

"You look awesome," Brittany said.

"I look like an episode of *What Not to Wear*. Pear-shaped woman in clingy A-line dress. Gasp."

Her sister was lolling on the bed, her shoes and jacket off. The scarf was back firmly in place, but every time Alexis looked at it, she got the heebie-jeebies. It was one thing for her to be having sex with a vampire, and getting bitten in kinky places, but her little sister? Eew with a capital *E*. File that under TOO MUCH INFORMATION.

But she was glad to have everything out in the open between the two of them. She didn't like anything that smacked of a secret being kept from her sister. Brittany seemed to be handling the whole vamp daddy thing pretty well.

"Alex, you look fantastic. If you would just stop wishing that you were five foot ten, you would recognize that you've always had a cute figure. Not every man wants a tall, skinny waif."

"What the hell planet are you living on?" Alexis tucked her hair behind her ears. Then untucked it. "Every man wants that."

"That's not true. A lot of men like big breasts."

"Strike two." Alexis pointed to her unimpressive chest. "And I have *never* heard a single man say he doesn't care about her breasts as long as she has a big ass."

She threw down the brush. "And why do I have to wear a cocktail dress anyway? It's a debate, not a party. I should be wearing a suit."

"Ethan said to wear a cocktail dress. And come on, this is Vegas. Any excuse to pull out the sequins works here."

"Two nights ago I was Barbara Bush, now I'm Hillary Clinton. This is starting to get scary . . . who's next, Betty Ford?"

Brittany laughed, which was easy for her to do since she was a tall, skinny waif.

"So now that Ethan's off doing his preparations—and I really hope they're not putting makeup on him or something—you can tell me the real story between you and Corbin." Alexis put chandelier earrings in. Maybe dangling earrings would elongate her stature when people looked at her.

"What do you mean?"

"I mean, you got all weird and skittish when we brought him up, yet you defended him like a mother tiger with her cub."

Brittany propped her head up with her hand. "Well, you know me. I get behind a cause and I can't let it go. But I have to admit, I'm not sure how I feel about Corbin. Having sex was very unplanned, and afterwards it was just totally awkward. I haven't seen him since, and I'm not sure that I will. He's really reclusive."

Alexis stepped into her shoes. "I'm not even going to pretend to give you advice. I know nothing about men. Never could I have predicted that Ethan Carrick would decide he has to have me, of all women."

"At first I think he was attracted to the fact that you didn't throw yourself at him."

"No. I kneed him in the nuts the first night we met." Alexis recalled the moment fondly. "But Brittany, you know you have the biggest heart in Vegas. I don't want to see you hurt, but if you want to be with Corbin, you know I'm here for you."

The thought of her sister hanging with a scientist who might be responsible for either eradicating vampires or multiplying their numbers tenfold didn't thrill Alexis, but she had learned you couldn't control everything.

Brittany's eyebrows rose. "Wow. You must be falling in love with Ethan if you're feeling this mellow. Normally you despise nine out of every ten men I date, and give me a laundry list of their flaws, followed by a background check."

"And a couple of times I turned up a prior conviction, didn't I?" Alexis wasn't about to let Brittany forget that.

Suddenly her sister's arms were around her from behind, cutting off her air. "Ack! What are you doing? You'll mess up my hair," Alexis grumbled but she gripped Brittany's wrists to hold her there.

Tears swam in Brittany's eyes in the mirror. "I love you, Alex. You're everything to me . . . I know it wasn't easy for you to take care of me when I was kid, but thank you for doing it."

She would not cry, she would not cry. Blubbering once a day was her limit, and she'd already dehydrated herself that morning with Ethan. A tear snuck out of each eye anyway. "Brittany . . . baby. You know I would never trade a thing about our time together. It was a privilege to help raise you, and damn, I can't even tell you how proud you've made me. I'd do anything to make you happy."

Ever since Brittany had surpassed her in height at age fourteen, she'd been slumping down and trying to insert herself into Alexis's hugs, and she was doing it now. It was Alexis's biggest regret about her height—she wished she could still be the bigger one when her sister needed comforting.

"Alex, do you know what would make me happy? Really happy? If you let yourself just enjoy a relationship. Let yourself take a chance on a man, marriage. I want you to let yourself fall in love with Ethan."

Alexis stepped forward, out of Brittany's arms. Fear clawed at her, irrational and unreasonable, just from Brittany's words. "I'm already in love with Ethan. But I don't know if I can trust him, or me, enough to make it work. I think about marriage and I just panic. I don't know if I can let myself be that vulnerable."

"If you don't take a chance, you'll be missing out on something amazing. After a thousand years of living, a man has decided you of all women are his soul mate. That's pretty damn romantic. I would jump at that."

Brittany sounded so sad, Alexis turned around and took her hand, wanting to cheer her up. "Maybe Corbin . . ."

"That was just sex." Her sister shrugged. "No big deal. I'm sure I'll find someone. After all, according to Ethan, I'll live to be a hundred." Brittany smiled, shaking off the ennui she'd been showing.

"Brit . . ." Alexis wasn't sure what she was going to say, so she hesitated.

"I'm going to go, okay? I didn't sleep at all last night and I've got a really full schedule tomorrow. Call me in the A.M. and let me know how the debate went." Her sister blew her a kiss. "You look great. Hugs, Alex."

"Thanks, Brit. I'll call you."

When Brittany left, Alexis sat on the bed, puzzled and deflated. Brittany's words had made her melancholy, bothered her, and she wasn't sure why.

The door to her suite opened. "It's just me, don't kick me," Ethan called.

Alexis didn't even move. She felt like the entire balance of her future was resting on the next few days. There was the safe, the usual, the lock-down of her emotions. Which meant flat, loveless status quo. Or there was the risky, the hopeful, the taking a chance. Which could mean disaster or could mean some really damn good years with Ethan.

He appeared in her doorway, wearing a gray suit and a blue tie. "Hey, everything okay? You look a little pale."

Before she could change her mind, Alexis stared at him and blurted, "I'll live with you."

Ethan froze. "What?"

Now that she'd said it, Alexis felt a thousand pounds lighter. "Yes, I'll move in with you."

"Alexis." He came toward her, bent down, kissed her hard on the lips. "Are you sure?" Then he shook his head, laughed. "God, what am I saying? I shouldn't give you an out. Not when you've made me so incredibly happy."

She was feeling pretty freaking happy herself. Grabbing on to Ethan's tie, she pulled him down for another kiss. "Ten years is better than one, right? I mean, I either get my heart broken then or now, so at least if we have some time together, I get some good sex out of the whole deal."

He grinned against her lips. "I'm so glad you're being logical about this."

Alexis flicked her tongue against Ethan's lower lip. God, he tasted so good. She couldn't even imagine walking away from him, a man who understood her, appreciated her strengths while respecting her weaknesses. A man who didn't patronize, or insult her intelligence. She breathed in his scent, light aftershave and crisp mint toothpaste. He had an obsession about brushing his teeth, and a constant toothpaste taste clung to him.

"That's me, all logic. Then there's also the fact that I'm completely and totally in love with you."

Ethan kneeled down on the carpet in front of her, pressing her legs apart so he could get closer to her. "That's a fact I'm glad you decided to share with me."

He wanted to inhale Alexis, press everything against her and show her how much this meant to him, that he understood the sacrifice she was making, how much trust she was putting in him to make the next decade or so worth the pain of separation.

"Alexis, I have waited over nine hundred years to find a woman I could love, and now that I have, I will do everything in my power to ensure you won't regret this." Ethan was supposed to be downstairs in ten minutes, but he didn't give a damn. Nothing had given him the sense of fulfillment that being with Alexis did.

Never had he felt himself to be lonely, but the thought of life without Alexis was agonizing. He was going to enjoy every moment he had with her.

Shifting her dress up, tracing his thumbs over her thighs, running his lips over her neck, he murmured, "Maybe I should resign the presidency. Let someone else run, so you and I can spend more time together."

"Are you insane?" Her breathing hitched when he nipped her breast through the clingy red dress. "We're not going to spend the next fifteen years just gazing adoringly at each other."

He noticed ten years had now stretched to fifteen. "No?" Her nipple rose for him behind her stretchy, seamless bra. He flicked his tongue across it.

"No. We both have careers, responsibilities. And when we split, we have to have something to go back to or we'll both just wander around in a stupor. No, we have to live normal lives, as normal as it can be for a prosecutor and a vampire president."

"Whatever you say." He didn't care what they did. He didn't want to argue, didn't want to do anything but make love to Alexis, find a wedding chapel, and put a hugely expensive ring on her finger. Because surely marriage was the next logical step.

He sucked on her breast, enjoying her moan, the feel of her fingers flexing in pleasure on his shoulders. Ethan moved her dress higher and higher on her thighs, stroked his fingers over the front of her flesh-colored stretchy panties. "Mmm, I like the way these feel. They give with you."

His thumb pressed into her, and the panties sank slightly into the dampness there, pulled back sticky and wet. Fangs down, lust raging alongside his love, Ethan could feel her heart racing, quickly pumping the thick sweetness of her blood. He scraped his fangs over her breast as she moaned, teasing himself, knowing he wouldn't bite.

She spread her legs farther apart for him, for his finger, a blatant invitation that he couldn't resist. He slid her panties down to her ankles, trailed his nose up the side of her calf, her knee, before sucking her skin into his mouth.

"If you're going to suck anything, you should aim for a little higher," she said, sinking back onto her elbows.

"Higher?" Ethan sucked her inner thigh. "Here?"

"That's not bad, but a little higher."

Nuzzling between her legs, Ethan parted her soft inner folds with his thumbs and scrutinized her. She was so damn beautiful, glistening with moisture, and giving little shivers of anticipation. "Here?" He sucked the button of her swollen clitoris, holding her down when she bucked against him.

"Yes, that's exactly where I was talking about," she moaned, collapsing back on the bed.

Her hot sweetness tightened as he pulled at it, the musky scent of her arousal surrounding him, filling his nostrils and blending with the scent of her mortality, her blood. His fangs ached with the need to taste her, his body cramped with sexual want, his erection thick and hard as it strained against his pants.

"Yes," she whimpered, clawing at the bedspread. Then she sat up, giving him a wicked, desperate look. "Bite me, Ethan. I know you want to, I can tell. Do it."

He pulled back, in agony. Once he started, he wasn't sure he could stop. He wanted to bite her everywhere, starting with those soft plump folds displayed so enticingly in front of him. "Alexis . . ."

She grabbed his head, shoved him down. "Please, now, I'm going to come, Ethan. Take me."

His vision sharpened as he groaned. That was an invitation he couldn't resist, didn't want to even try. Sliding his tongue up and down each side of her, he pushed a finger inside her right as he sank his teeth into her tender flesh.

The hot taste of her flowed over his teeth as she screamed out in pleasure, arching off the bed in a violent climax. Ethan's eyes sank closed as he took in her pleasure, felt it rush past him in a tidal wave of satiated ecstasy. His finger moved in her swollen flesh with slow, steady presses as she shuddered on and on, little whimpers assaulting his ears.

Forcing himself to retreat, Ethan swallowed hard, feeling the heat of Alexis's lifeblood scattering out to all his limbs, filling him with her essence, her strength, her love for him.

It was a good thing he was kneeling, because he wasn't sure he could stand on his shaky legs. She'd rocked him to the core.

A pounding filtered through his consciousness, and it wasn't the pumping of either of their hearts.

It was Seamus, knocking on the door. "Ethan! Jesus, where the hell are you? If you are in there, get your ass downstairs *now*. Donatelli will make mincemeat out of you if you're late."

Alexis gave a soft laugh, limp on the bed, dress shoved up past her thighs. "Oh, my God. He has the worst timing."

Ethan thunked his head onto the edge of the bed—once, twice, three times. "This is one of those moments where a man has to choose selfishness or responsibility. I have to have you or I'm going to die."

Alexis drew her legs together and fixed her skirt. "I don't want to take you from your duties."

She was starting to grin, the little tease. "Yeah, easy for you to say, you were on the receiving end here."

"No, the biting was all for you. I got nothing from it." She couldn't quite pull off the innocent look.

"Seamus can wait a minute. That's all I need." He started to unzip his fly and push to his feet.

The door pounded again. "Carrick! I know you're in there. I can hear you."

"Shit." Ethan stared at Alexis in agony. He wanted nothing more than to fill her with his hard flesh, pumping faster and faster into her, but he really didn't want Seamus standing outside the door listening.

Alexis sat up, looking more sympathetic than teasing now. "Don't worry. I'll make it up to you later. You don't want to rush it . . . It's more fun if we have all the time in the world."

"I'm going to die," he told her, most sincerely.

She grinned. "No, you're not. You're a vampire. Now stop being dramatic and go beat the crap out of the other guy in this debate. Then we'll sneak away for a little victory celebration."

Sighing, Ethan rezipped his pants. "I don't think you understand how much pain I'm in." He wasn't sure he could even walk.

"Since I don't want Seamus breaking that door down and walking in on us, we're just going to have to wait. Besides, that way I'll have time to suck you first."

Ethan groaned, his vision blurring, body tightening everywhere. "Alexis, you're torturing me."

"No, that comes later." She stood up, pushed her dress down, and headed toward the door.

He noticed she was still wearing her high heels and the thought had him groaning all over again. He could have done her with her shoes still on, damn that was hot.

"Hi, Seamus. Sorry to keep you waiting."

Bloody hell. Running his hands through his hair, he took a few tentative steps in the direction of the living area. His cock didn't break off and fall to the floor, but it ached abominably.

He needed to think about something else, divert his blood flow elsewhere.

"You're a sick man," Seamus told him when he walked in the room.

"No, just horny."

Alexis laughed.

Seamus flushed an ugly beet red. "Look, maybe you don't take this election seriously anymore, but I do. I've worked my ass off on this campaign and I'd appreciate a little cooperation."

That was enough to cause contrition and deflation. "Seamus, I apologize. I know how hard you've been working. I'm heading down now. But first you can offer us congratulations—Alexis and I are engaged to be married."

Seamus's eyes narrowed. "Really? Well."

He faced Alexis, who had turned a little pink. Ethan was amused. Getting caught in the act didn't embarrass her, but being engaged obviously did.

"Congratulations." Seamus's words were clipped and hard.

Too late, Ethan remembered Seamus supported an engagement to Brittany, not Alexis. He hoped this wouldn't cause a permanent breach in their friendship.

"We're not engaged," Alexis said.

Ethan took in her pale face, her stiff shoulders. Uh-oh. "But you said . . . you said yes."

"To living with you. Not to marriage. You never asked me to marry you."

Well, if she wanted to get technical. "But I'm going to."

"And if and when you do, maybe I'll say yes."

That almost sounded positive. "Really? You might say yes?" Ethan grinned at Alexis. She wanted to marry him.

His answer was an eye roll. "It's probable. Good odds, I'd say, if you don't tick me off in the meantime."

But then she smiled, softening her words, and Ethan felt like every cliché ever written. He was in love. He was a Celine Dion song waiting to be written.

Seamus made a sound of impatience. "Can we head down now?"

"Absolutely," Alexis said. "Sooner we go down, the sooner we can come back up." And she winked.

Ethan almost groaned. Damn, she was hot. Taking Alexis's arm, he followed Seamus.

"By the way," Seamus said, "we can't get an ID on the shooter. And Kelsey is missing."

"Missing?" Ethan frowned at Seamus, jerked out of his sappy and sexual thoughts.

"Well, no one has seen her since last night. She didn't show up for work today, but then Kelsey is known for late nights and partying. I just thought it was a coincidence since she was with the shooter that night."

They stepped on the elevator. "I don't like the way that sounds," Ethan said. "Kelsey was really frightened by him. I don't think she knows anything about him, but what if he thought she did? I suspect he was just an off-balance gambler, who lost a life savings or something, but would he hurt Kelsey?"

"Wouldn't she call for one of us if she were in trouble?" Seamus asked.

"True." Kelsey wasn't the best mind reader, but she could certainly project her fear or plea for help to them if she needed to. "Speaking of that." He squeezed Alexis's hand. "You need to learn how to call me with your mind if you need me."

"You can't read her thoughts?" Seamus asked in amazement.

"Not at all."

Seamus looked at Alexis with new respect. "You really are his chosen one, aren't you?"

Alexis looked at Seamus like he had serious body odor. Her nose wrinkled. "He may have chosen, but I had to agree to it, too, you know."

"I mean . . . never mind." Seamus crossed his arms. "You can teach her to project."

"You really should, Alexis. You can train yourself to open up to me only when you want to. That way if you're ever in danger, you can call for me."

"Sure. Like a mental cell phone. That's cool, as long as you don't enter my head without asking first." Her scowl showed what she thought of that.

"I wouldn't dream of it. Besides, I couldn't without you opening yourself for me."

That made her grin. "Sounds kinky."

Seamus made a disgusted sound. Ethan was starting to think Seamus needed to reinvent his social life.

"Okay, so just think of something that really brings out strong feelings in you. Something you despise." Ethan led her off the elevator.

"The grocery store."

"You hate the grocery store?" Ethan only went into one on occasion, to buy shaving cream or shampoo, but it didn't look that awful. Neat and tidy. Food was packaged and ready to cook, unlike in his youth when the castle cooks always had dirty fingernails from slaughtering animals.

"I hate it with a passion. It's like physical and mental torture. First you have to carve time out of your schedule to do it, then you walk in and are instantly surrounded by millions of choices. And every single item on every shelf requires you do something with it. Chop it or cook it or sauté it or remove it from gobs of packaging and microwave it. It's either fattening, which makes you feel temptation and guilt simultaneously, or it's good for you and tastes like crap, reminding you that you are five foot two on a tall day with slow metabolism and zero time to work out. Then for the privilege of all this fun, you get to pay outrageous prices for the food that had to be trucked across the desert to the over-air-conditioned grocery store near you, and all hopes of buying a new couch to replace the hideously ugly one you have evaporate in the checkout line."

"Wow." Ethan couldn't have begun to imagine. "Okay, so channel all that energy about the grocery store into one place in your brain."

They were walking down the hall side by side, Seamus in front of them, but that was just as well. She shouldn't really be looking at Ethan when she tried to give him her thoughts. "Now let me see it."

"The grocery store?"

"Yes. Let me see your thoughts, in your head, without talking. Push them at me."

Ethan heard and saw nothing.

Alexis made a funny growling sound. "You're not answering."

"I can't hear anything." Ethan tried to pick through her wall, but he couldn't get past it.

She giggled.

"What's so funny?"

"I'm thinking all kinds of dirty thoughts. I can't help it."

They reached the doorway to the ballroom where the debate was being held. He stopped and tried to give her a stern look. "Behave yourself. Don't try and project perversions to me when I'm in the middle of this debate."

"I wouldn't do that." She gave him a dignified look. "I'm a perfect political girlfriend. A lawyer. Logical. I'm going to have a really kick-ass pet cause, too. Maybe I'll overhaul campaign finance reform or Impure rights or something. First I'll have to figure out what's what, but rest assured I'll fix something."

"I look forward to it." He tucked her hand into his arm. "Ready? Smile for the vampires, Alexis."

"I'm ready." She took a deep breath and flashed him her pearly teeth.

Seamus opened the door and they strode into the packed ballroom, applause greeting them. Ethan raised his free hand and waved, smiling, giving the victory sign, and feeling damn proud Alexis was on his arm.

This was actually a lot of fun with a partner.

Nineteen

Alexis sat in the front row, heavily guarded on either side by Ethan's security team. Like someone was going to snatch her or something.

Seamus was two seats over from her, and she could practically smell him sweating. She felt a certain amount of guilt over stressing him out. Hey, she lived for her job, or had up until a week ago. She knew what it was like to put your heart and soul and hours of work into something, only to watch it fail.

It sucked. Failure was like physical pain. She was so Type A it was scary, and she could sympathize with Seamus. Leaning around the brawny henchman on her right, she whispered to Seamus, "I'm sorry for distracting Ethan. I'll do whatever is necessary to help him win the election. Just tell me your strategy . . . maybe we can schedule a meeting for tomorrow to get me up to speed."

He stared at her. "I think that's an excellent idea. We can verse you in proper protocol, such as not speaking during a presidential debate."

Tight-ass. Alexis sat back in her seat and studied the stage. She actually couldn't hear them all that well. "The acoustics in here are lousy," she told her bodyguard.

He glanced down at her, all dark hair and pale skin. "We have better hearing than you. It's not necessary to have it any louder."

"Well." So she would just sit there and admire Ethan's package in that gray suit. His opponent, Donatelli, was a very creepy dude. He wore expensive clothing, but his frame was so lean, he almost looked effeminate. Yet there was nothing gentle about the way he gripped that podium and fired accusations at Ethan.

He pointed fingers at the moderator, tugged at his tie, looked exasperated, and cast a cold, hard, arrogant stare across the entire audience. At one point, he said, "With all due respect, Mr. President, that is the most outrageous lie I have ever heard. We don't believe you, do we?" He held his arm out to encompass the audience. "We think it's time you told the truth to us."

That got Alexis riled up. "Bastard."

"Quiet," Seamus reprimanded her.

Right. She'd forgotten she was in a room with two thousand vampires, all of whom could probably hear her speaking if they tried hard enough. That was vaguely disturbing, but she'd better get used to it, since she was probably going to be spending a lot of time with this crowd for the next decade.

They all looked very normal. Acted very normal. It was all civilized. Just like an election in any other democratic country.

Ethan didn't look annoyed by Donatelli. He just smiled. "The truth is that we have prospered as a nation for the last forty years.

No deaths by mortals, zero poverty, low crime, and a stable source of blood through the banks we've established. I don't have to lie. The facts speak for themselves. Including your criminal record."

Go, Ethan.

Donatelli pounded the podium. "I am not a crook."

Hello, Nixon. Alexis fought the urge to roll her eyes.

"Read my lips." Donatelli turned to the audience. "I stand for your interests. No new laws, no new restrictions. No new taxes."

Alexis frowned and glanced down at Seamus. Did he notice anything odd here?

"My goal is to see a blood bag in every refrigerator."

The sudden need to giggle overcame her.

"We will bury you, Carrick."

Alexis slapped a hand over her mouth and smothered her snort. Now Donatelli was borrowing from the Cold War Russian dictator, Kruschev.

Seamus shot her a glare.

Ethan just raised an eyebrow and gave Donatelli a cool look of dismissal. He turned to the moderator. "Next question, please."

Thirty minutes later her butt was numb, but she had a whole new respect for her vampire lover, soon-to-be roommate. He handled himself with dignity and intelligence, and an excited Seamus actually smiled at her as Ethan and Donatelli left the stage.

"He did good," Seamus said, his shoulders sagging in relief.

She grinned back at him. "That's awesome. I'm sure all the prep you did with him helped quite a bit."

Now he was the one rolling his eyes. "You don't do well as a suck-up."

"Brittany's better at it than me. Maybe because she's sincere and I'm really not," Alexis admitted.

Seamus laughed. "I guess if Ethan finds it necessary to marry a mortal, at least he chose a lawyer. You should understand how to play politics."

"Yes, I do. And my sister's half-vampire. That should count for something."

"It does."

"Plus I sort of speak Spanish."

"Sort of?"

"Probably more than you," she defended herself.

"I speak English, Gaelic, and French," he said.

"Ooh, la, la." Alexis glanced around the room, noticing everyone was standing up and milling around. "What now? Can I leave? What's Ethan's schedule for the night?"

"He just needs to get his microphone off and speak to a few political analysts. Then he'll be heading upstairs to rest. We'll go over the results and opinion polls tomorrow night. And it would be smart if you're there so we can discuss your roll."

"Perfect." But tonight her roll was vamp vixen. She had the idea to hot-tail it upstairs and be ready for Ethan when he got back.

The idea of going down on the president had some real appeal. Too bad she hadn't been successful projecting her thoughts to Ethan. She could wing that one his way now that he was offstage.

"Okay, I'm taking off then."

"Take your guards," Seamus said firmly.

"Sure thing."

Donatelli threw down the mike in the dressing room Carrick had provided for him. He hated giving these speeches. He was much more persuasive one on one. And it had thrown him off when Carrick had strolled into the room with the sister of an Impure on his arm, looking very much a couple.

The crowd had lapped that up, and it had thoroughly irritated Donatelli.

After an early mistake he had never remarried because he'd rather cut his own head off than be latched on to a vampire wife for all of eternity. And mortal women were excellent for affairs, but he'd never enjoyed any of them enough to propose marriage, no matter how short term.

Carrick was a fool, in his opinion, if he intended to chain himself to a mortal. Then again, he'd always thought Carrick a fool. Which was why Donatelli needed to overthrow him and his concept of government. They were undead. Vampires possessed uncommon speed, skill, and agility. And what did they do? They hid among mortals, imitating their weak democracy.

Donatelli was going to restore the Vampire Nation to its previous glory, when men trembled in fear at their immortality and power was rightfully theirs. It would be his. All of it. Unless Carrick won the election.

The dressing room was well appointed, with buttery leather sofas and a minifridge stocked with blood bags. Carrick was ever the gracious host.

Donatelli wondered how gracious he would be when he went upstairs and discovered a corpse in his suite.

The thought of that was the only thing that kept him from flinging the glass coffee table through the wall.

High Stakes

Alexis ditched her bodyguards at the elevator when it stopped on the twenty-fourth floor.

"I know it's your job to escort me, but see, the thing is, I can't have you in Mr. Carrick's room with me."

"But Miss Baldizzi, that's what Mr. Fox told us to do. We're supposed to wait with you until Mr. Carrick returns."

"I know, but Mr. Fox isn't Mr. Carrick, and which do you think Mr. Carrick would prefer when he gets back? Me hanging around playing Scrabble with you guys or just me naked in bed waiting for him?"

Both bodyguards blushed profusely, their jaws dropping open, which was kind of cute. Alexis was getting rather fond of their silent, brawny presence, but she had to draw the line at the elevator door.

"Exactly, boys, just what I thought. Thanks for the ride, I'll see you tomorrow night." She waved cheerfully from the hallway, pushing the elevator button so the door closed and it started to descend. "Good riddance."

Swiping her key card, she entered Ethan's suite. She didn't have time to prep in her room, so she was just going straight for the kill. The minute she was in the door, she unzipped her dress and let it drop to the floor. Retrieving it so Ethan wouldn't trip on it, she gave a sigh of relief. The thing had been cutting her across the armpits all night long.

There were no lights on and she felt along the wall for the switch, hoping Ethan had closed his blinds since she was in her bra and panties. Not just any bra and panties. This was a red-hot push-up bra made up of a sheer material that showed everything and then some. A scrap of similar fabric that covered her in the front down south and nothing but a piece of red string masquerading as a thong in the back.

Impulse panties. Bought in one of those rare moments where she'd longed to get in touch with her femininity. Hopefully in about ten minutes, Ethan would be touching her femininity.

Her hand found the switch. She flicked the light on and squeezed her eyes shut reflexively at the sudden flood of brightness from the kitchenette. Saluting the hound dog standing sentry by the front door, Alexis strutted down the hall to the living area and tossed her dress on the wet bar, debating whether to leave her heels on or not.

Then the thought fled her mind altogether when she saw a body propped up against Ethan's glass balcony door. She screamed, a strangled shriek of horror that trailed off into a gurgle.

"Oh, my God." It was Kelsey, Ethan's secretary, the one who had been missing, according to Seamus.

Her stomach did a hideous roll, and she gagged at the sight of Kelsey's pale, bloodless face, her legs straight out in front of her, the strap on her dress slipping off her shoulder.

After a long horrified second, when Alexis battled back nausea, the lawyer in her took over. She'd seen many graphic crime scenes, both in photos and in person. She'd witnessed severely beaten rape victims getting medical examinations and she'd seen a five-year-old girl shot in the head by her stepfather. This wasn't any different—it had just completely caught her off guard, ripping her out of the frivolity of a seduction.

She scanned the room quickly, in her shock forgetting where

the phone was in Ethan's suite. Spotting it by the television cabinet, she realized it was too close to the body. She was going to have to go out into the hall and to her room so she wouldn't contaminate any possible evidence.

With shaking fingers, she reached down, feeling around to retrieve her dress before she remembered she'd thrown it on the counter. Then she sensed something as she stared at the body that had been a vibrant, energetic woman. Breathing. She could hear breathing other than her own. Was Kelsey still alive?

No, nothing about Kelsey looked alive.

Standing straight up, Alexis shot a nervous glance around the room. God, she wasn't alone, she just knew it.

Then she spotted him. Just a few feet from Kelsey's body, he was hunched behind a hunter green leather chair. Her eyes locked with his in the dim room, the glare of the light from the kitchenette flooding over into the living area. He moved so fast she wasn't even aware of it until his hand was over her head, pressing firmly, but not painfully. The glint of a knife flashed as he flicked open a switchblade.

Fear leaped up in her along with a rash of bile.

"Leave," he commanded. "You never saw me."

She tried to edge back away from him, but his hand cupped her head like a basketball. Alexis instinctively sliced out with her palm and gave a side strike to his flank. Using her spiked heel, she dug down into his foot.

He gave a startled roar and let go of her. "Bitch."

Immediately she realized her mistake. He'd been trying to wipe her memory of him and the incident. He would have let her go if she had faked confusion, acquiescence.

Maybe it wasn't too late. She groaned and grabbed her head, backing away from him. She was a shitty actress, but it was worth a shot, and he was between her and the door. If she could stumble around him, she could head for the hall slowly and carefully.

Too bad she didn't really know what the hell happened to someone under a glamour. She'd only seen the guy who'd shot Ethan sort of hanging there drooling when Kelsey had put him under one.

And now Kelsey was dead. Involuntarily her eyes darted over to Kelsey sitting there like a big stuffed doll.

A shudder wracked her.

The guy in front of her sucked in his breath. Alexis looked at him and realized what was happening. She had walked backward right into the glare of the kitchen light and the guy was ogling her breasts and everything else between her knees and neck.

Great. Just wonderful. She was going to die in her underwear, murdered by a henchman with a boner.

No way in hell was she pretending to be under a glamour now . . . He'd probably lick her or something gross like that.

Best tactic was surprise aggression.

"Ki-Hap!" She yelled her karate cry of strong energy, prayed for a little yong-gi—courage—and went at him, fists flying.

Smith had encountered any number of unusual situations in the two hundred years he'd worked for Mr. Donatelli, but he'd never been karate kicked in the knees and chest by a half-naked blonde.

She was fast and much stronger than she looked, but it wouldn't be any trouble to suppress her. Except he couldn't stop looking at her body. Every time she twisted, turned, lifted her foot to kick, he caught a new and fascinating shot of skin.

His brain couldn't seem to process why she was in her underwear in the first place, and he could only manage to defend himself with halfhearted blocks while gaping at the see-through red bra, her nipples puckered tight against the material.

And he didn't even flinch when she clipped him on the side of the head, because that extensive kick gave him a view that men paid good money to see every night in Vegas.

Distracting wasn't even the word for it. Smith was downright in awe, completely mesmerized, and only remembered where he was and what he was supposed to be doing when she tripped over the body he had planted.

She fell hard, her ankles flipping right over the sides of the high heels she was wearing. Pitching toward him, Smith instinctively moved out to subdue her while she was vulnerable.

The knife he was holding loosely made contact with the tender flesh below her ribcage. Horrified, he heard her gasp, felt her knees crumple, saw her eyes roll back in pain.

Uh-oh. This was bad.

Panicked, he tried to retract his knife, but it was caught on something—muscle or bone. He yanked and she groaned in agony, clutching at him. Shaking loose of her, he abandoned the knife and let her drop to the floor, falling right in front of the other girl. Smith headed toward the balcony, stumbling over the door runner as he yanked it open.

Damn it all. He'd just stabbed Carrick's mortal girlfriend, and he didn't think Mr. Donatelli was going to like that.

Even if it had been an accident.

Alexis wished she'd tried more seriously to open her mind to Ethan. Now she was screaming for him in panicked silence and it was nothing but a black, empty void. The pain in her side had faded into numbness, cold, cold, everywhere, like ice had crept over her hands and feet.

The clock in Ethan's bedroom was ticking, ticking, and Alexis lay on the floor, knowing she was bleeding to death, trying to move, but unable to get her body to cooperate. Brittany and Ethan hovered in the front of her thoughts and Alexis felt regret, for all the time she'd wasted, for all the things she wouldn't do or see.

Ethan, she screamed. *Help me.*

On the elevator to his room, Ethan was running through his schedule for the following night when he heard Alexis call out to him. In his head.

Alexis? He searched for the source, wondering if he had imagined it. She had sounded desperate, afraid. Lonely.

There was no answer, and only silence when he called out to her again. He didn't like this. Panicking, he willed the elevator to move faster. Seamus had said Alexis had gone upstairs with two guards, but he didn't feel at all reassured. Not until he saw her for himself.

He raced down the hall when the elevator opened, and fumbled with his key for a second before giving up and just shoving the door open, breaking the lock. Pausing in the doorway, he scanned the room, listening.

But it wasn't sound that assaulted him. It was the smell of blood. Hordes of it. "Oh, Lord." Ethan ran into the room and saw Alexis immediately.

She was on her side on the floor by the coffee table, eyes closed. Blood ran down her side, across her abdomen, and in a wide, wet circle on the carpet. Way too much blood. Falling to his knees, he pressed at her fleshy, gaping wound, afraid to check for a pulse, scared of what the answer might be.

"Alexis, love, what the hell happened?" Why was she in her bra and panties and nothing else? Who'd put the knife in her side?

"Ethan?" Her eyelids fluttered open.

"Yes, it's me." He brushed her hair off her face in agonized relief. "It's all right, I'm here now. I'm here."

"I don't want to die in my underwear."

He would have laughed if he weren't choking back tears. "You're not going to die in your underwear." Feeling in his pocket, he fumbled around for his cell phone. "I'm calling 911 and they'll patch you right up."

Except he could already tell by the pallor of her skin and the amount of blood she'd lost that it would be a miracle if they could save her. He felt his throat closing up, and he gathered her into his lap so he could wrap his arms around her, feel her warmth, hear her heart beat slow and sluggish. The knife in her side was twisted at an awkward angle, like she'd fallen on it. When he glanced around the room, he saw the missing Kelsey, drained of her blood, propped up against the glass door.

Good Lord. What the hell was going on?

Anger boiled in him, hot and fierce. He had finally found a woman he could love and she was being taken from him before he could even blink. He hadn't even had time to live with her, to make her his wife. And his cell phone wasn't in his pocket, damn it, not that he seriously thought she had a chance.

"You're crying," she said, sounding surprised.

"Vampires don't cry." But he felt the wetness on his cheeks, knew blood tears had fallen from his eyes. He gripped her closer, tighter, wishing he could give her his strength. "And you're going to be okay."

Her head went back and forth. "No. You've got to turn me. I'm dying." Her words were faint and pain-wracked.

"Turn you?" He stopped stroking her cheek and stared down at her, not daring to hope. "But . . . you said you didn't want to be a vampire. That you didn't want to drink blood or quit your job . . . or other things." He couldn't remember what else she'd said, didn't really care, but he wanted to remind her.

The temptation to take her fear and use it to his advantage was powerful, so he needed to be rational. Alexis hadn't wanted to be turned, and he couldn't be selfish and do it now when she was vulnerable and suffering with pain.

"Are you nuts?" she said, with characteristic Alexis attitude. "That was before I was dying. I choose living as a vampire over not living at all." Her eyes fluttered open, locked with his, clear and certain. "Do it. Please. I'm not ready to leave you and Brittany."

Hope flooded his chest, made him pull her closer to him. "Are you sure?" God, he wanted her to say yes. With Alexis turned, they wouldn't have to settle for ten or fifteen years together.

He could have her for the next thousand years, until he died of old age, an ancient vampire. She was his chosen one, and they could be together forever.

"I'm sure." It was barely a whisper, her lips moving slowly, white and cracked, but Ethan heard her clearly. "I love you," she said. "I want to be your wife."

That was all he needed to hear. "I love you, too, Alexis, for eternity."

Twenty

Ethan sent a call to Seamus for assistance, then bent to Alexis and whispered in her ear.

"It's going to hurt, love, I'm so sorry." Since he couldn't throw a glamour over her, or use pleasure to numb her senses, he was going to have to hope that she was in so much pain from her wound, a little more wouldn't matter.

He hadn't turned anyone since Seamus in the eighteenth century, and never had the outcome been so important to him. Closing his eyes, he lowered his head, while raising her limp body to meet him. Hovering over her shoulder and neck, he brushed his lips over her cold flesh and pulled the knife out of her side. The smell of death clung to her, her breathing a labored in and out, a soft rattling in the back of her throat.

"You'll suffer no more," he told her. "You'll be strong, powerful, my chosen one, my wife."

And he sank his fangs into her neck and drew what little remained of her lifeblood into him. She barely reacted to his invasion, giving only a slight shudder, and within a minute Ethan had drawn all that was necessary. Most of her blood had spilled on the carpet, down her side, over Ethan's hands.

Moving quickly, he punctured his wrist with his fang and sliced an inch-wide gash. Pushing her lips open, he let a few droplets touch her lips, pool on her tongue. Once she got the taste, she clamped on to him, her body going rigid as she sucked hard, drawing his life into her.

Ethan closed his eyes, felt the tug and yank throughout his body as she fed from him, a sexual flush rushing into his groin. It was an intimate act, one of joining, and while he'd certainly never felt it as a sexual desire with any of those he turned before, his feelings for Alexis were different. He loved her, lusted for her, feared for her, and with all of those emotions churning within, her eager sucking at him tugged at his soul, pleased and aroused him.

He cupped his hand over her breast, stroking her nipple, feeling it tighten for him, her mind flooding with pleasure. Locked together like this, her thoughts were flowing and mixing with his, the fear receding, while the pleasure grew and replaced the pain. Anticipation, excitement, love washed over him from her, and Ethan projected his own thoughts back to her.

Happiness that he'd found her, love, glimpses of his very long and lonely life were sent to her to show Alexis that she was special, the one, his only.

Knowing it was time—her grip strong, her body warm again, her eyes rolled back and dilated with pleasure—Ethan broke her suction on his wrist. She whimpered, but her eyes focused on him, and she smiled.

"I heard your thoughts."

"Yes." Ethan checked her wound, saw that it was healing already. "How do you feel?"

"Much better. The pain is going away and I don't feel so weak. And everything feels sort of sharp and neon . . . you know what I mean?"

He nodded, relief turning his stomach sour. He hadn't realized how fucking frightened he'd been until now, when it looked like she was okay. Ethan carefully hid those fears from her and gave her a smile. "I know exactly what you mean. You're going to have a few days of adjustment, but then I have a feeling you'll be enjoying your newfound vampire powers. Just think how fast you can karate kick me."

She gave a laugh, wiping at her mouth with her finger, catching a stray drop of his blood. The finger went into her mouth and she licked it, her eyes dilating with desire. "Mmm, I like the way you taste."

Ethan was shocked at how hard that made him. He'd never seen a mortal take to the change with such . . . nonchalance.

"Later, after you've rested, you can taste all of me."

Her fingers marched down his chest. "You wanted to do me, didn't you? I could feel Chief here . . ." She brushed over his erection. "And could feel in your mind that you wanted to get nasty on me."

"That's the first time that's ever happened to me during a change. You have a strange effect on me." Ethan tried to work up some embarrassment, but it just wasn't there. Relief, pleasure held top spot, followed by lingering shock, growing excitement.

She was his. Forever.

Alexis smiled, her normally green eyes sharpening to a sparkling emerald. "Good. Let's take a shower together and explore that strange effect." She was still smiling, her fingers working on him, but she also gave a rattling cough.

"You need to rest," he told her, stilling her touch on his erection before he moaned. "Your body has been through a trauma and needs to recover."

Currently, his body was going through its own trauma of lust, but he could ignore that for now. Even if his whole being urged him to take her, mate, push out all of the fear, the agony he'd just suffered watching her bleed to death, and join in desperate sex.

"Fine," she said. "But after I take a little nap, you'd better be prepared to initiate me in the ways of vampire sex. I have a very healthy curiosity. Can you hear my thoughts now? I want to understand all things vampire."

Ethan kissed her forehead. "No, only while our blood was mingling. And I'll show you all things vampire, have no fear. But the very first thing we're going to do is get married." He wanted to claim her, let the world know she was his, move her into his apartment and his bed permanently. "I'm holding you to your words, you know."

Before any of that, on a much less pleasant note, he needed to take care of poor Kelsey, as soon as he could force himself to let go of Alexis.

She wiggled in his arms. "I don't plan on reneging." Then she ran her fingers over his mouth and sighed. "Thank you for saving me."

"Trust me, it was my pleasure." Ethan bent down, touched her mouth with his. Love, passion, devotion poured from him into her, and she gasped as they tasted each other, blending teeth and tongue, blood and desire.

Vampire to vampire, mate to mate, this kiss was of tangled tongues, urgent relief, electric strength, and focused love.

"What the hell is going on?" Seamus asked in shock.

"It's about time you got here," Ethan said, turning to glance at his old friend.

Seamus ran his hand through his hair, his cell phone clutched in his grip as he took in the scene. "Oh, shit, I don't even want to know what happened here, do I?"

"Probably not," Ethan agreed. "But you have to know. Alexis had an appalling discovery." He gestured to Kelsey. "I need you to take care of Kelsey, please, and we need to know why she was put here like this. A vampire drained her."

"Oh, my God," Seamus said, his voice stunned. "Why?"

"And it was a vampire who stabbed me," Alexis said, sitting up and brushing her hair back off her shoulders.

Seamus made a choking noise.

Ethan took one look at the bra and panties Alexis was wearing and peeled off his suit jacket. Throwing it around her shoulders, he told her, "Why don't you go take a shower, love?"

"That's a great idea." She winced when she stood up, and shook out her ankle, but then she just clutched the jacket around her bloodied midsection and walked toward the bathroom as if she hadn't been injured at all.

"She was bleeding out," Ethan told Seamus. "There's no way EMTs could have saved her."

Seamus was glancing over Kelsey, checking her neck and shoulders for puncture wounds. "You don't have to justify yourself to me, Ethan." He locked his dark blue eyes on him. "Seriously. I'm sure you did what you thought was right."

"Thanks, Seamus. That means a lot." Ethan thought about a life without Alexis. "I know I did the right thing. I'm sure of it."

He knelt down beside his old friend and rubbed his jaw. "How long do you think Kelsey's been without blood?"

"Eight hours, maybe more." Seamus shook his head in disgust. "Who the hell would do this? It only looks like one vampire. Only one set of teeth."

"I don't know. And I can't imagine why either. Kelsey was absolutely harmless." Death in mortals was hard to see, but Ethan was used to it. But vampires . . . death was rare, and it hit hard, especially when it was someone as young and vibrant and full of life as Kelsey had been.

The brutality of the crime was shocking and offensive. "Someone wants to put this on me."

"Not if I have anything to do with it." Seamus pressed a finger to Kelsey's neck. "Don't worry. You deal with guiding Alexis through the change. I'll take care of Kelsey."

Ethan got up to do just that, but he paused. "Have you seen the Frenchman?"

"No. Why?"

"Just wondering." Ethan reflected on the bites on Brittany. On Corbin's research for the cure.

On why Atelier had been banished in the first place, and what that might mean for now.

Twenty-One

Alexis wished she could actually see herself in the mirror. So far, that was the only downside to the vampire deal. It was her wedding night and she couldn't possibly tell how huge her ass looked in the white sheath dress she was wearing.

Then again, maybe that was a good thing.

"Are you sure I look okay?" she asked Brittany for the twelfth time. "This is the only time I'm going to get married and I want to make sure Ethan doesn't scream when I come down the aisle."

"You look fabulous." Brittany pulled Alexis's hand off the back of the dress. "Stop touching your butt, you're making it bunch up."

Alexis dropped her hands and took a deep breath. "Okay, I'm cool. I'm fine. I'm just committing myself to one man for the rest of eternity. Somehow I never saw this twist in my life a month ago."

Her sister smiled, pressing the backs of her pearl earrings more firmly into her lobes. "I always thought you were the kind who would get married forever. You're loyal. Once you commit, you stick. I'll probably be the one who ends up divorced three times."

"Don't say that, Brit." Alexis watched her sister, still amazed that with her enhanced vampire senses, she could smell Brittany's skin and blood, shampoo and eye makeup, lip gloss and deodorant. It was a miasma of odors and her nose hadn't yet learned how to deal with them all. She also could hear, not necessarily thoughts, but feelings from people.

Brittany was happy for Alexis, but she was sad for herself. Alexis could feel her confusion, her loneliness, her worry that she was being left behind. Her fear that Corbin was responsible for what had happened to Kelsey.

"Have you seen Corbin?" Alexis asked casually, putting lipstick on with a hope and a prayer. She was probably creating the rings of Saturn around her mouth.

Brittany reached out and took the tube from her and applied it on her with swift, sure motions. "No, I haven't seen Corbin, and I don't think I ever will. He wanted blood from me and he got it. I think the sex was an accident, and I don't blame him or anything. I mean, I was the one who turned things in that direction. And I certainly do not for one minute think Corbin had anything to do with Kelsey. He's just not that kind of guy. Rub your lips together and pop."

Alexis obeyed, hating the feeling of wetness on her mouth. "Seamus thinks he did it."

"But why would he put her body in Ethan's room? That doesn't make sense."

"So he wouldn't get caught."

Brittany shrugged in her lime green sundress. Alexis couldn't believe any woman could pull that look off, but Brittany looked fantastic.

"Trust me, Alex. Corbin wouldn't do that."

"Ethan doesn't believe me that the vampire slayers are more than just a hoax." Alexis stepped into her shoes. "But last night I got a message saying I was being expelled from the group because I no longer fit the definition of a slayer. That's just too weird to be a coincidence. First they found me, now what if they know I was turned?"

The whole situation was alarming enough that it was preventing Alexis from truly enjoying her time with Ethan. It had only been a week since she'd almost died and had become a vampire, but it had been crammed full of activities and details like taking a brief leave of absence from work to recover from her injuries and to get married. She fully intended to stay at the prosecutor's office as an off-site legal consultant, at least for a decade or so, but she did need an adjustment period to the changes.

She had put her house up for sale and would be moving her furniture into storage for the time being. Living in the suite with Ethan was a temporary solution—she'd already informed him living in a casino was not going to cut it for her, and they needed to buy a house together.

In the midst of all those newlywed decisions, she was adjusting to a new fondness for nighttime, blood, and learning to control her strength so she'd stop ripping doors off the hinges. She had to admit, that was the coolest part. She was like the Bionic Woman, which more than made up for the fact that she was so damn short.

"I don't know how they could have found you, and if they really are vampire slayers, did they have anything to do with Kelsey and the attack on you?" Brittany readjusted her dress bodice. "You know, Ethan and Seamus aren't really listening to us on this one . . . I think we need to investigate on our own. I need to prove that Corbin didn't do this. Maybe I'm just an idiot, but I can't stand the thought of him being all by himself or worse, accused of a crime he didn't commit and punished. His work is really important and he needs to continue it."

"And I don't want you in any danger, Brit, which is what I'm worried about with these slayer people. I think you're right. We need to do some checking around on our own." Hell, she was an attorney. She knew how to gather facts.

"I tried to call Corbin but he's shut me out."

"You mean you can call him mentally? Telepathically, I mean, mental sounds kind of weird."

"Yes. Corbin can hear all my thoughts unless I concentrate really hard on shutting him out. And when I called him before, he came to me, but now he's not answering."

Alexis didn't like the way that sounded. "Maybe there's a reason he's not answering." Like he was injured or in danger or something. "Ethan can't read my mind at all . . . he's says I'm too stubborn."

Brittany didn't laugh like Alex was hoping she would. Alexis squeezed her sister's hand. "Don't worry. We'll find Corbin. But first, I guess I need to go get married before Ethan sends his goons after me."

Brittany managed a smile. "Those bodyguards of yours are really scary. But I guess when you're the president's fiancée, they're necessary."

"Yeah. Ethan still can't get over the fact that I sent them away the night I was stabbed." She shivered just remembering the fear, the pain. "But I keep telling him if I hadn't been so intent on seducing him, I wouldn't have been stabbed and wouldn't be a vampire now. So this really all worked to his advantage." She bit her lip and got the nasty taste of lipstick on her tongue. "Are you okay with me being a vampire, Brit? I know you wanted to save Ethan from eternal damnation and all that . . ."

Brittany gave her a hug. "That was before I knew that no one here is damned, or soulless. And I'd much rather have you as a vampire instead of not at all. I can't imagine life without my big sister taking care of me."

"Just let anyone try and hurt you now." Alexis embraced her in return. "I'd have kicked their asses before, but now I'll kick their asses and make them wet their pants in fear. It'll be great, though you might just want to tell your future boyfriends not to mistreat you."

Brittany rolled her eyes and pulled back with a smile. "You're all talk." She went to the door. "Now here comes the bride and all of that."

Alexis was going to try and really play this whole wedding/bride thing down, but she had to admit she was actually pretty excited. For a woman who'd spent half her life thinking she wasn't ever going to get married, she was really damn happy now that she was.

Ethan was . . . well, everything. He was amazing. Caring, considerate, intelligent, fair, sexy. Sexy. And sexy.

The vampire sex was killer. No pun intended. Every orgasm was like a regular one times twenty. And when he licked and bit her . . . well, she couldn't even think about it without getting turned on, which probably wasn't a good thing before facing the minister.

Since she wasn't all that great at differentiating between hunger and desire yet, she might wind up biting the minister and that wouldn't be cool.

She'd sucked down two bags of blood before getting dressed, but it was still probably better to just think pure thoughts.

"Okay, let's do this."

Ethan was experiencing blind terror. What if Alexis changed her mind and didn't want to marry him? What if he stumbled over his words and made a complete and total ass of himself?

Seamus clapped his shoulder. "Relax. She's not going to stand you up."

It was a testament to his nerves that he hadn't even bothered to shield his thoughts from Seamus. Wonderful. Maybe he could project his fears to the entire room while he was at it. That would be really attractive.

His best man, Seamus, was waiting at the end of the rooftop garden with him, next to the minister they'd gotten to do the service. One who didn't object to a quickie wedding conducted on the roof of a casino at night. One of the advantages of being in Vegas— the minister hadn't even blinked at the request. He was patiently waiting in front of their guests, holding a black leather-bound book, rocking on his heels.

The only people in attendance were Ethan's inner circle of friends and cabinet members, a handful of Alexis's coworkers, and a liquored-up middle-age woman who claimed she was his bride's aunt. Ethan wasn't entirely convinced that's who she was, but he couldn't exactly press her for ID, and she had an invitation.

Ethan inched away from the edge of the rooftop. He felt so idiotic and panicked, he didn't want to tumble over the side of the building or something embarrassing like that. This mattered a hell of a lot to him. He wanted this marriage—more than anything, even more than the urgency he'd felt to return to mortality, to a normal life, right after his change.

Alexis was his future, and if a vampire could throw up, Ethan would be doing it right now.

"Ethan." Seamus grabbed his arm.

"What? She's not coming, is she?" Ethan yanked at his tie.

"No."

"No?" Oh, God, this was his punishment for all those years of being a playboy. Now that he was finally in love, he was being tortured.

"No, I mean, I don't know. I'm sure she's coming. But look who just got here."

Ethan glanced toward the doorway, which had been decorated with some kind of arch, draped in a bunch of white fabric. Brittany had arranged for the chairs to be covered with slipcovers, flowers arranged strategically, and the arch to be transformed into what she called a grand entrance. All it did was prevent Ethan from having a clear view.

Shifting, he suddenly felt a strange sensation drift over him. Familiar, probing mental fingers invaded his mind.

"Gwenna," he whispered.

Then he saw her. Standing under the arch, a pale ethereal figure in an ivory dress that draped and clung to her thin frame, she stared at him with big, deep, solemn eyes.

High Stakes

You came.

Of course. It's not every day my brother takes a life mate.

I'm pleased, Gwenna.

He hadn't really thought his sister would come. As far as he knew, she hadn't left England in three hundred years. She hadn't even left her home in all that time either. He started toward her, but she shook her head.

Stay. I'll take a seat and we can talk later. You can tell me what finally made you step willingly into marriage.

Ethan yanked at his jacket sleeves. *Two things. A midlife crisis and finding the perfect woman.*

His sister smiled, a fragile, haunted tilt to her mouth.

"She looks beautiful," Seamus commented as Gwenna took a seat in the back row, apart from the other guests.

"Yes, she does." As did Alexis.

Ethan sucked in his breath when his bride stepped through the arch onto the dusky patio. She was wearing a clinging white dress, which flattered her curvy figure, and high heels that should put her at least to his shoulder. He didn't know why she obsessed about her height, when he thought she was so damn cute, but he'd learned not to call her that. Especially not when her fangs were accessible to a vulnerable part of his body.

Today cute didn't cover it, though. She was stunning, a wide smile on her face, a sparkle in her eye. And she hadn't changed her mind, thank God.

Brittany walked up the aisle in an eye-popping green dress, and then Alexis came confidently toward him, not with a serene bridal walk, but with an aggressive take-charge stride.

It suited her, just as she suited him.

When she reached his side, she gave him a wink and said, "Hi, sexy."

"Hey." Ethan wanted to grab her, and do something totally bizarre, like drop at her feet in worship. He settled for a hand squeeze. "You look amazing."

"Thank you. You're not too shabby yourself."

They turned to the minister, Alexis's hand comfortably in his.

After a few preliminaries, the owl-eyed man gave them both an encouraging smile. "I want to take this opportunity to remind you that marriage is the ultimate jackpot in the casino of life."

Ethan blinked. Was that a gambling metaphor?

Alexis stiffened next to him, a cough quickly covering a laugh.

"And that as a casino owner you understand that while there are risks, ultimately the house always wins."

Really. Risking a glance at Alexis, Ethan raised his eyebrow. She met his questioning look with one of amusement, and bit her lip. Hard.

God, he was going to laugh. At his own wedding. Ethan dug his fingernails into his thigh so he wouldn't lose it.

"And if you want to win big, you have to play every hand. When you argue, you have to know when to fold, and how to walk away without counting your money at the table."

What? He didn't even know what the hell that meant. And he was definitely going to laugh. Which would not be dignified, nor appropriate for an elected official.

A little desperate, Ethan blurted, "I do."

The man stopped speaking, startled. "You do what?"

"I do. Take Alexis as my lawfully wedded wife, for richer, for poorer, in sickness and in health, till death do we part. I do." He pulled the platinum band out of his pocket, relieved he could say the words without botching the whole thing.

"I do, too," Alexis added. "Take Ethan as my husband, plus all the other stuff he said."

Turning to Alexis before the minister started babbling again, he pulled her hand forward, slid the ring on, and looked into her eyes. "My love for you is like a circle—never ending."

The midlife crisis was over. He'd found contentment, happiness. Passion. Love.

The amusement on her face disappeared, and her eyes softened.

Alexis held her hand out to her sister and Brittany dropped Ethan's wedding band in it. She took it, rolling it around and around her finger, enjoying the cool feel of the smooth metal against her warm skin. Then with total confidence, she pushed the ring onto his finger.

"I give you this ring as a sign of my love and fidelity."

He kissed her then, barely waiting for her to finish speaking. Alexis closed her eyes and let him go to town, knowing that marrying Ethan was the smartest thing she'd ever done in her life.

And as cheesy as the minister had sounded, marriage could be a gamble. But she thought the odds were stacked in her favor.

Ethan whispered in her ear. "Now that this is done, it's time for our honeymoon, Mrs. Carrick."

"Ms. Baldizzi," she whispered back.

He pulled back, stared sternly at her. "Mrs. Baldizzi-Carrick?"

"Ms. Baldizzi-Carrick." With an eternity ahead of them, she couldn't let him get too cocky about their relationship.

"Mrs."

"Ms."

"Sparring match to decide? Most hits wins?"

"Deal."

To her surprise, he yanked her up into his arms, nearly taking out Seamus with her dangling legs.

"Ethan!" She laughed, waving and tossing her bouquet toward Brittany. "You're making a scene."

"I don't believe I care."

She didn't either. She felt too fabulous, too in love, to worry about what anyone thought. In two seconds Ethan had her under the arch. Two seconds after that he had her behind some potted lemon trees.

"Where are we going?" she whispered.

He wrapped his arms around her and jumped off the side of the building. "I'm going to embarrass myself by giving you the perfect ending."

The wind kicked her skirt up, exposing her backside to the bare air. Alexis yanked it back down. "That's your perfect ending?"

Ethan laughed as he flew them straight above the Vegas Strip. "I can't give you a sunset, but I can give you the night."

Alexis's heart swelled, as did her suspicions. "Did Seamus write that for you?"

"Nope. That one's my own. Seamus knows politics, but he doesn't know anything about women."

Then he kissed her, with the wind racing over her bare shoulders, and tossing her hair in all directions.

"Bring on the night," she murmured in encouragement.

"It would be my pleasure." And his teeth sank into her neck.